SET ME FREE

SET ME FREE is the cry from a woman's heart. Vicky, bullied and harried into a wrong marriage finds her life intolerable, and inevitably she falls in love with another man.

The theme of this novel will find an echo in the hearts of many readers. It is an absorbing study of a young girl pushed to the limits of her endurance.

SET ME FREE is a poignant exposition of an unhappily married woman's emotional life, and is one of the finest books which Denise Robins has ever given us.

SET ME FREE

Denise Robins

CORONET BOOKS
Hodder and Stoughton

Copyright 1937 by
Denise Robins

First published in Great Britain in
1937 by Ivor Nicholson &
Watson Ltd

Coronet edition 1990

British Library C.I.P.

Robins, Denise, *1897–1985*
  Set me free.
  I. Title
  823'.912[F]

ISBN 0-340-43080-X

Printed and bound in Great
Britain for Hodder and Stoughton
Paperbacks, a division of Hodder
and Stoughton Ltd., Mill Road,
Dunton Green, Sevenoaks, Kent
TN13 2YA, (Editorial Office: 47
Bedford Square, London, WC1B
3DP) by Richard Clay
Bungay, Suffolk

'The frost is gone;
  The south-west wind comes,
It comes leaping and shouting on the snowfields,
  Laughing at the ruin.
My spirit rushes forth again
  To meet the kisses of the South...

It shall speak for me,
  It shall sing for me,
It shall set me free.'

From a poem by Henry Simpson

For my brother

ADRIAN KLEIN, MBE., ARPS

*with my love and in admiration of
his years of work and unmitigating
faith in Colour-Photography*

1937

1

Mrs. Waide walked into the sitting-room carrying a large cretonne bag which contained her knitting, and was duly impressed by the sight of her eldest daughter seated by the window, bent over a pair of stockings which she was darning.

Mrs. Waide's eyes, always a little weak and watery, had in them a perpetual expression of anxiety, but they mellowed with the pride which she could not conceal when she looked at Freda. Dear Freda! Always a model girl! Never wasted time or money. There she was, using the last vestige of light for her work. Although it was not yet dark this mild May evening, it was high time the lights were put on and the curtains drawn. But dear Freda was so thoughtful about the electric-light bill. Thoughtful, too, about expenditure, knowing that her parents were not over prosperous.

Mr. Waide ran a bookshop and library in Norman Park. One of South London's garden cities. But in no profession is it easy to make or save money, these days. Freda appreciated that, and was never extravagant.

She looked up from her darning as the older woman entered the room.

'Hullo, Mother,' she said in a voice which was as lifeless as her appearance. She then bent over her work again.

When Mrs. Waide settled herself on the window-seat beside the girl, any onlooker would have been struck by the strong resemblance between mother and daughter.

Both gave out that extraordinary suggestion of lifelessness.

It might have been that forty-five years of domestic struggle, indifferent health, and lack of any real excitement or change accounted for the devitalising of the mother. Yet her daughter, aged twenty-four, seemed to possess little more vitality.

Both were fair and had anæmic complexions. The blondness of Freda's hair which waved naturally and was her one beauty, had in the mother's case turned to ashen hue.

Both women had 'buns' in the nape of the neck, and affected the same kind of clothes. Nondescript, neat, chosen generally for economy rather than beauty. During the daytime they often wore the rather 'arty' type of cotton smock, in which they did their share of domestic work.

Neither of the women used make-up; and since Freda's lips were naturally pale, it enhanced her 'dead' look. She considered herself superior because she avoided artificial colour. She shared her mother's opinion that lipstick and rouge were either fast or theatrical. Yet Freda considered herself up-to-date. She was of a hard-working disposition and had delighted the family by getting a diploma at a big London Domestic Economy school.

She was a domesticated, practical young woman. Mrs. Waide never quite understood why she was still unattached. She felt sure her Freda would make a perfect wife. She could never see that the overdose of efficiency in Freda and that touch of cold superiority in her were what kept most men away.

'Where's Vicky?' Freda asked her mother, looking up from her darning again.

At once Mrs. Waide sighed. That sigh was ever ready at the mention or thought of her other and younger daughter, Victoria.

'In her bedroom, I think.'

'Mooning about as usual, I suppose,' said Freda.

'She's in one of her "moods",' said Mrs. Waide. 'And as I told your father, before he went to business this morning, I am quite sick of Vicky's moods. Why can't she be more like you?'

Freda shrugged her shoulders.

'She isn't like anybody in the family. When Tom Collinson was here on Sunday, he said it was hard to believe that she was a Waide.'

Mrs. Waide sighed again.

'I really get worried about Vicky, Freda. Tom's right. She isn't like any of us. Your father seems to think she takes after his mother. I never saw her, of course. She died before I married. But you know she was a mixture of Irish and French, and there you are—it's a wild strain and it's skipped a generation and come down to Vicky. She ought to have been a boy—I say so every day of my life. Then her father could have thrashed some of the nonsense out of her. *I* don't seem to have any control over her these days.'

'It's a shame,' said Freda. 'Poor Mother!'

'Well, I've always got you,' said Mrs. Waide. 'And I must say I need some backing up. Your father is much too inclined to be soft with Vicky. He says she has an artistic temperament, and ought to have gone on the stage.'

'A lot of rot,' said Freda. 'I'm surprised at Father. And I think its frightful, the way Vicky goes on about films and film stars, and the rest of it. She never seems to me to want to sit down and do anything sensible.'

Mrs. Waide's face once more creased with anxiety. Vicky was *such* a worry! Her mother had never understood her even when she was a small girl. Instead of being an easy little thing like Freda, subservient to control, the second daughter who had arrived when Freda was four, had speedily shown herself the antithesis. Difficult, passionate, *different* . . . with a superabundance of vitality which at times had taken her listless mother's breath away.

When, as a small child, Vicky had been naughty or

11

shown temper, she had received the stereotype treatment—nagging, slapping, petty punishments. And always Mrs. Waide hoped that Victoria—thus named after her paternal grandmother—would quieten down and develop some of Freda's quiet, studious tendencies.

But nothing like that had happened. Vicky had been a rebel from birth. A rebel she remained. She did not seem to be able to fit in with this life which the rest of them were prepared to lead in their quiet suburban home. And for the last year, since her twentieth birthday, she had been pestering the family to allow her to go out and take a job.

Now had Freda wished to leave home and get a job, Mrs. Waide would not have minded. She was sure Freda was to be trusted and would be as excellent and decorous in her work as she was at home. But Vicky! . . . Heavens! . . . They'd be crazy to allow her to escape the shelter of her home and the authority of her parents. Her head was far too full of foolish romantic notions. And she was much too pretty. Mrs. Waide had to admit that Vicky scored over Freda in looks; although Vicky possessed the type of beauty which Mrs. Waide understood and appreciated as little as she did her younger daughter's gay, impulsive nature. No amount of nagging prevented Vicky from using a lipstick, and some powder. But even without it she had so much warmth and colour that it made Mrs. Waide quite uneasy to look at her. She had a mysterious flame-like quality that drew men to her as swiftly and readily as they were chilled by Freda.

Take Tom Collinson, the mother thought, now, as she embarked upon the wool-cardigan which she was knitting for her husband. Tom was a good, steady fellow, the son of one of Mr. Waide's oldest friends, and with a flourishing poultry farm down in Sussex. One would have thought that he would have seen in Freda the ideal wife. But, no! It was Vicky who had attracted him since she left school. He had proposed to her half a dozen times and been turned down. More was the pity. Tom was an optimist if he thought Vicky would make him happy, but

12

at least if she married him the family could feel that she was out of harm's way, in safe keeping for the rest of her life! And perhaps marriage and one or two children would calm her down; knock a few of those absurd, independent ideas out of her head.

The droning sound of a mowing machine made Mrs. Waide open one of the casements and thrust out her head.

Into view came the small coatless figure of a thin little man with shirt-sleeves rolled up, and a hat set incongruously on his head. He was pushing the mower doggedly. His wife screamed above the noise of the machine:

'Stan-ley! You ought to come in. The dew is falling, and you will get your bronchitis again.'

Mr. Waide paused. He pushed the hat back on his head, wiped his streaming forehead, and nodded to his wife. Under shaggy brows he had small sad eyes, like a monkey's. He was a kind little man, easily managed. At his business he showed an efficiency and superiority worthy of his eldest daughter. But at home he was retiring and dominated by his wife—and Freda.

He did not want to leave his work. He enjoyed mowing the lawn on a mild May evening. He liked to see the stars come out in the tranquil sky, and to gaze upon the fine Darwin tulips which he had planted with his own hands, and which were flaunting their gay colours in all the beds. He liked the peace of the garden, and the promise of the spring. But he was too used to doing what his wife wanted to dream of making a protest when she called him. Besides, there *was* his bronchitis. He had had it two years running, and he did not want it again.

'Stan—come in!' Mrs. Waide called again.

'Yes, dear,' he said, and turned the mower in the direction of the toolshed.

Then from an upper window came another voice. Not a sharp, nagging voice; but a warm vibrant one which had music in it.

'Daddy, darling! I've got a surprise for you. Go into the

13

drawing-room and see what you shall see!'

Mr. Waide looked up at the window. That was Vicky. He could just discern the outline of her face and figure. He was too short-sighted to see more, but his whole face softened.

'Just going in now, dear,' he called back.

He was so fond of Vicky. Fonder of her than of anyone else. She was warm and pretty and alive. He knew, of course, that she was difficult; a little too modern and go-ahead, maybe. And he knew that her mother and sister were good, God-fearing creatures. But there were times when he had to confess to himself that his young Victoria was the one human element in the home. Like his lovely, madcap Irish mother whom he remembered in the days of his boyhood. Ah! But she'd had a wild streak in her. It made one feel a bit anxious about Vicky who was so like her. He hoped the child would come to no harm. She had a generosity and a sense of humour which those others in there did not possess, though he felt guilty for admitting it. There were plenty of times when he longed to back her up during some of the rows, but he dared not. It wouldn't be loyal to her mother, and Freda had such a sharp tongue. Peace at any price was his motto.

He washed his hands and joined the family in the drawing-room. The curtains had been drawn now and the lights switched on.

'Well, well,' said Mr. Waide, sinking into a chair, and feeling in the pocket of his coat for a pipe. 'It's a grand evening. Vicky says she has got a surprise for us and is just coming down.'

'What *does* she mean?' asked Freda.

'I don't know, I am sure, my dear,' said Mr. Waide.

'Perhaps she is bringing down a bit of mending,' said Freda; 'that *would* be a surprise.'

'Oh, Stanley!' said Mrs. Waide in an aggrieved voice, 'you've brought mud in on your shoes. Can't you ever remember to scrape them properly.'

'Sorry, dear,' said Mr. Waide, and looked with a

14

childish dismay at the marks on the carpet pointed out to him.

He was thirsty, and would have loved to have taken a long draught of beer after that mowing. But Gracie did so dislike him drinking. He had become almost teetotal for her sake. He suggested that she might ring for Edith, their maid, and ask for some lemonade.

Mrs. Waide clicked her tongue.

'You know it's Edith's night out.'

Freda laid aside her stockings.

'I'll get it,' she said.

Mr. Waide gave her a timid smile.

'Don't worry, dear.'

He was always a little afraid of Freda. She could be surprisingly caustic for one so young. But before Freda reached the door, there came the sound of Victoria's warm voice.

'Family! You will not go to the films, so I bring the films to you. *Behold!—Dolores Del Rio!*'

Mr. Waide looked expectantly at the door. So the 'surprise' was to be one of Vicky's theatrical 'turns'. She adored dressing up—dissolving herself into some glamorous personality of the film or stage. And very good she was at it. She made him laugh.

Mrs. Waide's face retained its anxious expression, Freda merely looked bored.

Into the room came Victoria Waide; shut the door and stood with her back against it. The other Waides stared at her. She never seemed to be really one of themselves, and in this disguise she was a stranger. 'Dolores Del Rio', she called herself. Well, it was not a bad impersonation. But it irritated Freda: as though that radiance and beauty were a reproach to her own pallor and negativeness.

Grace Waide felt a fleeting pride that she was responsible for so much charm and loveliness. Albeit the pride was speedily tempered by a total lack of understanding, and her inveterate feeling of anxiety.

Against the white-painted door stood Vicky, slim and

15

alluring in an old black velvet evening dress which Mrs. Waide had bought in which to attend a business dinner of her husband's two winters ago and which she hadn't worn since. She hardly ever changed into full evening dress. Vicky had drawn it tightly about her, and wound a red scarf about her hips. Over her shoulders was an old Spanish shawl which had belonged to her grandmother. Between her teeth, an artificial rose; one slender hand upon her hip, the other brandishing a cigarette. Her whole attitude was Southern and abandoned. It would have caught and held the attention of any film producer in a studio. It was so full of natural grace.

But all that was alive and magical in her face was lost upon her family, who saw only a ridiculous mask of lipstick and rouge. Yet against the ivory paint of the door, her face was exquisitely chiselled and her hair, parted in the middle and sleekly combed off her ears, looked like black satin. Black hair, wide blue eyes, high cheekbones, and curling red lips, gifts bequeathed by that grandmother who had passed on to Victoria Waide some of the mystery of Ireland, much of the glamour of France, and made of her something that these people to whom she belonged found inexplicable and even embarrassing.

2

Vicky retained her pose only for a few seconds. During those few seconds she *had* been Dolores Del Rio, to herself, prepared to enact a scene of passion and beauty for these people who were her flesh and blood, yet strangers to her.

Then the spark grew cold and flickered out, extinguished by what she saw before her. Freda's cold, pale, rather disgusted face. Her mother's anxious, uncomprehending one. Her father's—more kindly than the rest, but with a pathos that hurt Vicky because it suggested that although he could not quite understand her, he, himself, went through life equally misunderstood. Poor henpecked little man!

Vicky's slim body relaxed. With a sweep of her hand as graceful as any of her gestures, she took the rose from her lips and flung her cigarette into the fireplace.

'Well, that's that,' she said.

And her brilliant eyes took on that mixture of dissatisfaction and defiance which 'the family' could always bring into them.

'Dolores Del Rio' was gone. In her place was just Vicky Waide, born and bred in Norman Park, educated at a local mediocre 'school for young ladies', never having known any of the real thrills of life beyond those which were depicted for her in film and play and book. One in a million girls. Yet one out of a million who could not settle down at home and wait drearily until some ordinary man married her and put her into a similar home; one who could not willingly accept the dull routine, the common

17

tasks, the total lack of originality and colour and warmth, things which she knew life held somewhere—*somewhere* outside this place, beyond these people.

There was a spirit inside Victoria Waide which was like a wild bird beating its wings against a cage. But now that her moment of thrill, when she had first struck her dramatic pose, had passed, she was just a young, restless, disappointed girl, 'dressed-up', out of place, quite aware that she looked a little ridiculous in the eyes of her family.

Freda returned to her darning and said:

'I don't know why you waste your time like that.'

'I don't know why I do,' said Vicky coldly.

'You look very nice, dear,' said Mr. Waide.

'I didn't say you could put on my dress,' complained Vicky's mother.

Through narrowed lids, Vicky looked at them all. Her red lips curved disdainfully. She said:

'It was just a bit of fun. I tried to impersonate Dolores Del Rio as she looked in that film the other night.'

'I can't say I approve of these films,' said Mrs. Waide. 'They put a lot of stuff and nonsense into young girls' heads.'

Vicky folded her arms.

'My dear Mum, the other day you were saying you were more modern than most people.'

'So I am!' said Mrs. Waide. 'I'm not at all old-fashioned—am I, Freda?'

'Certainly not,' was Freda's retort. 'But Vicky thinks you've got to be thoroughly fast if you want to be modern.'

Vicky crimsoned. She looked lovely with that burning colour on her high cheekbones.

'Dear Freda! I suppose you wouldn't enjoy anything but educational films and the Newsreel. You never were romantic, dear. But, thank goodness, I am.'

'Now you two, don't start nagging each other,' said Mrs. Waide plaintively.

'She makes me tired,' muttered Freda.

'Not as tired as you make me, Freda,' was Vicky's swift retort. 'Everything I do or say is wrong, and if I want to have a good time I'm just *fast*. I'm sick of it! And as I'm always annoying you all, why don't you let me go away and find a job?'

'Now don't start that again, Vicky,' said Mrs. Waide. 'We're not going to have you leaving home, so get it into your head once and for all, please.'

Vicky's wide blue eyes, which had such big pupils that they looked almost black when she was excited, flashed angrily at her mother.

'All right! Keep me here if you want to! I shouldn't have thought you'd want to. But you can't force me to stay once I'm twenty-one.'

'Meanwhile,' said Freda, in her most freezing voice, 'I suppose we've got to put up with this sort of misery for another year.'

'Well, you're such a comfort to everyone,' said Vicky. 'It ought to make up for what I lack—my God!'

'Tut, tut,' put in Mr. Waide mildly. 'Strong language, my dear.'

Vicky made a gesture of exasperation, turned, and was about to fly out of the room when the door opened and revealed a tall, fair man standing in the hall. He wore a tweed coat and grey flannels and held a hat in his hand. So busy had the family been with their bickering, they had not heard his approach.

'Why, hullo, Tom!' said Mrs. Waide, rising from her chair.

Tom Collinson answered her greeting, but his gaze was directed at Vicky. In an astonished way he regarded her theatrical dress.

'What's all this?' he said, with a laugh.

Vicky, still hot with rage against her sister and against life in general, controlled herself sufficiently to speak to the young man whom she knew was in love with her.

'Oh, good evening, Tom. I was just doing a bit of dressing up for fun.'

'Sort of Spanish, isn't it?' said Tom, and advanced farther into the room.

Freda had put her darning away and was looking at the visitor eagerly. The only time when her face became at all animated was when Tom Collinson appeared on the scene. But only for an instant, then her features resumed their cold rigidity. What was the use of an extra heart-beat at the sight of a man who was in love with someone else? Freda thought it hard and cruel that Tom should love Vicky, who didn't care a fig for him, and treated him so casually.

Freda would have given much for a chance with Tom. She had always admired him. The fact that he was stolid, dull, and typically British in his reserve, his dislike of betraying what he felt, appealed to her just as much as it irritated Vicky. Freda knew that she would have made a good wife for Tom. He was mad to want that foolish, headstrong sister of hers, with all her queer ideas.

'I'll just go up and change my clothes,' said Vicky. 'You'll be staying a while, won't you, Tom?'

'You wouldn't like to come out for a walk, would you?' he asked, twiddling his hat between his fingers.

Vicky hesitated. A walk with Tom wouldn't be an excitement. Just another proposal, stammered with his usual difficulty in expressing himself, and followed by her refusal.

Tom was a good sort, but as far removed from the romantic lover of Victoria Waide's dreams as the earth from the sun. However, she was fed up with the family and staying indoors just to listen to their nagging. She might as well take a walk with Tom.

'All right,' she said, 'I'll come out.'

Freda went back to her chair and her darning. She applied her needle furiously, conscious of a jealousy which made her almost hate her young sister.

'Sit down, my boy, and have a smoke,' said Mr. Waide.

Tom took the cigarette that was offered, and the two men then entered into a discussion about the price of eggs, which was Tom's subject of the moment.

He was heart and soul engrossed in his poultry farm. He was returning to it tomorrow, having stayed up here in Norman Park for two or three days with a married sister.

It was at a local Christmas party that he had first seen Vicky, then a mere schoolgirl of sixteen, with a satin black plait of hair tied with a pink bow. And somehow her unusual dark, sulky beauty, that strange glamour with which she surrounded herself and which set her apart from all the other girls in the party, had captivated the young farmer completely.

He was a man without much imagination. He had been brought up in a narrow and conventional house up North. His people had a little money and had given him a sound education. He had studied agriculture and farming. He was more interested in his work than anything else, and women had never played much part in his life, except that he always knew he would one day want a wife and children.

Seeing Vicky had meant falling in love for the first time. Her strange attitude toward life, her love of excitement and her restlessness, did not annoy him as it did her family. Although he had no sympathy with her views, he thought them just an exuberance of youthful spirits which would soon simmer down. He did not see why she should not settle down on the farm with him and make him a good wife.

The sensual side of him was stirred by her beauty, whereas Freda left him cold. He had seen Vicky regularly for the last four years, and although she had turned him down several times, he was not without hope. He was a phlegmatic, patient young man, and he hoped that in the fullness of time Vicky would change her mind. He had no intention of changing his, unless she married somebody else.

Just how cruel or wrong it would be of any man to take her glowing youth and loveliness and shut it away in a farmhouse given over entirely to the raising of chickens and selling of eggs, never entered his mind. It was quite a flourishing little farm, and he had a bit of money saved up. He could make Vicky comfortable. What else could she want? He was twenty-seven—seven years older than she was—but that didn't seem too much, added to which he had a pompous idea of his own worthiness, and was pleased to think that he had always led a very straight, decent life. He was sure Vicky would marry him—in time.

Upstairs in the little bedroom which was her haven, her refuge from the rest of the family, Vicky took off the velvet dress, the red scarf, her one and only pair of evening shoes, and cleaned the make-up off her face.

Angrily, passionately, Vicky removed every trace of artifice, then put on a skirt, a green woolly jumper, and some walking shoes. She was so slim and small that she looked very young in such clothes—younger, too, now that her hair was done in the usual style, combed back from her forehead and tied round with a piece of ribbon. The black, glossy hair was just long enough to pin into a little bun if she wanted to, but generally she let it loose, and it fell in dark curls to her neck.

She looked gloomily around her bedroom while she dressed. Here she could think quietly and dream her dreams, undisturbed; write her letters or read her books without acid comments from Freda or mother. But even this room was beginning to be a prison from which she felt that she must escape or go crazy.

She had a natural taste for good things, for beauty and art. This was the home which she had always known, and it was familiar to her, yet unfamiliar to the Vicky inside herself—the Vicky who lived in a world of romance. And that Vicky disliked cheap houses, and bad limed-oak furniture which Mrs. Waide prided herself was 'modern', and the one-and-threepence a yard cretonne curtains in here. Most of the colour had long since been washed out of them; *and* that 'art-silk' bedspread which had been picked up in a sale! . . . the colour screamed with the curtains.

Oh, there was another room in which Vicky dwelt—big, spacious, softly lighted, full of rare old furniture, brocades and velvets, shimmering satins and silks, and flowers. Always masses of flowers, and lovely scents, music, dancing, and the dream man whom she had pictured a thousand times.

Handsome he was, but not only that—good fun! He would make her laugh. It was so necessary to laugh and see the joyous, funny side of things. He would take her in his arms, and they would laugh together, then grow serious when he told her how lovely she was and how much he adored her. And she would whisper:

'Darling, I've been so unhappy—I've wanted you so long!'

Crazy dreams. Secret longings. They meant nothing to anybody but herself, and she could never even speak of them to anybody. Outside this room there waited for her life in the family circle, constant irritations and misunderstandings—and Tom! Good old Tom, who often sat beside her in a cinema, to which he went only to please her, oblivious of her rapture and ready to quench it by remarking that the picture was 'a lot of drivel'.

Perhaps it *was* drivel. Perhaps life on the screen wasn't real at all; and reality for Vicky meant domestic routine, economy in clothes, dull days and nights; an occasional holiday in Scarborough with father's relatives who lived there; somebody coming in to tea or supper—and the wireless! That might be all—all that life would ever hold for her. And marriage, with a man like Tom.

But something fiercely alive and creative in Victoria Waide rebelled more fiercely than usual against such beliefs tonight, as she went downstairs and told Tom that she was ready for their walk. Her mother's voice followed them into the garden:

'Don't be too late, Vicky!'

Vicky thrust her hands into the pockets of her coat and made no answer. She hated the coat as much as she hated everything else to-night. It was of cheap blanket-cloth, and had once been white, but was now well-worn, shrunken from dry cleaning, and discoloured. It had been bought for a local tennis tournament in which Vicky had played with the same vigorous enthusiasm that she attacked anything in life. She hadn't won. Sports were not in her line. But it had amused her to enter the competition, and she had felt proud when in the local paper she saw her photograph in the group that had been taken. There was some satisfaction in knowing that amongst all those rather ham-faced, dull-looking, thick-ankled girls, her own slim beauty stood out arrestingly.

Tom Collinson took a cursory glance at Vicky's face, just discernible to him in the spring dusk. He could see her fiercely-knit brows and the passionate rebellion in her mouth. It worried him. He didn't know what to do or say. He wasn't really capable of dealing with Vicky's moods. He made some trite remark about the fine weather and the stars, to which she answered in monosyllables. Then he said, rather foolishly:

'Where shall we go?'

Vicky looked down the street. On either side there were little uniform houses with their little gardens and gates. There were lights shining behind blinds and curtains in most of the downstairs rooms. Here and there was a dark, empty house with boards up: 'To Be Sold.'

It struck her, not for the first time, that all the houses were of an appalling similarity. Yet each owner had made a pathetic attempt at planning something a little 'different' in his garden. Here, there were standard rose trees. There, a rockery. And everywhere, tulips vying with each other for colour and design. Here, a gate bore some stereotyped name: *Homeleigh* or *Bella Vista*, or *The Hollies*. There must be thousands of them in garden cities all over England, Vicky thought. Occasionally someone had tried to think of a more unusual name. They passed one gate marked *Jullundur*. No doubt the owner had been to India in his time and had retired, and this was his sad little effort at keeping fresh the memory of those other days. More glamorous days than any he could spend in Norman Park.

Vicky understood that. She could understand anybody wishing to get away from a place like this, even in dreams.

'Where shall we go?' repeated Tom Collinson.

She answered:

'Where is there except up and down streets like this? They're all the same.'

'You are a queer girl,' he said.

'Oh, don't talk about me,' she said. 'How's the farm?'

He cheered up. That was more in his line. He could talk at length about his poultry farm. He had talked about it so many times that Vicky felt that she knew the place. But she never wanted to go to it. Tom rarely touched on the one subject that appealed to her—the beauty of Sussex, and the old Sussex farmhouse in which he lived. It could only be lovely outside, not inside, if decorated and furnished by Tom! Tom was no artist, poor dear, and a thrifty man, at that. Most of the stuff would probably be massive and Victorian, bequeathed to him, by grandparents and aged aunts. He didn't talk much of the house. Only of his land—those acres spread with wire-netting, wooden houses, and thousands and thousands of stupid, senseless chickens, jerking their scrawny necks, gobbling their food, laying their eggs.

Tom ran his show on the intensive system. Lit up the houses at night so that the fowls laid twice as many eggs, because the poor idiots thought it was daytime again.

There was an outhouse in which the men washed and weighed the eggs, and packed them ready for despatch to London. Vicky knew that room very well by heart. Tom often said:

'You must come down and help wash the eggs sometime.'

As though she would like it! As though he were holding out a big temptation. It interested him of course. It was his whole life, that farm. On all other subjects he was dumb. Tonight he tried to add a touch of romance to it all, in his

25

awkward, simple way.

'You ought to see the incubators now. Hundreds of little fluffy chicks coming out. You can pick 'em up in handfuls. You'd like them, Vicky.'

'I'm sure I would,' she said, absently.

'We've got some new kittens, too.'

'Any puppies?' she asked.

'Some on the way,' he said. 'It'll be my spaniel's second litter. She's a good little thing. Best gun-dog I ever had. We've got a young foal, too.'

'There seems to be nothing else,' said Vicky, 'but giving birth, down on your farm.'

He was rather shocked, but laughed.

'That's the way of things, you know.'

'The spring, I suppose,' said Vicky.

He wasn't sure whether or not she was laughing at him. She really was a queer girl. But provocative. The beauty and nearness of her stirred his pulses. He slipped an arm through hers and tightened it against his side.

They stopped on the street corner.

'When are you coming down to see the farm, Vicky?'

'One day, perhaps.'

But her eyes were fixed on a hoarding which they had just reached. In the lamplight the big black letters stood out.

DANCE COMPETITION
NORMAN PARK TOWN HALL. JUNE 1ST.

In smaller print there followed details. Prizes were to be given, and the judges included a well-known film actress and a Mr. Paul Dallas who would give an exhibition dance with his partner, Dinah . . . late of Monte Carlo and the Argentine.

What visions that conjured up! The South of France. South America! All the exotic splendour of Southern nights, palms, orchids, and sleek men and women dancing to the lilt of a first-class band.

Vicky wanted to see the exhibition dance—and the film star who was judging the amateurs. She would have liked, passionately, to have entered for that competition. But she had nobody to dance with. She knew no young men except Tom, or that frightful spotty youth next door who could do nothing but take wireless sets to pieces and fail to put them together again. And one or two other dull, unenterprising young men who couldn't dance properly at any time, let alone go in for a competition.

Tom Collinson became aware that his companion was hardly listening to his rhapsodies on the farm. He followed her gaze to the poster.

'What's this—a local dance?' he asked.

'Yes,' said Vicky, and sighed.

'June 1st, eh? A Saturday—h'm——Perhaps I could leave Jones, my head-man, to see to things and drive up in the old Ford and take you to the show,' he said, anxious to please her.

She turned luminous eyes to him, her whole face lighting up.

'Oh, Tom, *would* you?'

'Yes, I'd like to, if it would amuse you. Of course, I can't dance much, but——'

'But I'd be able to see it all,' she broke in. 'Oh, I'd *love* to see the exhibition dance. The dancers must be good. They've been to Monte Carlo—and the Argentine.'

Something in her voice, her face, made him catch his breath. He wasn't concerned with the thought of the dance or the dancers and the fact that her imagination was fired by it. But he did know that he wanted this girl for his wife and that she was in his blood like a fever. Whether she was the right woman for him or the wrong, he didn't care. He wanted her, and he had always got what he wanted in his rather stolid, stubborn fashion.

He caught both her hands and said:

'Vicky, give me a chance—let's be engaged. Won't you, dear? I'll try to make you happy. I swear I will.'

The light died from her eyes and glamour faded. Here

27

she stood at the corner of Acacia Street in Norman Park, listening for the fourth or fifth time to a proposal from a man who meant nothing to her, except as a friend, and not a very intimate one at that. She and Tom were poles apart in thought and she was not in the least moved by him physically.

She supposed that some girls would think him good-looking, because he had a tall, straight figure, and broad shoulders, and he looked fit and strong and clean. But she did not like his tow-coloured hair, which was cut short and stood up in a rather bristly way on his head. Nor that scarlet complexion, and the rather pale eyelashes, and big, stupid mouth. His eyes were nice, blue, and kind. But it *was* a stupid face. There was no getting away from that. And when Vicky looked at his throat—he had rather a long neck with a very prominent Adam's apple—she felt a ridiculous inclination to laugh, because he really reminded her of a chicken. There were times when he thrust out his head in the same way. There was 'poultry farmer' written all over Tom. She couldn't marry him. She didn't love him. She could never love him.

She drew her hands gently away from his big, muscular fingers.

'I'm so sorry, Tom dear. You're so awfully nice to me. I do appreciate your offer. But I can't marry you. I don't care for you in that way, as you know. Please let's go on being friends.'

He looked bitterly disappointed, but had himself, as always, well in control. He coughed and cleared his throat.

'I do wish you'd change your mind, Vicky.'

'I can't, Tom. I don't want to get married, anyhow. Not yet.'

He looked down at her a trifle wistfully, then shrugged his shoulders.

'Oh, well—there it is. But I'm not going to give up hope.'

She sighed. She wished he would. But she was a little

28

touched by his insistent devotion. He said:

'I'll take you to the dance, if you want, anyhow.'

'It's frightfully nice of you,' she said, 'and I'm really grateful.'

They turned and walked back toward her home. She felt that it hadn't been a very profitable walk from his point of view, but grand from hers. It would be a thrill to go to the dance, even if she couldn't enter for the competition. It was something thrilling to look forward to.

When she got in, she found that her parents had retired to bed, but Freda, wearing glasses, was diligently working out some household accounts which she had been asked to do. She looked up at Vicky, and felt a stab of jealousy at the sight of that flushed and glowing face framed in the dark, silky curls. The child looked as though she had enjoyed her outing. Had she by any chance accepted Tom this time? But Vicky was quick to explain the reason for her excitement. She told Freda about the dance on June 1st.

Freda sniffed.

'Tom's much too nice to you—coming all the way up from the farm to take you to that silly thing.'

'Why don't *you* get someone to take you?'

'I don't want to see exhibition dances,' said Freda. 'I've other things to do.'

Vicky gave a long sigh, and shut her eyes. She wanted to shut out the sight of Freda's unfriendly face. She tried to visualise Paul Dallas . . . A nice name, Paul . . . She imagined that he would be slim and handsome, and move with incredible grace. He would enrapture Norman Park as he had enraptured the sophisticated crowds at Monte Carlo and in Rio. She wondered if he would notice her. What dress would she wear? She would have to beg that black velvet off Mum. She couldn't wear her own old blue taffeta rag which had lost all its colour in the process of being cleaned, and was splitting everywhere. If only Paul Dallas would see her, *notice* her, and ask her to dance. If only she could talk to him about getting a job, like his partner. She knew she could do it if she tried. She opened her eyes and looked down at her feet, which were small and arched, and at her little ankles, which were about half the size of Freda's. They were dancer's feet. If only they could carry her over shining floors miles and miles away from Norman Park, and the family, and poor old Tom!

Freda picked up her account books, rose, and cast a dark glance at Vicky.

'What have you got that silly look on your face for?'

'Mind your own business!' said Vicky hotly. 'I'm thinking about things which wouldn't interest *you*, anyhow. But one of these days you're not going to think I look silly. You're going to be sorry you've been so beastly to me!'

In her own room, she stood a moment, breathing fast, looking at the black velvet dress which she had worn earlier this evening, for her impersonation of Dolores Del Rio. She thought:

'I shall wear that, and I shall *make* Paul Dallas dance with me. I'm going to show Freda and the rest of them that I'm *not* so silly. I'm going to make something of my life. I am! I *am*!'

3

The exhibition dance given by Paul Dallas and his partner, Dinah, was the big hit of the evening at Norman Park Town Hall.

It was a very polished performance, and nobody appreciated it more than Victoria Waide, who sat beside Tom Collinson, the pupils of her eyes dilated with excitement, her lips parted, her heart beating at twice its normal rate.

She concentrated on every movement of that dance. And on the sleek and handsome young man who glided over the floor with such grace and ease that it took her breath away. Passionately she envied Dinah. They moved together so perfectly that it was as though they were one figure, the slender body of the girl in her white dress which sparkled with diamanté, held lightly yet firmly against the young man.

He was very debonair in his 'white tie and tails'. Like Fred Astaire, thought Vicky; slim and supple and with such nimble feet. Was he English or foreign? He had a touch of the South about him—glossy black hair, almond eyes, very white teeth. He fascinated her. She tried to imagine herself as Dinah, his partner, and thought how thrilling it must be—to dance like that so perfectly with him—always in the limelight—hand in hand, receiving the rapturous applause.

She wondered if he was in love with this Dinah, married to her, or just a friend. She had an immense curiosity to know something about their lives behind the scenes.

Now and then she made some excited little remark to

Tom, who answered in his fashion, slowly, and without much comprehension of her excitement.

'It looks all right to me,' was all he said when she exclaimed:

'Tom, isn't it *marvellous*?'

But his lack of enthusiasm and appreciation could not chill her own ardent pleasure this evening. She was adoring it all, even though she was disappointed that she could not enter for the competition.

Later, after the platinum blonde with diamond bracelets all the way up her arm, and who was supposed to be a well-known film star, had given away the prizes, and made a suitable speech, everybody danced.

Tom offered to do a waltz with Vicky, but she refused. Too well she knew his stumbling steps, his clumsiness. She did not want Paul Dallas to see her being pulled around by Tom, and having her toes trodden on.

But her moment came when she saw several young women going up to Paul and Dinah, asking for autographs. So she was not alone in her love of glamorous people, she thought. She wished she had an autograph album, but she had not. It had always seemed to her rather stupid and futile, collecting signatures. But she had a little programme with the names of the competitors and it suddenly flashed into her head that she could ask Paul Dallas to sign that. She saw him standing on the platform at the end of the hall from where the prizes had been given. He was talking to the man who played the drums in the band. Vicky suddenly stood up and said to Tom.

'I'll be back in a second.'

She threaded her way through the crowd of dancers, up to Paul Dallas. And now she was quite composed. She told herself that she must not appear like a foolish schoolgirl. She held her head high and took the last few steps toward him with almost studied grace.

Paul Dallas suddenly became aware of Victoria Waide. He took the cigarette from his lips and watched her approach. Ye gods, he thought, here was something far removed from those other badly made-up, cheaply-dressed young women in this suburb. What a little beauty! Moved divinely, had hair as black as his own, and a face which immediately arrested attention. Those shadowed cheekbones—like Dietrich's—very alluring. And what a pair of eyes! Unexpectedly blue with that black hair. Who the devil was she? He was quick to note that her velvet dress was shabby, but it fitted tightly enough to show the lovely curves of her young body.

Now she had reached him and was holding out a slip of pink paper.

'Mr. Dallas, will you sign this for me?'

'Why, of course,' he said, and gave her a flashing smile.

He was more flattered by that request than he had been by any of the others which had come his way this evening. He had been very bored. Besides, he had had the hell of a row with Dinah before they drove down to Norman Park. She was a bad-tempered little swine and their partnership wouldn't last much longer. It had been all right while they were lovers. But lately she had been attracted by an American with some money, and she was freezing up on him, Paul. He was fed up with her.

He scribbled his name on the programme and handed it back to the girl in the black velvet dress. How seriously her big blue eyes regarded him! He knew women—was experienced with them—but he felt that although this little suburban girl might be very young and naïve, there emanated a queer, but definite attraction from her. He gave her another charming smile and said:

'You didn't enter for the competition, did you?'

'No—I didn't . . .' Vicky folded the programme and pushed it nervously into her bag.

'But why? I'm sure you should have done so.'

'I hadn't a partner.'

'Are you here all alone, then?' Paul Dallas was far from bored now. This child was not only beautiful, but dead serious. Nothing flimsy or flirtatious about her. How the devil she had got to Norman Park, he did not know. She ought to be in the West End, dressed by an artist, on the stage or the films, dancing.

Vicky was explaining that she was not alone, but that her 'friend' could not dance. He ran a poultry farm and didn't have much chance to practise steps. Paul grimaced to himself. A poultry farmer. She *would* choose friends like that. Obviously she was longing for a thrill. Well, he would darn well give it to her.

'You mustn't go through the whole evening without a dance,' he said. 'I'm sure you're pretty good at it. How about having one with me?'

Vicky went crimson. Her eyes were enormous. Paul Dallas was intrigued by that surging wave of colour. He didn't know any modern girl could blush like that. How divinely shy and old-fashioned.

She said:

'Oh, I—I'm sure I couldn't—*with you*!'

'But yes, please!' he murmured, and put his cigarette under his foot. 'Your—friend—won't mind, will he?'

'I don't mind if he does,' said Vicky, with a little laugh that had a husky note to it.

'Now that's talking,' said Paul Dallas. 'Come along.'

Vicky pushed a truant black curl away from her flushed cheek. She felt intoxicated with excitement. She had *meant* the exhibition dancer to notice her. She had promised that to herself. But she had never for a moment thought that she would get a dance with him. That really was heavenly. What *would* the family say? Wouldn't Freda be sick with jealousy? No, perhaps she wouldn't care. It wouldn't mean anything to her. But it meant a lot to Vicky. And when Tom saw her—what would he say? Well, he would have no right to be cross. She didn't belong to him just because she had come to the dance with him. He knew he couldn't dance decently, himself.

Paul Dallas had thrown a hint to the band. They played what he wanted them to play. A new fox-trot. He took one of Vicky's hands, put an arm about her, and led her on to the floor.

For a moment she was terror-stricken. She was sure she would stumble, trip over him, make a little fool of herself, have him laughing at her. But she didn't do anything of the kind. So superb and expert was he, that she could not make a mistake. Skilfully he led, and somehow or other she managed to follow. She had never had such a dance. She wondered dizzily how they looked. She was like Dinah—merging into one with him as they moved. She had forgotten the very existence of Tom Collinson, and did not even bother to look in his direction as she passed his seat.

Paul talked to her while they danced. She liked his voice. It was smooth and a little mesmeric, like his whole personality. She had never known anybody quite so different from Tom. Tom was a big, blundering, awkward sort of fellow. Paul Dallas was a finished product of the world. His eyes did not avoid hers shyly. They were searching and intimate. It was very exciting. And the things he said were exciting, too.

He asked a lot of questions about herself, and she told him that she had lived with her family here in Norman Park most of her life. When he ventured to remark that it must be dull, she agreed, ardently. Yes, it *was* dull, and she was simply fed up with it.

'I can well understand that,' he said, 'because you're different. You're not like the other girls in this place. I can see that.'

'What do you think I'm like?' she asked, with an excited little laugh.

And to her immense satisfaction he answered:

'You remind me a little of Dietrich or Dolores Del Rio.'

She was enchanted.

'Do you know I've sometimes thought so?—I've often tried to impersonate Dolores—I think it's my cheekbones—and the way my eyes are set. But of course that's terribly conceited. I'm not like her really. I couldn't hope to be.'

'You might be anything if you tried,' he said.

'Do you think I could ever become an actress?'

'Go on the films, do you mean?'

'Yes. The thought of it has always fascinated me.'

'You might,' he said, 'or you might be a dancer. Like Dinah.'

Vicky looked round the room. She saw Paul's partner dancing with some man quite close to them. In the distance Vicky had thought her beautiful. Close up she did not think so. Dinah had good features and platinum fair curls, but her face was mercilessly hard. A mask of paint and powder.

Paul Dallas followed Vicky's gaze. He echoed her thoughts.

'Dinah doesn't look so good close up, eh? But she's effective with a spotlight on her.'

'Oh, if only I could dance like she does——' exclaimed Vicky.

'You've got to be trained,' he said, 'and I'm going to tell you something. I've never danced with any amateur who moves like you do. You're wizard.'

'But do you really think so?' The blood mounted to her face again.

He held her a little closer.

'I do. Little Miss Victoria.'

'Oh—h!' she laughed. 'How funny that sounds.'

'It's a grand name,' he said, 'and look here, I want to see some more of you. I know talent when I see it. You're no ordinary dancer. You know how to move. You've got lovely feet. You're rather lovely altogether, if you don't mind me telling you so.'

She didn't mind at all. She was enraptured. The evening had worked out in a big way for her. Of course she knew she mustn't believe half he said. It was just a lot of idle flattery. But it was terribly exciting, and so was this dance. She wished that it need never end.

'Why don't you train to become a dancer?' he was asking her. 'I could help you. I know everybody in the trade. It's a darn shame you haven't been working at it for the last four or five years—since you were a kid. But you say you're twenty now. That's not too late. A little hard work and you'd soon get to the top. I'll let you into a secret. My partner's thinking of getting married to a fellow in New York. I shall be looking for another girl. And then——' He paused and smiled down into her eyes significantly.

She was quite pale with emotion now.

'You're just laughing at me,' she said. 'You know I could never be your partner.'

He did know it. He was perfectly well aware that although this girl was a better mover than the average amateur, and damned attractive, she could never perform in public like Dinah, or one of her kind, who had trained for stage and ballet since they were small children.

But he saw no harm in encouraging Victoria Waide of Norman Park to change her mode of living. He was sorry for her—darned sorry. He hated to see a good thing wasted. It was a shame that such a lovely kid should go on living in a horrid little house in a garden city with nothing to look forward to but being taken out by a dreary farmer, or one of her family.

He, personally, was quite successful at his job—danced here, there, and everywhere, and although they were always second-rate appointments and he could never get into the front line, he liked to think of himself as a 'big noise'. Certainly he was a big noise to a girl like Victoria Waide. She wasn't to know that originally he came from the Ghetto, and was born of a poor Jewish family. That he had been in turn a chorus boy, a gigolo, a dance-instructor in the Argentine, and once—when he couldn't get anything else—a waiter in the South of France.

Sometimes starving, sometimes rich enough to live in a smart hotel, go to parties, meet a lot of chic people, and buy a lot of expensive clothes. He had his wits about him, an artistic sense, a flair for social climbing, and he was certainly a good dancer. For the last year or two, he and the girl, Dinah, who had joined him, had not wanted for engagements.

Today he liked to pose as a young man who came of good family, with a touch of Spanish blood which, he told people, accounted for his dark eyes and hair. He professed the greatest antipathy for the Jews. (Thanking God that his hair was not too curly and that his nose was straight.)

He was a good talker. He filled Vicky's ears with sensational stories of his dancing triumphs in Europe and South America. He told her in so many words that Dinah meant nothing to him except as a dancing partner, and that he was fancy-free. That intrigued Vicky, as he intended it should do. She saw no reason to disbelieve what he told her, and she felt that here was somebody who knew how to *live*, and who realised what she was missing. He suggested that she should learn to be a professional dancer. Well, why not? He would help her, he said. With the help of a man like Paul Dallas, surely she would be all right, Vicky thought. She would get somewhere. Even though that business about being his partner was just nonsense.

He said that he wanted to see her again; asked her to meet him in London. Why not? The family would kick up a fuss, but she wasn't going to be bullied and nagged into staying at home all her life. She was nearly twenty-one. It was time she took a firm stand with the family and told them that she intended to do what she wanted. Let Freda rave and rant if she wanted to. This was the most thrilling thing that had ever happened to Victoria Waide. This meeting, this dance with Paul Dallas. This chance that he was offering to help her make a career for herself.

'There's no reason why you shouldn't let me introduce you to a few people, anyhow,' Paul was murmuring in her ear. 'Give me your address when this dance is over and I'll get in touch with you.'

'All right,' said Vicky breathlessly, 'I will.'

The band was playing a waltz now. Paul Dallas smiled down into her luminous eyes.

'Like to go on?'

'If you—if I'm not a bore——' she stammered.

'A bore!' he repeated, 'but you're charming.'

She was very close to him now. His cheek rested against her hair as they waltzed languorously through the hall in which the lights had been effectively lowered.

As she listened to the tune, her heart leaped. *Glamorous Night*. This was, indeed, the most glamorous night of her life. Something that she had dreamed of and wanted.

> *'Fold your wings of love around me——*
> *Fold them close till they have bound me.*
> *I'm your slave and your defender.*
> *I surrender!'*

Paul's dark almond eyes were looking down into hers, a little warm and blurred.

'I think we were fated to meet,' he whispered. 'I shan't forget you, little Victoria Waide.'

She could not answer. She was dumb with ecstasy. But she knew that she could *never* forget him! And she was going to see him again. He was really going to help her dance for a living. What a triumph it would be. She would defy the whole family—all of them!

The waltz ended, and Paul Dallas had to let her go. Dinah was wanting to be driven back to London. He managed to scribble Vicky's address on a card. And he gave her his. She took it in trembling fingers and looked at it.

MR. PAUL DALLAS,
Palm Beach Club,
London, W.1.

Palm Beach Club! That sounded exciting. He explained that it was a little dance club just off Piccadilly, and he used it for a business address. He had no settled home. He was often abroad. But if she applied to the Palm Beach Club, she could always find him.

'Mind, I'm not going to wait for you to get in touch with

me,' were his parting words. 'I'm going to ring you. Or if you're not on the phone, I'll write, and you must come and have lunch with me and talk over your future.'

They said good-bye. He looked long and warmly into her shining eyes, took her hand and carried it to his lips in Continental style, bowing, clicking his heels together. Vicky had never had her hand kissed before. She had only seen it done on the films. She was glowing with a sense of her own beauty and success, and a renewed belief in the thrills of life, when she returned to Tom Collinson.

Tom had been sitting, smoking his pipe gloomily, watching Vicky dance with the 'dago', wondering how the devil she got to know him and feeling decidedly peeved that he had been left by himself.

The sight of Vicky's happy face and all the youthful enthusiasm that radiated from her did not have any effect on Tom, except, perhaps, to annoy him. He frowned at her.

'Well, you've been gone a nice long time.'

She sat down beside him and pulled out her powder-puff.

'I'm terribly sorry, Tom. But didn't you see who I was dancing with? That was Mr. Dallas, who gave the exhibition dance. Wasn't I lucky?'

'Were you?'

'Well, Tom, he's a frightfully well-known dancer—he's given exhibitions all over the world.'

'Well, that's no reason why *you* should make an exhibition of *your*self.'

'Oh, don't be so silly, Tom. I only danced with him. Didn't we look nice together?'

He thrust his pipe into his coat pocket.

'You always look all right to me. But I hate that sort of fellow. Oily sort of lounge lizard.'

The light died from Vicky's eyes. Her lips hardened.

'That's just being rude. Mr. Dallas isn't an "oily lounge lizard". He's a very clever dancer and famous. And just because he gave me a dance, I don't see why you should be so beastly, Tom. Anybody would think you didn't want me to enjoy myself.'

Tom looked at her awkwardly and ran his hands through his tow-coloured hair.

'Of course I do, Vicky, but——'

Vicky made haste to interrupt. She had an awful feeling that another proposal of marriage was coming from Tom at any moment. Quickly she said:

'Let's go home, shall we?'

He took her home. They boarded a bus, and rode in it in gloomy silence. Vicky hated that bus. It typified all the narrow economy of her life. Just as she hated the blanket-coat over her evening dress. She ought to have an ermine cape around her shoulders and be taken home in a taxi or a luxurious private car. Paul Dallas had a car. He had driven down from town with his partner. Her thoughts winged to the exhibition dance. She forgot about Tom Collinson. She shut her eyes, and in an ecstasy, remembered her dance with Paul, the way his dark, intimate eyes had looked into hers, and the way he had told her that they were 'fated to meet'.

Perhaps it *was* fate! At any rate, she had that little card with his address, inside her bag. She was going to see him again, and talk over her dancing career. She *must*.

When she had said good-night to Tom, he began to stammer an apology for being boorish. She cut it short and assured him that she had had a lovely time, and that she was grateful—oh, so much more grateful than he knew—that she had been taken to that dance. She knew that Tom would like to kiss her, but that was the last thing she wanted. She managed to get away from him, and let herself into the house.

She was still thinking about Paul as she groped her way up the dark little staircase. Then a door opened, and a shaft of light revealed the thin figure of Freda.

Vicky looked up at her sister almost pityingly. Poor old Freda! What was she ever to know of the warmth and excitement of life! Would any man ever tell her that he was 'fated to meet her'? If she looked dull and insipid in the daytime, she looked worse like this, in the white glare of electric light, wearing that unbecoming dressing-gown which she had made out of blue ripple-cloth, virtuously concealing a nightgown of shrimp pink 'art' silk. (She thought it quite dashing!) Poor Freda! Tight-lipped, shiny-nosed, disapproving as usual.

'You're very late!' she said in a hissing whisper which should have awakened her parents, if it didn't.

Vicky was much too enthralled with her night and her prospects for the future, to do otherwise than smile at her sister.

'The dance has only just ended,' she whispered back. 'Oh, Freda, it was grand!'

'H'm, well, I think it was very good of Tom to take you.'

The sisters were close together now, face to face. The one anæmic, thwarted, out of tune with life. The other vibrant, glowing, lovely. They looked into each other's eyes and understood nothing of each other. Sisters yet strangers. Scarcely even friends. When Vicky leaned forward to kiss Freda, she got the usual response. Freda turned a cheek, kissed the air, and grunted:

'Better not, I think I've got a cold coming.'

She always did that. She seemed to hate kissing anybody, and pleaded a perpetual cold.

Vicky went into her own little room, shut the door, and then took the card out of her bag.

MR. PAUL DALLAS,
Palm Beach Club,
London, W.1.

While she gazed at it her vivid imagination was working. She saw not this meagre bedroom, but a lovely ballroom with a polished floor, lights, and flowers. The sparkle of jewels. The lilt of a dance band. And herself in a glittering dress, such as Dinah had worn, floating into the spotlight, in Paul Dallas's arms. She heard the thrilling swell of applause as they bowed to the audience. And there were posters all over Norman Park. No, not Norman Park: London—Paris—New York. *Paul and Victoria*. No, that wouldn't do. *Paul and Vicky*. That sounded more modern. Or she might spell it with an 'i'. Like Vicki Baum, whose books she adored.

Paul and Vicki.

What a superb thought! And hadn't Paul hinted that it might be so? He had said that his partner was getting married, and that she, Vicky, must meet him in town and learn to dance professionally.

With a little long-drawn '*Oh-h-h-h!*' Vicky folded her arms around herself and gave herself a little hug. Life was good! Or, rather, life was *going* to be good. All the dreams she had dreamed were going to come true. The family, Freda, Tom . . . that would all fade into the background, and one day they would be forced to acknowledge that they had been fools to try to hold her back, to laugh at her, to make her settle down to this life which was no life at all, in Suburbia.

Vicky went to sleep that night feeling that she could hardly wait for tomorrow, and all that it might bring.

4

'It is obvious to me,' said Paul Dallas, 'that if you do not take a firm stand with your parents, you will get nowhere. And it is your duty to get somewhere. It is wrong for anybody so young and lovely as yourself to get into a rut and stay in it.'

Vicky listened to this piece of worldly wisdom breathlessly, as she had listened to all the other words which had been flowing smoothly from the lips of Paul Dallas during the last half-hour.

They were sitting in the lounge of the Regent Palace Hotel. It was the first time in her life that Vicky had ever been there. It seemed to her magnificent, breathtaking, so full of lights, of people, of sights and sounds far removed from the atmosphere of Norman Park that it was enough to make her forget that outside the sun was shining, the sky was blue, and that summer was nearly here. Everything was a thrill in this huge, gilded room, and particularly the sleek, handsome young man beside her, who was trying to tell her the way that she should go.

It was just over a week since she had seen him dance with his partner, Dinah, down in Norman Park. During that week she had seen him twice. She had been immensely satisfied and flattered when he had kept his word and communicated with her within twenty-four hours of their first meeting. Twice she had made some suitable excuse to get away from the family, and taken the electric train up to town at Paul Dallas's bidding.

The first time she had lunched with him, the family had thought she was up here for the day with an old school-friend. She hated lying, but it had to be done, otherwise she knew she would never have got away. She had been so excited and so shy at the same time, that she had hardly known what to say when Paul tried to persuade her to start out on her own and take up a career.

The next time, he had been rehearsing and only able to give her half an hour for tea. Now, here she was again, and much too enthralled by Paul and his philosophies to be interested when a waiter offered her a big tray covered with little sandwiches, or a grand choice of cake and pastries which she was still young enough to enjoy. Paul was asking her to leave home and become a dancer. She wanted to do it. Not only because she liked the idea of dancing and was completely enamoured of the prospects of leading what she thought would be a marvellous life, but because she wanted to be with Paul.

She *would* be with him. He had told her so many times, his dark almond eyes fixed upon her with that intimate tenderness which made her heart miss a beat. He said that she would be under his tuition, and that they would practise together, and always he hinted that one day, *one day* . . . she might step into Dinah's glittering little shoes.

'I know what you feel about quitting home,' Paul said to her this afternoon. He could be exceedingly tactful and sympathetic when he chose. 'But you owe it to yourself to make something out of your life. They have no right to hold you back. You say your sister isn't like you and that she is quite content down there. But you couldn't be. Why, you're so alive—such a beautiful, vital child——'

He broke off with an expressive gesture of a slim hand. He had an onyx ring on the little finger. (A ring which had been given to him by an infatuated, elderly woman in Monte Carlo.)

Victoria Waide bit her lip because it trembled a little. Paul was the most wonderful young man she had ever dreamed about. She was beginning to wonder whether *he* was the man whose idea she had cherished in her imagination ever since she first began to think about love.

It seemed to her miraculous that this successful dancer with his glamorous personality should worry about her—a little 'nobody' from the suburbs. At the same time, she felt assured now that she had not been such a little fool as the family thought her, to immerse herself in dreams of beauty and success. Hadn't she always told them at home that one day she would be *somebody*! Hadn't her mirror also told her, silently, what Paul Dallas never failed to say when they met. That she was beautiful. *Different* from other girls.

She felt an agony of embarrassment about her clothes. She had nothing really smart in which to meet Paul when she came up to town. She had asked her mother for a new hat, but met with no success. Mrs. Waide had told her to get last summer's straw cleaned and reblocked. She hated it. It was a flat sailor shape and she didn't think it suited her. So she carried it, confident that she looked better so, with the sleek blackness of her silky curls uncovered.

Her dress was last summer's too. Beastly cheap— picked up at a sale—a sort of sponge-cloth with no cut about it, pulled in at the waist with a patent belt, and with a little coatee. It was pale yellow. The colour suited her, and she had been extravagant enough to buy a bunch of violets at the station and pin them on her shoulder. She was glad she had done so, because as soon as he saw her, Paul had told her how sweet the violets were, and how symbolic of her.

'Divine shy things,' he had murmured. 'So very sweet!'

She had liked that, but she didn't want to be thought shy and sweet and like a violet. She wanted to become like Dinah—only more so. To be a subtle, sophisticated flower—like an orchid—and oh, Paul understood what she wanted. Nobody else had ever understood so well as he.

The young man beside her sipped his tea and looked at Vicky through his long, rather womanish lashes. He felt fairly confident of ultimate success in that quarter.

He was a man of moods, of sudden acute desires, of

equally sudden hates. At the moment he was quite infatuated with this little girl from Norman Park. An expert on feminine attire, he had seen at once that she was dressed about as cheaply and badly as she could be. That was the parents' fault. Give her the money and opportunity and she would show the taste. But despite what she was wearing, she was the loveliest girl in the place. And about as lovely as any girl he had ever met, anywhere.

He had never seen such eyes. The blueness, the brilliance of them, and those marvellous upcurled lashes! The dazzling complexion—she needed no rouge—and the passionate curve of her lips! She was a delicious combination of child and woman, of innocence and sophistication.

He half-believed that he was in love with her. At any rate he intended to become her lover. Whether she became a professional dancer or not was another question. But he harped on that subject because it was obviously the one which would draw her like a magnet into his arms.

Suddenly he said:

'Look here, Vicky, we'll have to come to some decision soon about you, because I'm leaving town.'

'Are you?' asked Vicky, aghast; and the dismay in her eyes was immensely flattering to his vanity.

He handed her his cigarette-case. A thin gold one. Another memento of his gigolo days. Vicky took a cigarette because she supposed she would be thought a baby if she didn't. But of course at home she never smoked. Mrs. Waide disapproved and Freda considered it a 'bad habit'. Not that they could have stopped her from smoking, any more than they prevented her from using lipstick. But she couldn't afford to buy cigarettes. She was kept so short of money.

Paul Dallas lighted her cigarette and for a moment his sleek black hair was very close to hers. He whispered:

'Sweet thing! Don't you want me to go away?'

The colour rushed to her face in the sensitive way which intrigued him.

'Of course I don't. You're the first—the first boyfriend I've ever really had.'

He drew back, laughing.

'What about the boyfriend who keeps chickens?'

'Oh, Tom!' said Vicky with a grimace. 'Tom's a friend in a way—but not——'

'But not the same as I am, eh?'

'No, not at all.'

'And what am I—to you?'

Her lashes drooped and the hot colour surged into her face again.

'Oh, I—I don't know.'

'Just somebody who wants you to take up dancing, eh?'

'Not . . . altogether . . .' she stammered.

He leaned near her again.

'I know what I'd *like* to be, Vicky. One day perhaps I'll tell you.'

She raised her eyes to his. They were such clear, candid eyes that the man felt a momentary twinge of conscience. Such conscience as he possessed. She was such a baby, really. Might be sixteen instead of twenty. It was money for jam. The easiest thing in the world to get Vicky completely under his influence. He wondered if he ought to do it. But compunction was short-lived in Paul Dallas. He had a twisted mind, and he twisted it now until he made himself believe that he would be doing her a good turn, not a bad one, if he could get her away from that family of hers. Out of that rut which was her present existence. Yes—a good turn. It would be a shame to go away and do nothing for her. But for the moment he'd better leave love-making alone. Obviously she was very sensitive and one false move might drive her away. So he adopted a more practical manner.

'Ah, well, one day I'll tell you a lot of things,' he said easily. 'But not just now. It's your career we want to think about.'

Vicky recovered herself. She had been on the verge of losing her emotional balance, thinking that Paul Dallas was going to make love to her. She respected him because he did not. She said:

'When are you going away?'

'In about a fortnight.'

'Where to?'

'Paris.'

'Paris!' she repeated, and sighed. There was magic in that name for her, just as there had been for centuries, for the women of England. The Paris of gorgeous clothes, chic little hats, jewels, cafés, and nightlife with a spice of wickedness. The city in fact which was not Paris at all, but a manufactured playground for the tourist.

Vicky had seen nothing of the world. Nothing much beyond the limits of Norman Park. She knew little of London, really. Perhaps once a year the family went there to do a matinée or Christmas shopping, or attend a celebration lunch given by a relative or friend. There were undreamed-of possibilities in London, for Vicky. But Paris meant the Continent—and she had been brought up to believe that anything that came out of that city was particularly choice. If a hat was a 'Paris model' it meant an extra half guinea, which put it out of her reach. Oh, yes, Paris was chic, the *dernier cri*, paradise for a pretty woman.

And Paul was going there! Of course Paul had often been there, danced there. Entranced, Vicky looked at him and said:

'You *are* lucky!'

He toyed with the idea of asking her to go with him, but said nothing. He flicked the ash from his cigarette and smiled at her.

'Before I leave London, you've got to make up your mind whether you're leaving home or not, little Miss Victoria.'

She said:

'Well, I can't go on like this . . . I mean just deceiving Mum and Dad right and left. I think I must tell them about you and about your suggestions for my future. I

49

must give them a chance to help me. Oh, I know you've offered to finance my training, but that I really couldn't accept. I must try to persuade Daddy to let me train. After all, he paid for Freda to go to the Domestic College. He should do something for me.'

When she said those things, they merely bored Paul. But of course he knew that Vicky had been brought up in the suburbs by narrow-minded people, who kept her there, and it was only natural that she should be suburban and narrow-minded, herself. But he'd soon alter *that*.

'Well, what do you want to do?' he asked.

'I want you to come to my home and meet the family,' she said.

Paul very nearly said: 'Heaven forbid!' but controlled himself.

'What good would that do?'

'Well, you might be able to talk them round.'

He was amused. He couldn't see himself talking the Waides round. He wouldn't understand them any more than they could understand him. But it was a piquant situation. He got a bit of a kick out of it. He had had so many devastating affairs with women all over Europe. It was something new to be interested in a girl like Victoria Waide, who, instead of being ready to step out and lead her life as she wanted, still submitted to the authority of her father and mother.

Vicky hung on his answer.

For all her intense desire to get away from Norman Park and spread her wings, she had that instinctive feeling that she belonged to her family and could not just walk out against all their wishes. Paul was wonderful—a marvellous talker. And it would be so perfect if he could persuade them to change their minds. Then she could set out on her dancing career without unpleasantness, or complete disruption from home.

'You really want me to go down and see your people?' Paul murmured.

'Yes.'

'All right then, I will,' he said.

'Oh, Paul, I can't thank you enough.'

His hand stole out and closed over hers, squeezing it surreptitiously.

'But you can.'

She was filled with ecstasy. Her fingers returned the pressure of his. She felt gloriously awake, *alive*. She felt that it was the most wonderful thing in the world that Fate should have thrown Paul Dallas across her path. If only poor old Tom knew what he had done when he had taken her to that dance! She tried to imagine how the family would receive Paul—what effect he would have upon Freda. Of course, she might hate him. But he was so charming. Freda wouldn't be flesh and blood if she didn't like him. He was a gentleman and looked like one in his smart suit and suede shoes and with that rose in his buttonhole. He had marvellous manners. No doubt he would win them over all round.

Vicky felt a growing sense of excitement and hopefulness. She was in the highest spirits when finally Paul said good-bye to her outside the Regent Palace. He had to go to a rehearsal, he said. But on Sunday—the day after to-morrow—he would come down to Norman Park and meet her people. She must ring him up at the Club and let him know whether or not they would receive him.

'They might tell you they won't have me in the house!' he smiled. 'And then what?'

'I won't let them do such a thing,' said Vicky. 'They've *got* to see you. There's no reason why they shouldn't.'

Paul's lips curled a little sardonically. There was every reason. But Vicky wouldn't know about that. What a kid she looked, standing there in the sunlight with her sailor hat on her black curls. He wanted to kiss that sweet, provocative mouth with its serious upper lip. Instead of which he took her hand and kissed it.

'*Au revoir*, Vicky. I've adored seeing you. Let me know about Sunday, and don't waver, my little one. Strike out on your own. This is the age when parents should take a back seat and youth should come into its own.'

Her eyes danced at him. He always said such wise, marvellous things. And that kiss on her hand had been just a little warmer, longer than his farewell salute at their last meeting. She could not help being thrilled by him. He held the golden key to the golden gateway which could open and admit her to an existence which she had consistently wanted, planned, built up in her mind.

When she left him, she was filled with the resolution to do as he said, to 'strike out' . . . take a firm stand and not let the family crush her down. This resolution stayed with her all the journey home, as did the memory of Paul's handsome eyes and caressing manner. So much so that she was sufficiently inspired to take courage and speak of him to the family that very same evening.

During supper—they never had late dinner because Mr. Waide had a weak digestion, and Edith, being a daily, went home early—Mrs. Waide noticed that Victoria had an unusually high colour and ate very little. She remarked upon it.

'You haven't got a temperature, have you?'

Vicky smiled and shook her head. Poor Mum! She never attributed anything about anybody to mental causes. All ills, in her eyes, were physical, and to be dealt with by thermometer, aspirin, and a variety of patent medicines which were tried out on the family at intervals.

Freda helped herself to a second poached egg, Vicky having declined it. Considering the amount of food that Freda consumed, it was astonishing she remained so pale and thin. But she always had a big appetite, added to which she abided by that proverb: *Waste not—want not.*

'What did you do up in town?' she asked her younger sister. 'You haven't told us much.'

Mr. Waide, who put on gold-rimmed glasses for the purpose of seeing his food, looked over the rim of them at Vicky. He, too, noticed her almost feverish colour.

'Been doing your face up for some show, my dear?' he asked mildly.

'No, Daddy,' said Vicky. 'Just a bit flushed.'

Then she was seized with courage. Her throat felt dry and her heart thumped. But she came into the open bravely.

'I met a young man in town today,' she said.

The other Waides laid down their knives and forks with one accord and looked at her.

The effect of such a declaration had the immediate result of creasing Mrs. Waide's face with the most anxious lines. Freda said sharply:

'What young man? Where?'

Vicky pushed back her chair and got down to her confession thoroughly. She told them everything. She explained that this young genius of an exhibition dancer had danced with her down here a week ago and was confident that she should train for the job. She had seen him twice in town (she saw no reason to add that she had never met her school-friend at all!) and that she had seen him again this afternoon, and that he wished to come down on Sunday to meet them and talk things over.

When she finished speaking, there was a momentary silence. Freda's pale, censorious eyes turned to her mother. She nodded her head once or twice in an *I-told-you-so* fashion. Mrs. Waide looked bewildered. Vicky's father, alone, seemed unconcerned, and he was the first to speak.

'Well, well, fancy that!' he said. 'You are a young monkey.'

'Young monkey!' repeated Freda. 'I should call her something else.'

Vicky swung round on her sister.

'There's no need for you to start being horrid. I haven't done anything criminal, have I? I suppose I'm allowed to make friends outside this house if I want to? Oh—I know you've none of you wanted me to have a career. But you can't stop me. I'm going to have one, and it'll be your fault if I do things behind your backs. I've told you the truth now, and I want you to meet Paul and talk to him. That's

53

quite above-board isn't it?'

Mrs. Waide found breath.

'Really, Vicky, there's no need to speak in that cheeky way.'

Vicky's eyes flashed.

'Mum, what *do* you think I am? A little girl at school?'

'I shan't say what I think,' came from Mrs. Waide, and immediately proceeded to do so. She broke into a tirade against her young daughter. Dad could be lenient and call her a 'young monkey', but Freda was right—there was another name for her. Meeting young men up in town without saying a word! Imagine it! A professional dancer, too, and she was already calling him by his Christian name! Thoroughly fast, it was, and anybody would agree.

Vicky listened in silence. She didn't think anyone would agree except Freda. She felt nothing but contempt for her family. One couldn't be decent and honest without getting into a row. They were the most un-understanding narrow-minded crowd. She felt sick and tired of them, and when her mother finished reproaching her, Vicky as good as told her so.

'You keep on at me,' she exclaimed, 'but I can't see what I've done that's so frightful. Honestly, it's ridiculous in these days. And heavens! It's a waste of time for us to nag at each other. Why can't we be friends and talk over things like reasonable people?'

Here Mr. Waide took off his spectacles and timidly ventured to interfere.

'The child's right, Gracie. Folks should be reasonable and able to discuss things, and she hasn't done anything so terrible.'

'Oh, of course you've always got Dad as a champion!' Freda sneered.

'Now, now,' said Mr. Waide. 'No quarrelling.'

'Well, all I ask,' said Vicky, 'is that you should see Paul on Sunday.'

'Paul what?' asked Mrs. Waide.

'Dallas.'

54

'What's the good of him coming here?' interposed Freda. 'Vicky won't be allowed to go on the stage.'

'It's nothing to do with you!' said Vicky.

'But we've told you you're not to take a job away from home,' said Mrs. Waide. 'And I think it's very wrong of you to have met this young man without our knowing it.'

'Well, that's your fault,' said Vicky bitterly. 'You see what I get if I do tell the truth and ask you to meet any particular friend of mine.'

'Mr. Waide helped himself to a chunk of cheese.

'The child's right, Gracie,' he repeated. 'If she wants us to meet the young man and talk to him, we should do so.'

'Do you want your daughter to become a professional dancer?' demanded Mrs. Waide.

'No, dear, I never said I did. Of course it's non-sense——' he coughed. 'But we can tell Mr.—er—Dallas that we'd rather Vicky didn't earn her own living, and must give up any idea of dancing.'

'Then I see no object in meeting him,' said Mrs. Waide.

Vicky pushed her chair back and stood up. Her face was hot with resentment.

'It isn't fair! I just won't have my life arranged for me like this.'

'Aren't we behaving nicely!' sneered Freda.

Vicky swung round on her sister.

'Oh, *you* don't want to dance, do you? *You* don't want to see life or live it as it should be lived! You just like sitting down to work out household accounts or knit a new jumper or—oh, because you feel like a glass of lukewarm milk, I don't see why I should!'

Freda flushed. She, too, stood up.

'Lukewarm milk, eh? You rude little beast!'

'Children! Children!' said Mr. Waide.

Then Mrs. Waide put the finishing touch to the scene by beginning to cry dismally into her handkerchief. Between sniffs and gulps, she accused Vicky of having wrong ideas, of being rebellious and ungrateful, told Freda that she was no help, and left no doubt in her husband's mind that he was of less use than anybody on the earth.

Vicky, having lost her temper, soon recovered it. She was warm-hearted and naturally affectionate. She did not want to make her mother cry nor be the cause of trouble. She tried cajolery. With an arm about her mother's shoulders, she begged for sympathy.

'I know I may be disappointing, Mum, but I have got something in me which makes me feel I just *can't* sit down and do nothing. And even if you don't let me learn to dance, will you please see Paul Dallas and let him talk to you.'

Freda said no more. She maintained a hostile and disapproving silence. Mrs. Waide thawed a little to Vicky's demonstrations of affection. She did not get much, even from her favourite daughter, and when she allowed herself to be human, she could not help loving Vicky. She told herself that perhaps Stanley was right. She ought to see Vicky's friends—particularly if they were male—or she would only have herself to blame if the girl went behind their backs.

'All right, we'll see this Mr. Dallas,' she said. 'You can ask him to tea on Sunday. But we're not going to allow you to be a professional dancer, and we shall tell him so, so get that into your head once and for all. Now please help clear away the things, because we're late, and Edith ought to be away by now.'

Vicky was as thrilled as a child. She kissed her mother's cheek, embraced her father, and started to collect the dirty crockery.

Her eyes shone with victory. She would ring Paul to-morrow from the Post Office call-box, she thought. She would tell him that the parents were willing to see him. The rest she would leave to him. She was certain that his powers of persuasion would take effect—even with her mother. Freda didn't count—wouldn't be allowed to count. She was an old stick-in-the-mud, anyhow.

Her heart sang within her:

'Sunday—and Paul! Sunday—and Paul!'

She felt happier than she had been for weeks, and glad that she had put everything on a right basis. The future could take care of itself.

5

But the enthusiastic heart of Vicky ceased its singing when that all-important Sunday came.

From the beginning, everything went wrong. Vicky's mother never ceased to remark that she 'thought she was making a great mistake' in having Mr. Dallas in the house. Freda was both freezing and sarcastic about it, and what Father said didn't matter, anyhow, so it couldn't disturb Vicky.

Even the weather was against them. It poured. Vicky had got up early to pick some of the first roses of the year for the drawing-room. But after a night's soaking they were bruised and bedraggled. Nothing in the garden was at its best. It was cold, too. It might have been March instead of June. Vicky knew that Paul was used to central heating—the luxury of modern flats and hotels. She dared to suggest that they might light a fire. Mrs. Waide looked at her as though she were mad.

'Fires in June? My *dear* child!'

Vicky, torn with anxiety that everything should be lovely for the wonderful young man who had brought such warmth and colour into her life, such new ideas and aspirations, felt exasperated.

'It may be June, but it's freezing! Why can't we have a fire? I'll pay for the coal.'

Then of course Freda had put in her spoke.

'You know the chimney's been swept and we don't light fires again till the autumn.'

Vicky pursed her lips.

'All right! Stick a fern in the grate, and I hope you perish!'

'Now don't start quarrelling on a Sunday,' said Mrs. Waide in an aggrieved voice.

Freda, removing the overall with which she had covered her best skirt and jumper, whilst she helped Edith make a few cakes, threw a withering look at her young sister.

'Oh, it doesn't matter, Mother. Being rude doesn't get anywhere with me. And all this fuss just because this young man's coming to tea! Humph! If our home isn't good enough for him, why did Vicky ask him?'

Vicky left the room without replying.

She was still too excited about Paul's coming, to let her irritation against the family get uppermost. But everything *did* look grey and drab, and she *did* wish the sun had been shining.

When Paul's car—a black and green racing saloon—rolled up outside the gates of the little house, Vicky's pride and pleasure made her heart pound. But an unaccountable nervousness came over her.

Supposing the visit wasn't a success! Supposing Paul didn't win the day. Everything would be lost. Oh, but it couldn't be! Something must be achieved this afternoon. The parents *must* be made to realise that she couldn't go on living here, doing nothing for the rest of time!

Edith let Mr. Dallas into the house, no doubt impressed by his faultless suit (grey flannel with a pin stripe), his slightly brown pointed suede shoes, the green hat which he removed from a glossy black head and handed to her with his hogskin driving gauntlets. A very smart young man who might have come off the stage, so Edith thought. So Vicky thought, too, when he stepped gracefully into the drawing-room. Her cheeks were hot. Her eyes shone as she held out her hand.

'Oh, it *is* good of you to come——' was all she could stammer.

'Hullo, Beautiful,' he said airily. And his almond eyes looked down into hers with an expression which made her young blood race through her veins. He made it so obvious that he was glad to see her.

The greeting, however, did not go down well with the family. Freda 'froze' on the young man the moment she looked at him. And Mrs. Waide was horrified by the intimacy of the manner in which he had addressed her young daughter. Mr. Waide, who only heard half that was going on, peered over his spectacles and said:

'Come in, come in! Nasty day for a drive, eh?'

'Filthy weather,' drawled Paul Dallas. 'I had a lousy run down.'

Mrs. Waide's eyes met those of her elder daughter. *Lousy*! Not a gentlemanly term.

Paul gave Mrs. Waide what was meant to be his most attractive smile. He was all for winning over 'the old girl'. But he got little response. Her fingers were limp as he pressed them, and when he looked at her pale, peevish face, he began to wonder how she had ever managed to produce a glowing, vital creature like Vicky. As for that elder sister—God, but she gave him the bird—the frozen mitt, all right! Acid-looking spinster! No wonder Vicky wanted to get away from such people and her home-life.

What a depressing little house. Frightful furniture. It depressed him. Secretly it reminded him that he had come from a home a lot worse than this, and he didn't wish to be reminded of *that*. He only wanted to remember that he was Paul Dallas; that he belonged to the over-heated hotel-lounges and ballrooms and an artificial atmosphere which was soothing to the senses—even if hard on the bank balance!

He sat down—gracefully—he couldn't do otherwise—crossed his long legs and accepted the cigarette which Vicky offered him!

Freda rang for tea. Vicky was left to break an embarrassing silence by remarking that Paul's car was 'a beauty'.

He liked to be impressive and to dramatise himself. He didn't tell them he had borrowed that car for the day from a pal. He talked 'cars' for the next twenty minutes, wishing to leave no room for doubt in the minds of these simple people that his next purchase would be a Rolls-Bentley. He believed in making a good start and letting them know right at the beginning what a fine fellow he was . . . what a success . . . what a condescension it was, sparing the time to come down to Norman Park.

With the exception of Vicky, the Waides were unmoved by anything that Paul Dallas said. They were not impressionable people. They didn't understand him, his method of speaking, or the aura with which he surrounded himself. To Vicky it meant glamour, glamour, *glamour*! To her, everything he said was right and wonderful.

Tea was not the triumph she had hoped it would be. The cakes were over-baked and not worth eating. The bread-and-butter was too thick. The tea much too strong. There came a paralysing moment when Paul asked if he could have China tea. Mrs. Waide stared at him blankly. China—at three shillings a pound—what next? Freda told him, icily, that they had none. Vicky, overcome with shame, said:

'But I do so agree with you. China is so fragrant and refreshing after this kitchen brew.'

'There are a great many people who prefer what you call "kitchen brew,"' said Freda; 'and I haven't noticed you ever wanting China before to-day, Vicky.'

Vicky cast her a furious glance. She was sure Paul must think them very second-rate people. But he cast her a liquid look from his handsome eyes and murmured:

'It doesn't matter, really.'

Freda, handing her mother a cake, whispered in her ear:

'Poisonous young man.'

Vicky, however, went on adoring her hero of the hour, and when tea was over, brought the conversation round to dancing. That was where the fun began. Paul started to rhapsodise about dancing, and on Vicky's budding genius.

'You've no idea how divinely she dances,' he told the family. 'She really shouldn't waste her time down here.'

Vicky stirred a trifle uncomfortably. She thought that that was a false move. And, indeed, it brought a snort of indignation from Mrs. Waide.

'I didn't know that Vicky *had* been wasting her time, Mr. Dallas.'

He spread out a slender, deprecating hand.

'But when she can dance so exquisitely—she should be trained—go to Paris——'

'Paris!' cut in Mr. Waide, pricking up his ears. 'No, no, I wouldn't let Vicky go abroad, and neither would her mother. We're neither of us lovers of the Continent. England's our home and good enough for all of us.'

'But, Dad,' protested Vicky, with crimson cheeks, 'Paul says there's a wonderful training school for dancers in Paris, and that's where I ought to go. After all, Freda had a training at the Domestic Economy School. Why shouldn't I——'

'I don't think you can quite compare a French dancing school with a college for Domestic Economy,' interrupted Freda.

Paul Dallas looked through his long lashes at Vicky's elder sister, and loathed her about as much as she loathed him. He began to feel impatient. He couldn't waste his time arguing with these senseless clods, he told himself. Vicky saw that he was irritated and her heart sank. If only the family would listen to Paul and not be so stupid and stubborn!

The next half-hour was as futile as it was unpleasant. None of Paul's arguments availed. His pictures of Vicky as a professional dancer held neither charm nor interest for the Waides. Mr. Waide loved Vicky dearly, but even he was not to be persuaded to give his permission to what he called 'a lot of stuff and nonsense'. Finally, Paul rose to his feet and declared aloud that he had wasted his time.

Mrs. Waide looked a little anxious. She did not like Mr. Dallas, but she had no wish for it to be said that she had not received Vicky's friend graciously, and been the perfect hostess. She began to murmur that she was sorry that they could not 'see eye to eye'. Freda, however, had no compunction about being downright rude.

'I should have thought Vicky would have known better than to bother you to come, if it was only to ask if she could be a dancer. The sooner she gets that idea out of her head, the better.'

Vicky, shaking with anger and disappointment, flashed at her sister:

'Oh, what *is* it to do with you?'

Paul shrugged his graceful shoulders.

'I don't think Miss Waide approves of me,' he murmured.

Freda kept her lips tightly shut and did not argue the point. Paul walked out of the room, and asked for his gloves and hat. Vicky gave them to him. She was near to tears.

'I'm so terribly sorry! Absolutely fed up with Freda for being so rude. And you've been so kind—and coming all this way——'

She broke off, biting a quivering underlip like a disappointed child.

Paul, whom the Waides had put in one of his worst moods, looked down at her and softened again. He saw no hurt, bewildered child, only a very alluring woman. God! but what a figure she had, what skin, what eyes! And was that all to be left down here in the suburbs to wilt and decay, to bloom for no lover other than her poultry farmer? It seemed to Paul a crime. He knew that he ought to let her alone—go out of her life and leave her to settle down as best she could. But he was much too selfish and greedy, added to which he still convinced himself that he would be a Good Samaritan if he got her out of Norman Park.

'Poor little Vicky,' he said tenderly. 'Walk to the car with me; it's stopped raining.'

She went with him, miserable, dependent on his every word. She dreaded his going—certain that he would never come back. He was the only worldly-wise, attractive young man she had ever come up against. And he was a well-known dancer. He could give her *her* chance. Was he to be allowed to vanish, just because the family could not understand him any more than they understood her? Just because Freda had been horrid, and the parents determined not to allow her an individual life of her own?

'I don't think it's fair!' she broke out passionately, as she and Paul reached the car. 'Do you?'

'That you should be bullied and hampered like this? No, I think it's most unfair,' he said. 'And you'll be crazy if you stand for it.'

She put her hands to her hot, flushed cheeks.

'What can I do?'

'Get out of it, of course.'

'But how? They won't pay for my training. They won't let me——'

'Don't worry about them,' he interrupted. 'Let me deal with this for you, Vicky.'

She looked up at him, breathing fast.

'But how? How?'

He took her arm and squeezed it.

'Listen, you funny little thing, you mustn't bury yourself down here. You don't want to live and die in Norman Park, when there are such lovely places in the world—heavenly places in the sunshine—where life is full and flowing, just as it should be for a gorgeous girl. Vicky, you mustn't stay here. You know that, don't you? And if you want to get away from it, you must have courage, my dear. Courage, do you understand?'

She nodded, half-suffocated by a mingled feeling of rapture and fear. Yes, she understood. Wasn't that how she had always felt? He was wonderful to know so much, to bother so much about her.

His hand moved down her arm to her wrist, and then closed over her hand.

'Listen, Vicky, be brave and step out of it—with me.'

'With you!' she repeated.

64

'Yes. To Paris next week,' he said dramatically.

Later, when Vicky went indoors, and the green and black racing car had roared away from the little house down the rain-soaked road, she was no longer trembling or glowing. She was rather white and silent.

The moment she entered the drawing-room, the family with one accord began to voice their opinions of Mr. Dallas.

'Dressed-up young puppy,' was Mr. Waide's comment. 'Shouldn't think he's ever done an honest day's work in his life.'

'No,' agreed Mrs. Waide. 'And fancy Vicky preferring such a boy to a good fellow like Tom Collinson.'

'*I* don't think much of her taste,' put in Freda.

Vicky looked at them all through half-closed eyes, her expression one of profound contempt. She said:

'I've never heard anything so ridiculous. You call him a dressed-up young puppy just because he's got nice clothes. You say he doesn't work, yet he's a well-known exhibition dancer, and a dancer's life is admittedly one of the most strenuous anybody can lead. As for my taste, I prefer it to yours, that's all.'

'Say what you like,' said Mrs. Waide, 'I wouldn't let you have anything to do with that young man, whether you wanted to learn to dance or not.'

Vicky clenched her hands. She didn't want to work herself into a rage. It was so futile. She said:

'You don't understand Paul any more than you've ever understood me.'

'*I* understand you all right,' said her mother grimly. 'What you want is a good talking to, Vicky, and it's a pity your father doesn't give it to you.'

Mr. Waide pulled his ear.

'Oh, well, the child's still young, Gracie,' he mumbled, 'and I don't suppose she means any harm. But of course it *is* a lot of nonsense, this wanting to dance for a living.'

'A lot of nonsense, is it?' said Vicky, her voice ice-cold. 'Well, we shall see about that.'

She turned and walked out of the room.

Up in her little bedroom she stood for a moment at the window staring across the little patch of lawn. The rainstorm had been heavy. There were puddles everywhere. The sun was just breaking through ragged clouds. A sudden gleam of gold before twilight. And it seemed to Vicky like an omen.

After the storms, the setbacks, life was going to be sunny and good. She could have everything that she wanted *if she was courageous enough to take it*. That was what Paul had said. Paul was right. One never got anywhere by sitting down and waiting for plums to fall into one's lap.

She would never get anywhere if she stayed here with the family and let them direct her life in the narrow, dull, heavy way in which they directed their own. Out there in the road, just now, she had told Paul she would let him take her away. She had given her word. A tremendous undertaking, but she had given it in a moment of terrific emotionalism. That was the only way to do things—on the spur of the moment—without too much thinking or scheming. She didn't want to lose courage, back out and consign herself to all the miseries and monotonies against which she had been fighting for months.

The parents refused their sanction to her training as a dancer, so she must set to work to make her career without asking permission. Real artists, Paul had said just now, fought their way to the top through hideous difficulties. She might be miserable or homesick or afraid, sometimes, that she had taken a wrong step, but it would come right in the end. She would see. When she became a world-famous dancer, she would realise how well worth while were all the early sacrifices. If, on the other hand, she listened to the voice of conscience and duty, and clung to the old shibboleths and customs, it would prove that she was no artist—that there was nothing vital in her.

She didn't want to do that. And Paul said that he would help if only she would trust him and put herself in his hands.

He was not asking her to do anything wrong. There was no suggestion of him playing the lover. He was just going to take her to Paris and put her into the care of a woman-friend whom he said was a first-class teacher. Later, when she began to earn money, she could pay him back.

Vicky had argued wildly at first. She could not take his money. But he had been subtle in his counter-arguments, and finally had made her feel that she owed it to the great art of dancing itself, to take this chance; to give the world the dancer for which it had been waiting. She would be greater than Dinah, he said. As good as any of Fred Astaire's partners. She would get well beyond him, Paul, in time, if she forged ahead.

She found it hard to credit half that he said, but she believed some of it; enough to convince her that she should not miss this opportunity, no matter what it cost her to take it.

Of course he had hinted that he, personally, was deeply interested in her, not only as a dancing partner, but as *Vicky*—and that one day he might want her to be more than Dinah had ever been—his wife, in effect. Yes, he even hinted at marriage. But over that subject he had skimmed lightly and delicately, knowing that it was better not to scare her with more than that suggestion of the great physical appeal she had for him. It was the word 'art' which he used all the time. Playing upon Vicky's vanity and her theatrical sense; through that, winning her confidence.

She had promised to get a passport, meet him in London next Tuesday, and go to Paris with him, to his friend Madame Simone.

Dinah would not be crossing with him. She was going at a later date, Paul said. So he could take care of Vicky, until he got her safely into Madame Simone's hands.

At first Vicky wanted to tell her parents outright that

67

she intended to leave home. But Paul was quick to dissuade her from that. He respected her desire for honesty, he said, but she was not yet twenty-one, and if the parents liked to make a fuss, they could stop him from taking her across the Channel. Once there, it would be so much more difficult for them to make a row. If she wished, she could send them a wire from the boat. Once they knew that she had gone and was determined to go her own way, they would resign themselves to it.

Vicky agreed to everything. Yet now, when she thought it over, it all seemed overwhelming! Frightening! She, who had never been away from her family for longer than a few hours, to leave them altogether—to go to France—in the care of a young man whom she had only met three or four times! Wasn't it an awful risk?

She was not an ignoramus. She knew that girls had to be 'careful', and that sort of thing. But she was sure that she could take care of herself. It was Vicky's very self-confidence which was her worst enemy at this moment in her career. She was so certain of her own judgment. Paul was all right, Paul wouldn't let her down. He was interested solely in her *art*, and that was what she was going to pursue.

What *would* Dad and Mum and Freda say when she'd gone? They'd be horrified. Mum and Dad would be terribly upset. Freda, probably, wouldn't care. She'd say: 'Good riddance to bad rubbish.' Anyhow, it would be an awful moment when they got her wire. Poor dears! Vicky pitied them. She didn't want to hurt and worry them. They'd always been kind, according to their lights. And there was Tom. Poor old Tom would be very cut up. He was such a faithful suitor. But when she compared Tom with Paul—it was Paul who won every time.

It was no hysterical impulse which led Vicky to carry out her scheme, and gave her courage to see it through. It was her very real belief in herself and the career which Paul prophesied would be hers. She had never really been calmer, more self-possessed, nor on more friendly terms with everybody in the house than during those forty-eight hours preceding her departure. So meek and mild and friendly was she, indeed, that Mrs. Waide congratulated herself that Vicky had taken a turn for the better and was settling down, although Freda sarcastically remarked that her younger sister couldn't be well because she was being so agreeable.

Mr. Waide, as usual, saw nothing that was not pushed under his nose. But it was the little kindly, simple man for whom Vicky had the greatest affection, and whom she most hated to leave. She was glad, when the time came, that she had taken Paul's advice, and slipped away from the house before anybody could realise that she was gone.

6

It is a dismal fact that nine-tenths of the things to which human beings look forward intensely, disappoint them in the end. In other words, anticipation is invariably more exciting and wonderful than realisation. But these were things which Vicky, like everybody else, had to discover for herself in the fullness of time.

When she set out for France with Paul Dallas, she was still in the throes of wildest anticipation. Her common-sense, her judgment were warped. Her vision was blinded by the veil which the unscrupulous young man had deliberately thrown across her eyes.

She left Norman Park, and the family whose control she had accepted for so long, believing implicitly that it was for the best—that she was taking the courageous line directed by Paul, and that it would lead her straight to glory.

But some of the anticipatory thrills faded within a few hours of running away. The escape was a terrific excitement. Stealing through the back door on Edith's after-noon out, with a suitcase (it was impossible to get away with a trunk, but she would ask the family to send that on), running down the road to the bus, getting to the station, then being met at Victoria by Paul, who was charming, obviously delighted with her for taking the plunge, and ready to bear her off on the night-boat to Paris.

She could take a sleeping-bunk in the women's dormi-tory, he told her, and rest until they reached Dieppe. They would be in Paris in time for breakfast. Paul had chosen the Newhaven-Dieppe route, because although it was the longest, it was the cheapest. Thence in Paris to Madame Simone's house. Then she could dance with him, and Madame would see how good she was.

So the great adventure began, and Vicky was so stimulated by the whole thing and by the word 'CAREER' which Paul tactfully quoted on every occasion, that she felt scarce a pang at leaving the family. She would miss them in a way, of course. No matter how dull home life, one was bound to miss the habits and customs of a lifetime. But if she felt any real distress, it was for them. She knew how appalled they would be when they got her wire. For that she was truly sorry. But for nothing else.

For Paul she felt warm gratitude and admiration. A shy, half-awakened emotion trembling on the brink of something much more breathless and exciting than mere platonic friendship. But there had been no time in her mind for emotions of that kind except in the vaguest way. At the moment, nothing mattered but dancing, and Paul Dallas was the central figure around which her young ardent hopes whirled and circled impetuously.

So long as she was with Paul, she was all right. He was a charming cavalier, attentive and ready with flattering words, always encouraging. He would not let her get depressed.

'You've done the right thing, my dear,' he told her, as they sat in the boat-train, 'and you will never regret it.'

'But I do hate knowing that you're paying for my fare—for everything,' Vicky said with a sigh.

'Money doesn't matter to me,' said Paul in his most lordly way.

But he was considering in his mind how much he was prepared to spend upon this girl. He was mean to everybody except himself. For the moment his desires were concentrated upon Victoria Waide. It was really himself he was considering, when he carried her off from her home.

71

With cool, critical gaze he summed up her appearance, despising her cheap tweed coat, her handbag which looked as though it had come out of a third-class sale, and those cheap shoes which he particularly loathed. For those little slim dancing feet, there should be high-heeled Paris shoes. And for that perfect figure, lovely dresses, furs and jewels (one could buy marvellous imitation jewellery in Paris!). He would spend a bit on her over there. Make her a fitting companion for Paul Dallas. And once he got her to that gay city, he would use all his fascination to get across that touch of the prude in her.

He knew that she wouldn't be easy, but that appealed to him. He was sick of the elderly women who flung themselves readily into his graceful hands. His jaded fancy was no longer stirred by professional dancers such as his partner, Dinah.

But Vicky was fresh, sweet, and wholesome. Very alluring, because there was nothing of the bread-and-butter miss about her. She had depth and mystery. He would have that black silky hair perfectly cut at Antoine's in Paris. He would choose her lipstick, rouge, face-powder, eyelash-shadow. She could become a raving beauty in experienced hands. But he wasn't going to do it if she turned the traffic signals to 'Stop'. She must learn to be charming to him. Well—time would tell. And between here and Paris he would have to think of the lies that he would have to tell and the excuses, once he got her to Paris and she discovered that Madame Simone was no dancing instructress, merely the proprietress of the small, flashy hotel at which Paul usually stayed when he was there.

He could work cleverly upon Vicky's imagination and did so while they were together. But some of her high spirits evaporated once she separated from him, and went down in the women's dormitory at the bottom of the boat.

It was her first experience of a Channel crossing, and the night was none too good. The weather was playing pranks, and on this June night there was no moon to cast a tender benediction upon Victoria Waide. A brisk wind lashed the waves to a most unpleasant choppiness, and with it came a driving rain. A truly British crossing, singularly hard on an inexperienced traveller.

Vicky speedily discovered that she was not a good sailor. The dormitory was indescribably hot and stuffy. No portholes could be opened because of the rough weather. The waves dashed against the glass, booming and splashing as the boat pitched and tossed. Everybody was ill, and Vicky was no exception.

During those three and a half hours, she lay on the narrow bunk, covered with a blanket, cold and shivering one moment, hot the next, and unutterably miserable. Sea-sickness is no aid to cheerful reflection. The worse she felt physically, the lower Vicky's spirits drooped. Until, just before the boat put in at Dieppe, she had become a wretched, rather frightened young girl wondering how she could have been so mad. The gay, brave adventurer had vanished. Even the thought of Paul and his glowing promises for her future could not comfort Vicky. She turned her face to the hard pillow and cried a little, half wishing she was back in her bedroom at Norman Park, with Mum and Freda within calling distance.

Mum was pretty good when one was ill, and oh heavens, she felt ghastly! Her head was splitting. And the sounds of misery issuing from women in all directions increased her sense of disgust and discomfort. What *had* she done this thing for? When *would* the boat stop rolling?

In the early hours of the morning Victoria Waide, feeling and looking a wreck, struggled off her bunk on to the floor, thanking God that the stewardess had announced that they were just coming into Dieppe harbour. Certainly the boat seemed steadier. She could stand without feeling giddy. All the other women were struggling on to their feet, too. There were a good many mutters of: 'Thank God *that's* over!' in both French and English. A child was still crying dismally in its mother's arms. Vicky pitied the mother. It was bad enough to have

73

to look after oneself. She wondered if Paul, in the men's dormitory, had been ill.

She glanced in her pocket mirror and was aghast at her appearance. She looked green. She tried to comb her hair and powder her nose, and put a little colour on her pale lips. What *would* Paul think of her?

When she struggled on to the deck and found Paul, she was still far from happy either in mind or body. It was a gloomy young face which she presented to Paul when she discovered him. She was surprised to find how little he was affected by the crossing. He seemed to have spent most of the night smoking, drinking, and playing cards. She felt rather resentful because he was so airy and nonchalant.

'Haven't you enjoyed your sea voyage?' he asked.

'Oh! It was awful!' she groaned.

'Never mind,' he said. 'We'll be in the boat-train for Paris in a moment. Have a drink.'

She shook her head.

Paul looked at her with some distaste. He hated sickness in any shape or form, and there was nothing very glamorous about Vicky's appearance just now.

She saw his expression and felt more miserable. She wished he would be a little sympathetic. She was conscious of an ever-growing presentiment that she had done the wrong thing by coming away with Paul Dallas.

'Did you send that wire off to my mother?' she asked in a low voice.

'Of course I did.'

'I wonder what they're thinking now.'

'What do you care, Beautiful?' he laughed.

She did not join in the laugh. In a way she *did* care. She was not as cold-blooded as all that. Paul was not a patient young man. He was spoiled and exacting. He would not waste the time coaxing Vicky into a good humour. So he let her alone, and spoke to a man with whom he had been drinking. Vicky felt altogether wretched as they passed

74

through the Customs and into the boat-train for Paris.

Once the train had started, Paul, who had had plenty to drink on the boat, settled himself in a corner, put his well-shod feet on a suitcase, and announced that he would sleep.

Vicky, in the corner opposite him, felt not at all sleepy; just nervy and wideawake. A little more colour had come back into her face. Paul turned his attention to her. Something very young and sweet about her roused him to as much tenderness as he was capable of feeling. But it was a tenderness which took a selfish form. He wanted to recapture her absolute belief in him, and prepare her for what was to come.

He leaned forward and took both her hands.

'Poor little Vicky. She isn't enjoying her journey.'

A lump stuck in Vicky's throat.

'Oh, yes, I am—quite. It's all right now I'm off the sea.'

'We're lucky to have this carriage alone,' he said significantly.

She looked on either side of her at the windows. The blinds were down. Certainly they were alone. They were leaving Dieppe behind and gaining speed into the night. Heading for Paris! Some of the thrill returned to her. Her fingers tightened over Paul's.

'I'm lucky altogether, I know,' she said.

'So am I,' he said, 'to be alone with you like this. . . . *like this . . .*'

He was pulling her slowly toward him, and the next thing she knew was that he had drawn her right down into his arms. He took off her hat, and threaded his fingers through her hair. His lips were very close to hers.

'Can't I make you forget that lousy crossing by telling you how lovely you are—how made for love—my little Miss Victoria.'

She was momentarily too surprised by his love-making to answer. But she sat stiffly in his embrace. No man had ever touched her—like this. She was not sure that she

75

liked it. Yet he was attractive. Those handsome dark eyes of his looked swimmingly down into hers. Was this love? The passionate and enthralling romance of which she had dreamed? Was Paul in love with her? A host of bewildered questions chased through her mind, leaving her confused, uncertain. She hadn't really come away with him expecting to be plunged into a love-affair. At the moment she only wanted to make her career.

But Paul was fired to passion by the softness, the sweet youth of her. Losing his head a little, he pulled her head down to his shoulder and closed those red, half-parted lips with a long kiss. The first real kiss of passion Vicky had ever received.

It woke in her a dozen conflicting sensations. She was half thrilled, wholly afraid. She did not surrender. She did not fight. She received that kiss passively, still asking herself whether she had meant this to be included in their programme. Then the insistent pressure of his hands and lips became unutterably embarrassing and she could no longer bear it. She knew in her heart that she was in love with love, with the thought of a dancing career, rather than with this young man himself. She pushed him away and slid back to her own seat, her face crimson, her breath coming fast.

'You mustn't—really!'

'Mustn't what?' he asked in an aggrieved voice.

Her lack of response had annoyed him. He liked to believe that a caress from him would send any girl into a delirium.

'Mustn't make love to me,' she said, swallowing hard.

'Why in heaven's name not?'

'Because I—you—oh, I don't know,' she stammered.

Paul gave her a long look, pursed in his lips, then settled himself down and crossed his arms over his chest.

'Anybody would think you didn't like my kisses.'

She remained silent. She wanted to please him. And he did attract her. She might so easily have been in love with him if he'd treated her in the right way.

76

But he was too inflated with his own sense of importance and fascination to make a good lover for a shy girl,
and too used to women like Dinah who received kisses
and caresses in the same spirit in which she accepted
cocktails.

'We do live up to our name, don't we, Victoria?' Paul
suddenly sneered.

'Oh, Paul, don't be cross with me, please. But I——'

'Don't worry,' he broke in; 'I'm going to sleep. I don't
wish to force my attentions upon any woman.'

His eyes closed. He said no more. Feeling rebuffed,
Vicky stared at him. She saw that she had offended him.
After all his goodness to her, she hated having done that.
But somehow she had not been able to respond to his
passion.

She hated him to be curt and sarcastic. After all, she
had left home and come away with him and she had
nobody else in the world to talk to, depend upon. She felt
suddenly unutterably alone, sitting there in the train going
to Paris with Paul. She had never been more conscious of
the fact that he was a total stranger and that she really
knew nothing about him or his character. His face in
repose was sculptured, handsome enough with the long,
dark lashes curving against the ivory pallor of his cheeks.
It was almost effeminately beautiful, but there was a touch
of cruelty in those lips, of coarseness in the flared nostrils.
Vicky turned her gaze away. The frightened feeling that
she had had in the boat was coming over her again.

What did Paul really expect of her? Ought she to allow
him to be her lover if he wished to be? But she couldn't if
she didn't love him that way. If she wasn't *completely* in
love. Hadn't she laid herself open to this sort of thing by
travelling alone in his company and at night? She really
had only herself to blame if it was so. But she was very
disappointed, because, in England, Paul had given her no
reason to believe that he expected love from her or wished
to give it. Certainly he had hinted that one day . . . but
only *hinted* . . . and it was to help her become a dancer

77

that he had *really* taken her away.

She began to wonder what his attitude would be once they got to Paris. It was going to be awful if he wanted more than friendship in return for what he was doing. It must be remembered that he was paying for her journey and her training.

Vicky put a hand up to her lips. She was on the verge of tears. And she was slowly but surely getting a proper perspective of Paul, herself, and the whole mad thing that she had done. That it was complete folly, she now realised, but it was much too late to turn back. She must go on.

She could never go home and confess that she had behaved crazily and that she could never make a career for herself. She *must* learn to dance: and she must manage Paul, too; not offend him again, and endeavour not to let personal feelings upset the whole apple-cart.

But the memory of his lips and of his hands upon her destroyed her peace of mind. She knew that she was *afraid*.

She felt suddenly unable to sit here and go on thinking while Paul slept serenely, egotist that he was! Her tears were flowing now, and she could not restrain them. She did not want him to open his eyes and see her crying. He would only have further cause for sarcastic comments upon her 'Victorian' outlook.

Quietly she made her exit from the carriage into the corridor and shut the door behind her. The train whistled shrilly, rattling through the blackness—bringing her nearer Paris—and what? If only she knew! If only she could get back her feeling of confidence in Paul, and that gay, adventurous thrill with which she had started out.

Suddenly Vicky lost mastery, and putting her face in her hands, she wept heart-brokenly.

After a pause, she felt a touch on her shoulder. A man's pleasant, cultured voice said:

'I beg your pardon, but are you feeling ill? Is there anything I can do?'

She looked up, pressing a handkerchief to her mouth. She felt overcome with shame that a stranger should discover her crying like this, in a corridor of the Paris express.

She found herself looking up at a man whom she thought at first to be much older than he was, because he wore horn-rimmed glasses, had a touch of grey in his hair, and a rather lined, thin face. She discovered later that he was only twenty-eight, but had lived many years in the tropics where a good deal of malaria-fever had aged him.

He was not handsome in the accepted sense, but had a distinguished look and kind, clever eyes. His manner inspired confidence. Vicky, badly in need of human contact at this moment, did not obey the instructions she had always had from her mother 'never to speak to a strange man'.

She said:

'It's very nice of you—but I—I'm all right, thank you.'

'Are you sure?'

'Um,' she said, and blew her nose rather forlornly.

It was the forlorn gesture and the sight of tears in the most beautiful blue eyes into which he had ever looked, that made Digby Farnel's heart go out to the young girl.

She seemed such a child—he judged her to be about fifteen or sixteen—seen in the dim light of the corridor, with her black curls and her tears.

Digby Farnel was a man of strength and decision, ruthless with himself and with those whom he disliked. For the very young and helpless he had the utmost sympathy. Children or animals in distress, he maintained, always made a fool of him.

He said:

'I don't think you're all right at all. I think you're feeling thoroughly miserable. Are you by yourself?'

Vicky, the handkerchief still against her mouth, glanced at the carriage in which Paul was slumbering. There was a growing resentment within her against Paul.

79

'M-more or less,' she said on a sob.

'Going over to France to school or something?'

That made her smile. He saw how lovely she could look when she smiled. He was intrigued by her high cheekbones, the blueness of her eyes, and the blackness of her hair. An Irish strain, he judged. Poor little thing, she looked simply wretched.

'No, I'm not going to school, exactly. I'm going to learn to dance.'

'Well, it doesn't seem to be making you very gay,' said Digby Farnel. 'And if you're more or less alone, how about coming and having a chat, and let's see if we can't cheer you up.'

'Oh, no, I couldn't possibly!' said Vicky.

Digby took a packet of cigarettes from his coat pocket and looked at her over the tortoiseshell rim of his glasses.

'Oh? Why not?' he asked.

'Well—I—I *am* with somebody.'

'Chaperone?'

Vicky felt she must explain herself.

'I'm not a kid, you know.'

'Aren't you? How old are you?'

'Twenty.'

He paused in the act of lighting his cigarette.

'Good lord, are you really? You must have thought me very impertinent, but looks are so very deceptive, and it's none too light in this corridor.'

'That's all right,' said Vicky miserably.

He wondered who she was and whom she was with. Twenty. Out here weeping alone in the corridor! He still felt she was only a little girl and that he ought to do something for her.

'Is there anything to prevent you having a cigarette with me and a talk?' he asked.

'I—it's very kind of you—but I don't think you could do anything to help. I—I'm just a bit worried about my future. As a matter of fact I've just run away from my home, if it interests you.'

It did interest him vastly. He said:

'I'd like to hear about it. Look here—I'm in the next compartment to yours. Can't you tell whoever you're with that you've met an old friend and want a chat?'

'You're not exactly an old friend,' she said, with the ghost of a smile.

'Then let me be a new one,' he said, and smiled back. 'Digby Farnel, at your service. I don't think I have a card. But my address in London is the Oxford and Cambridge Club.'

His was a very boyish and charming smile. It transformed Digby Farnel's face into something more than mere good looks. Vicky was not much of a judge of character, but she did feel a queer confidence in this stranger, with his grave, yet tender eyes and that delightful smile. He was so much older than she was. Older than Paul. Oh, quite different from Paul. There was nothing sleek, handsome, or exciting about him. But he gave one a feeling of power, of knowledge, of *security*.

'It's awfully kind of you,' she said; 'but I think I ought to go back to my own carriage. My—my friend might wake and be cross, if I talked to you.'

Digby Farnel felt suddenly worried about this girl. Who was she with? Where did she come from? What was the trouble? They were on French soil. He was an Englishman, and this girl was English, and inspired him to an almost patriotic wish to protect her if she needed protection.

'Just tell me one thing,' he said: 'Are you in need of any help or advice? You say you've run away from home. Would you think me impertinent if I asked you to tell me just a little more before you go. You make me feel quite anxious, you know.'

That made her smile again.

'It's awfully nice of you. But I'm all right. At least I think so. My—my friend is—Paul Dallas. He's a well-known exhibition dancer.'

Digby Farnel did not know the name. But then he was

not interested in exhibition dancers. He liked the Russian Ballet, and if he attended a dance himself, he enjoyed it. But he had never met any of the professionals. His brows met in a frown. He lit a cigarette, took a breath of it, and peered through the dimness at the girls' face. It was strangely intriguing in this light, and heavens, what lashes she had! Like a child's, silky black, curling upwards.

'Oh! So you've run away with a professional dancer, have you? Is it an elopement, then?'

He saw the blood rush to her cheeks.

'N-no . . . I mean, not really. He's going to introduce me to somebody in Paris who teaches dancing. I want to train.'

Digby Farnel's interest grew. So that was it—the little girl had left home in the company of a professional dancer who was going to help her 'train'. It didn't sound quite right to Digby. He felt a swift, intuitive fear for this pretty child. He said:

'Look here, I must talk to you. I do a lot of photography in my spare time. I'm going over to the Photographic Exhibition in Paris. I shall be at the Hotel Edouard VII. You can get me there. If you need any help, will you ring me up?'

She stared at him.

'Why should I need help?'

'I don't quite know, but—oh, look here,—do you know a lot about this fellow you're with? Is he English? Do your people know about him?'

Vicky felt a queer tremor of nervousness at the mention of her 'people'.

'They'll have had a wire by now. I sent a wire telling them I'd gone. I—I haven't known Paul very long, but I have every confidence in him.'

Before Digby Farnel could answer, the carriage door behind them suddenly slid back. For a moment the light from the carriage caught Digby's glasses so that he could not see very well. Then, shading his eyes with a hand, he saw standing before him the willowy figure of a young man in an atrocious, grey striped suit. So over-elegantly was he attired, in general, that he made Digby feel quite sick. This must be the little girl's exhibition dancer? He exuded a strong perfume of hair-pomade. Digby's immediate summing up of Paul Dallas was:

'Frightful cad!'

But Paul, very much on his dignity, looked from Vicky to the man with the horn-rimmed glasses, and drawled:

'So here you are, Vicky! I wondered where you'd gone. Who's your friend?'

Vicky began to stammer something inaudible. She could see that Paul was angry. Digby said curtly:

'My name's Farnel. This young lady and I were both taking a breath of air in the corridor. Pretty hot in those carriages with the steam heating full on, isn't it?'

'Lousy,' said Paul.

He then turned from Digby, took Vicky's arm, more or less pushed her into the carriage, followed her, and shut the door in Digby's face with a crash that was as rude as it was intended to be.

7

Alone in the carriage again with Paul, Vicky had none too good a time. He was sarcastic and even insulting about Mr. Farnel.

'What the devil did you want to speak to him for? Bored with me? Looking around for a new boyfriend already.'

Vicky was horrified. She began to wonder if Paul had had too much to drink on the boat. He was so uncivil, so unkind. She was seeing him in a totally different light. With as much dignity as she could muster, she said:

'I didn't think I was doing any harm, Paul. You've always told me I was too Victorian! Surely nowadays one can say a word to a stranger without all that fuss.'

'What did the fellow want, anyhow?'

'Nothing.'

'Well, you're much too young and pretty to talk to strange men,' said Paul in a mollified voice, and taking her hands, he drew her toward him, adding: 'I didn't mean to be cross, angel. Give me a little kiss.'

She hesitated. She really did not want to kiss Paul. And so plainly did she exhibit that fact that he flung himself into one of those nasty moods which always seized Paul Dallas when he was thwarted or annoyed.

Pushing her away from him, he shrugged his shoulders and became icily unpleasant.

'Ho—ho! I do seem unpopular. Well, run along, back into the corridor, my dear, and kiss the gentleman with the horn-rims. What is he? A commercial traveller?'

Vicky, who had never in her quiet, ordinary life at

home had to deal with such a situation, nor cope with a man like Paul, stared at him blankly. Her face was scarlet, her eyes full of tears again.

'I think he was a gentleman and very nice!' she stammered.

'The old school tie, and all that,' sneered Paul. 'Well, you thought me very nice, in England. I don't know what's come over you.'

She shook her head dumbly. She didn't quite know, herself, what had come over her. Except that she mistrusted this young man and resented his method of speaking to her and dealing with her. As though he had the right to say, 'Come here' or 'Go there', 'Do this' or 'Do that.' Perhaps he felt that she had given him that right because she had taken his money. That was what was so mad of her—to have let Paul pay. But he had been different at home—beguiling and persuasive, not at all dictatorial, and he had assured her that he would regard the money spent on her as a loan—that it was all on a business basis.

Paul was saying:

'It's damn dull for me to have you this way—I thought you were more amusing. It seems to me we shall be scratching each other's eyes out by the time we get to Paris.'

Vicky looked at him appealingly.

'Why should we? Why can't we be friends? Of course if you're bored with me when we get to Paris, I must just carry on with my dancing, and you needn't be bothered with me.'

He flickered his long lashes angrily. He could see plainly enough now that he had been a fool to spend money bringing this girl over. There was sure to be trouble. She would kick up a hell of a fuss when she found out that the career was to be of secondary importance to the love-affair. He was half inclined to tell her to take the next train back whence she had come. There were plenty of lovely girls in the world for Paul Dallas. Then he reminded himself that there were not many like Vicky. She was exceptional. And perhaps she'd be a bit more fun once they got this journey over. She was just tired and a bit homesick. That was what was the matter with her. He decided to be magnanimous.

'I'm a swine,' he said. 'Sorry, Vicky. I was just jealous when I saw you with that fellow.' He held out a hand in his most appealing fashion.

Vicky was quick to respond. She put out her hand to meet his. He then became very friendly and solicitous. Insisted upon tucking her up in a corner with his rug, turned down the light, and told her to go to sleep and forget that they had 'had a few words'.

She felt a good deal better and happier after that. But she could not sleep. Her head buzzed with thoughts. And some of them were circling round the man with the horn-rimmed glasses, who had been so kind out in the corridor. He was the sort of man Dad would have liked. Sort of trustworthy and quiet. Like Tom. No—not like Tom. Much more cultured and talkative. She was sure Mr. Farnel would be very interesting if one got to know him. And despite the fact that Paul was being nicer now, she could not altogether banish her fears, and with them a sensation of real relief that she knew somebody in Paris. Digby Farnel. If she wanted help she could always find him at the Hotel Edouard VII he had said. Somehow that was worth knowing, although she could not exactly explain why she felt like this.

If she could have seen Mr. Farnel at this moment and heard what he was saying, she would have been surprised, and not a little flattered, to discover that he was concentrating on the thought of her.

He was discussing her at length with the man in whose company he was travelling to the Photographic Exhibition. He and Jack Morgan had been friends for many years, and were both intensely interested in colour-photography. They had first met in their early twenties, in South America, where for some years Digby had had a job and Morgan had been his assistant. Since then Digby's father had died and left him a considerable amount of money, which meant that he need no longer work. He was free now to pursue his favourite hobby.

Morgan had married unhappily. His wife had left him in Rio, and he was back in London in a job.

Digby, having recently been out in West Africa, photographing the coast, had organised this week's holiday for himself and his friend, in Paris.

If there was one man in the world for whom Jack Morgan had a profound respect and affection, it was Digby Farnel. In the days when his wife's departure had hurt him profoundly, it had been Digby who had helped Jack get through the difficult days. Digby, with his sound unswerving judgment, and his great enthusiasm for life and beauty.

Digby himself, in his quest for beauty, had never yet been sufficiently attracted by a beautiful woman to lose his head or his heart. Once or twice he had found a passing attraction, but never a serious one. He did not altogether believe in matrimony. And Jack Morgan's catastrophe had not encouraged him.

Jack was somewhat amused now to hear his friend enlarging on the attractions of a young girl whom he had spoken to for ten minutes in the corridor.

'You seem to be quite *épris*, old man,' he said.

Digby looked sheepish.

'Well, I wouldn't call it that,' he laughed. 'But she was a charming little thing. And I don't like the look of that fellow she's with one scrap. My God, he was a bounder! The sort of dago these women seem to admire. And she's run away from home with him. It doesn't look good to me.'

'Is it a love-affair?'

'Well, that's what I thought, but she says "no"—he's just taking her over to train as a dancer in Paris.'

'Bit fishy, eh?'

'Well, she's such a kid. I made an awful fool of myself,

87

treating her as though she were just out of school. Then she told me she was twenty.'

'Really pretty?'

'Take a good look at her, Jack, when we get off the train, if you get a chance. It's a face I'd like to photograph. She's got marvellous bone—like Dietrich and Garbo—lovely structure.'

'Well, well,' said Jack Morgan, 'fancy you doing Knight Errant to a weeping Marlene on the Paris express. I think I'd better keep a close eye on you.'

'My dear fellow, I don't even know her name or where she is going. It's just that I'm not altogether happy about her. She looked damned scared to me when that fellow pushed her into the carriage. I hope she'll be all right, poor little thing.'

'I'm always an accommodating friend,' said Jack. 'Would you like me to sleuth her for you, when we get to Paris?'

'Good lord, no,' said Digby.

He then proceeded to settle himself down in a corner and snatch some sleep.

But he found himself remembering the girl's tear-filled eyes—unimaginably blue—the alluring contour of her arresting face—that lovely line from brow to chin, and the way her black curls tumbled to her neck. He wished he knew her name. And he wished she wasn't running away with that frightful Paul whatever-he-called-himself.

Digby Farnel had never been more attracted by a passing face nor more anxious about the fate of a girl who was an entire stranger.

In the morning when the express steamed into the Gare St. Lazare Digby made a point of trying to see the girl again. He caught sight of her as they stepped out of the train. She was taking a suitcase which her companion handed her. Digby touched Morgan on the shoulder and said:

'Jack—look—there's the girl—in the red beret and tweed coat.'

Morgan looked and raised his brows in appreciation.

'*Ravissante*. Is that object in the striped suit the hero she's run away with?'

'It is.'

'Lord help her.'

'That's what I say,' said Digby, and with his suitcase in his hand, pushed forward through the crowd toward the barrier, and tried to get close to Vicky. He wished he knew her name. He managed to catch her eye at last. She broke into a timid little smile, but immediately looked away again and started to talk to her companion.

Digby fell back, shrugging his shoulders. Absurd for him to be interested in the girl. He would never see her again in his life. And what became of her was none of his business. But he could not forget her. Her intense young face, seen in the light of the summer morning, was as beautiful as it had been in the dimly lit train. What a shy, funny little smile she had given him. A bit as though she was afraid. That was what worried him, that she *was afraid*. He couldn't bear to think of that fellow doing her any harm. He felt quite depressed once the slender, childish figure was lost in the crowd.

Vicky, hurrying with Paul to get a taxi, was wishing that she could have spoken to Digby Farnel again, but she had not dared to throw him more than that brief smile, in case Paul got jealous. He had been nice and friendly since their row in the train. She did not want to upset him again. Digby Farnel had given her such a friendly glance, she thought, sighing. He had wonderfully kind eyes.

'Well, here's Paris, Sweetie,' said Paul Dallas.

She drew a long breath.

'Yes, here it is!'

She felt tired and in need of a bath and some rest, after that trying journey. However, she was thrilled at the sight of the gay capital of France, thrilled to find herself in the swiftly-moving taxi which seemed to rush through the traffic so much faster than the English taxis. Down narrow, cobbled streets they went, along the wide boulevards, giving her here and there a glimpse of famous buildings. The Arc de Triomphe under which the unknown soldier was buried. She must go and see that some time. How beautiful it looked against the clear blue of the June sky. And Paris was beautiful in the sunlight. Most of the shops were barred and the houses shuttered. It was still early, but there were plenty of people moving about, women in black shawls, men in coloured blouses and berets, going to the market. This was France. And oh! what a long way from England and Norman Park it seemed. She wondered what on earth Mum and Dad and Freda would be saying about her at this very minute. They wouldn't be having a very happy breakfast.

'Where are we going?' she asked Paul.

'To a little hotel I know.'

'Where's Madame Simone?' she asked rather anxiously.

'In the hotel,' he said, and yawned.

They came to the place, a typical Continental hotel in a cheap quarter in Montmartre. Grey, shabby, with tall, narrow windows opening on to little balconies. It was too early for many people to be up, but a sleepy concierge greeted Paul and Vicky in the lounge, wherein there was a strong smell of roasting coffee mingling with the stale tobacco of last night.

It all looked strange and a little unfriendly and uninviting to Vicky's eyes. She took Paul's arm and whispered:

'I'd like to see Madame straight away.'

'She may not be up,' said Paul.

Vicky's heart sank.

Now that she was actually here, in Paris, in an hotel with Paul, she was frightened—even more frightened than she had been in the train. Career or no career, she would have given a lot to be back in London—and even in Norman Park.

Paul said:

'I'll book a room for you and you can go up and have a sleep if you like.'

Vicky looked around her with apprehensive gaze.

'Where do we dance? Has Madame some sort of studio?'

'Huh-huh,' he said.

So non-committal was he, so unconvincing, that Vicky, for the first time since she had gone away with Paul, had a strange and terrifying belief that he was lying—and had lied all the way along. She was also convinced that this was not a place in which one learned to dance.

Paul, with his usual insensitiveness to any girl's feelings, suddenly took Vicky's arm, leaned down to her, and whispered:

'Shall I come up with you and help you unpack?'

Vicky went white as death.

'You know you can't do that, Paul.'

'Oh, Victoria!' he jeered and laughed.

'Don't keep on saying that sort of thing,' she exclaimed with heightened colour and a growing sense of anger and misery. 'And why can't I see Madame?'

'Because——' began Paul.

Then he paused. For a shrill voice interrupted his little contretemps with Vicky.

'*Allo! Mon cher, Paul. C'est toi, enfin!*'

Vicky looked up. She saw an enormously stout woman wearing a rather dirty satin dressing-gown trimmed with torn lace, her hair in curlers, her fat dirty fingers bejewelled with rings. She came down the stairs, and waddled toward them.

Paul greeted this apparition as 'Madame'.

Vicky knew enough French from her school-training to translate a little of what passed between them. Madame Simone embraced Paul, kissing him on both cheeks, and welcomed him to Paris. Paul responded effusively in bad but fluent French.

A sense of complete dismay seized Vicky. She had visualised a clever, attractive teacher of dancing. How could this mountain of flesh, whose hair obviously should be white and not that dyed scarlet, teach anybody to dance?

Every instinct in Vicky cried out the word *'Danger!'* now.

She swung round to the concierge, who was still standing by, grinning stupidly, with hers and Paul's suitcases in his hands.

In the best French that she could muster, she whispered:

'Who is that lady?'

He answered that she was Madame Simone, the proprietress of the hotel.

'Does she teach dancing?' Vicky questioned him rapidly.

The concierge crackled a laugh.

'*Mon Dieu*, but no—Madame does not teach dancing. She is far too busy cooking the meals!'

Vicky turned back to Paul and the woman with whom he was still conversing. She felt ice-cold. The palms of her hands were moist. And she knew definitely, now, that Paul was not only a liar but something *worse*. . . .

Paul smiled at her. She had a curious flash-like memory of this same young man smiling in the same way in the dance-hall at Norman Park when she had first thought him so wonderful. How secure she had felt that night with Tom! *With Tom!* Dear God, but she had it in her this moment to wish that dull, stolid old Tom were here beside her so that she need not go on feeling this horrible sensation of panic.

'Come and say "How do you do?" to Madame,' said Paul.

Before Vicky could move or speak, she felt two fat soft hands seize her shoulders. She was drawn to the woman's bosom, smothered in lace and the odour of cheap perfume. A shrill voice was attempting to 'croon' over her in broken English.

'Such a nice leetle girl. Going to be friends with Simone, eh?'

Vicky pushed her away and swung round to Paul. Her eyes were enormous in her white face.

'Paul, where am I? Why have you brought me here? Who is this woman? The concierge says she doesn't teach dancing. Nobody teaches dancing here.'

Paul's smile vanished. His mouth curled downward with an ugly sulky look.

'Now, Vicky, don't be a little idiot——'

'I wish to know,' broke in Vicky, 'why you lied about this. Where is the dancing studio? Where am I to have my training?'

He laughed and took her arm and pressed her to his side.

'I think I shall have to undertake that myself, little wild-cat. You are so ready to spit, aren't you?'

She broke away from him.

'I don't like this place, and I don't want to stay here. I don't know what you've got in your mind, but it isn't what you led me to believe at home. I am not going to stay with you, Paul.'

'Now look here,' he said angrily, 'you might remember that I paid for your passage out here and that I've taken a lot of trouble over you, one way and another. You can't just walk out on me like this.'

'I am sorry I ever let you pay for me!' she flashed, 'and I wouldn't have done it if I hadn't thought you meant all you said.'

'I did mean it.'

'Then why did you tell me Madame Simone taught dancing, when she's only the proprietress of an hotel?'

'Oh, *la! la!*' put in Madame, her fat body wobbling with laughter. 'The leetle English girl doesn't like poor Simone.'

Paul came closer to Vicky. His eyes looked down into hers furiously.

'Shut up making all this fuss, Vicky. There are plenty of people in Paris who do teach dancing, even if Simone doesn't. Now look here, we can't go on like this. I brought you here and I admit a certain amount of responsibility. You can't just quit cold. You've got no money. You can't

93

go back to England, and I should think you'd be too proud to wire for help to the old homestead, wouldn't you?'

Vicky was silent for a moment. Her breath was spasmodic and her eyes bright with the shame of her thoughts. But there was a certain truth in what Paul said, which sank into her mind. It cast her down to the depths of despair. He was right. She had no money and she couldn't get home, and it would be the most frightful humiliation to have to wire to Mum or Dad and say that she was destitute in Paris, and that all the hateful things they had said against Paul were true. She couldn't bear to go back and be subjected to their crowing over her. Freda would never stop laughing at her, jeering, or Mum saying: 'I told you so.'

Paul took her arm again.

'You're just getting yourself worked up over nothing, my sweet. Let Madame take you to a room, and we'll talk things over.'

She had another lightning memory of Paul in the train . . . his hands and lips upon her. His attempts to establish an intimate relationship. And she knew that she could not and would not stay here with him, and that whatever she did, she must not be persuaded to go upstairs.

She had a trapped feeling. Every instinct warned her to run away. And run away she did. In blind panic. Without even waiting to take her suitcase which the concierge was holding, standing open-mouthed, understanding nothing of what was going on.

She turned and ran out of the odorous, sinister lounge, into the street. Into the sunshine which was now flooding Paris. It was such a beautiful June morning, soft, warm, and windless.

Vicky heard Paul calling her.

'Vicky! Vicky, come back, you little *fool*.'

She paid no heed. She knew that Paul was running after her. She ran faster. And while she ran, her breath coming in great gasps, she remembered the man in the train: Mr.

94

Farnel, with his glasses, his kind, clever face, his gentle voice, and the words he had spoken to her.

If she needed help, she was to let him know, he had said, and he had given her his address. In her wildest imagination she had not thought she would ever need it. At the same time she was profoundly grateful that she knew him—that there was one person in Paris to whom she could appeal for protection against Paul. Oh, it was horrible that she should need to be protected from the young man she had thought her friend. Utterly sunk and dead now were her hopes of embarking upon a grand career as a dancer. And any feelings of admiration she had ever entertained for Paul Dallas had been killed stone dead within the last twenty-four hours.

She reached the corner of the street, looked back over her shoulder and saw Paul coming towards her. Breathless, sick, but determined to escape him, she ran on until she saw a passing taxi. She hailed it—the driver pulled up. She said:

'Hotel Edouard VII.'

'Edouard VII . . . *oui*,' he nodded.

She jumped in, slammed the door, and the taxi wheeled round and moved off with that rapidity for which Paris taxis are famous.

Vicky sat huddled in a corner, her face in her hands, her breath coming in great gasps. Her whole body was shaking. She felt wild relief that she had got away from Paul. Or *had* she? Would he follow? She looked out of the back window, but saw nobody in view. At this early hour there were not many taxis. She had been lucky, and perhaps Paul, even had he wanted to follow her, had not been able to get a vehicle.

Gradually she calmed down. She was being taken right across Paris, into the better part of the city. Under happier circumstances, Vicky would have thrilled at the sight of the Seine, silver-bright in the sunlight, at the beauty of the green trees in the Bois de Boulogne, at that splendid giant tracery of ironwork, the Eiffel Tower, pointing up to the blue sky.

But she saw nothing. Her mind was a confusion of doubts, fears, and a sense of utter hopelessness. For what was she going to do when she reached her friend of the train? What lay in front of her except humiliation; the prospect of a return in disgrace to Norman Park?

Yet before Vicky reached the hotel some of her old spirit revived. Some of that independent feeling that she could not, and would not, stay the whole of her life in Norman Park. She must get some sort of work over here. Any work. Nothing would induce her to admit such utter defeat.

The taxi deposited her at the Hotel Edouard VII. She had just enough money in her bag to pay the fare. And now she found herself in a smart and very different type of hotel from the one from which she had just run away. But it was a miserable Vicky who asked the porter timidly if she might speak to Mr. Digby Farnel. He said that he would send her name up to the gentleman, who had only just arrived, and asked her to wait.

8

Digby Farnel was just about to step into a much-needed bath, when his friend Jack Morgan knocked on the door, and called:

'Hi! Come out of that, you old rascal! The girlfriend has turned up.'

Digby seized his glasses, wiped the steam from them, enveloped himself in a dressing-gown and thrust his head into the bedroom.

Jack Morgan grinned at him, holding on to the hand-microphone of the telephone.

'The hall porter says that a young lady named Miss Waide wishes to see *M'sieu*.'

'Miss Waide!' repeated Digby, 'never heard of her.'

'Must be the girl in the train.'

'Impossible,' said Digby; but his heart gave a sudden jolt. It was a feeling of hope. Above all things he wanted to see that girl again.

'Well, tell them to ask her to wait and I'll be down again in a minute,' he said.

'What about your breakfast?'

'That can wait.'

Jack grinned again.

'*Vive l'amour*, but I'm for this excellent coffee and an omelette.'

Digby dressed with more rapidity than usual, got into grey flannels, and took the lift downstairs into the lounge.

It was still early for Paris and there was nobody in the writing-room into which they had shown his unknown visitor. The moment Digby saw her—the slim little figure, and that lovely young face which had haunted him since he had first seen it—he knew that Miss Waide *was* the girl of the train. Quite ridiculously pleased, he walked toward her and held out a hand.

'Why, hullo! This is an unexpected pleasure.'

Vicky, having waited for a quarter of an hour alone, over-tired, hungry, and unutterably wretched, then behaved in a most childish manner and burst into tears.

So for the second time Digby found himself comforting the weeping stranger. She collapsed back into her chair, her face hidden in her hands.

He drew a chair beside her and pulling a blue silk handkerchief from his pocket, pressed it into her fingers.

'Take this—it's a nice clean one,' he said gently, 'and don't cry like that. Things can't be as bad as they seem. I'm awfully glad you've come along. I hoped you would.'

Vicky tried to stifle her sobs. She found herself using the nice blue handkerchief. She was glad of it. She had lost her own long ago. She felt like a small and rather naughty child. To Digby Farnel she looked pathetically young. He took the beret from her head and touched the dark untidy curls with a forefinger.

'Poor child! You are just feeling all-in. I am frightfully sorry. You must have something to eat and drink, and then tell me all about it.'

Vicky said into the crumpled handkerchief:

'I couldn't—eat—anything——'

'Oh yes, you could, and you are going to—with me.'

Vicky managed to recover herself. She wiped her eyes, and with the handkerchief pressed to her still trembling lips, looked at this friend in need. She was horribly ashamed of herself. Ashamed of the whole situation. It was such a dismal affair. And when she thought of Paul Dallas, she felt almost physically sick.

'I don't know what you must think of me, Mr. Farnel,' she said, 'but I had to come to you because I know nobody else—not a soul.'

He pulled out a cigarette-case and handed it to her.

'I wanted you to come. I told you to. I had a sure feeling something was going wrong. A sort of presentiment. Now have a cigarette. It will soothe your nerves.'

She shook her head.

'Not just now.'

Digby lit a cigarette for himself and returned the case to his pocket. He smiled and looked at Vicky in his characteristic fashion—over the rim of his glasses.

'You look much too young to smoke, anyhow.'

Vicky laughed in a very forlorn fashion.

'You mistook me for a schoolgirl in the train, and now you must think I'm just a regular cry-baby. I am terribly sorry to be so stupid, but I think it was mainly relief because I've got away.'

'From the fellow you were with?'

She nodded.

The nod and the expression in her eyes were eloquent to Digby. He wondered what the devil that howling cad had done to the child. But he insisted upon her taking some food before she launched on any explanation.

'You are worn out, you must really have some breakfast with me and talk afterwards.'

The difference between his method of treating her and Paul's was marked. She felt that here was somebody who was not only concerned with himself. Not selfish and horrible and *dangerous* like Paul.

She found herself, at length, drinking delicious coffee, and eating an omelette in the dining-room of the hotel, at a little table alone with Digby.

Jack Morgan remained tactfully upstairs.

After the much-needed refreshment, Vicky felt better able to cope with life in general. She was afraid that she was looking 'a sight' even though she had powdered her nose, combed her curls back to order, and put a little colour on her lips. But Digby thought, as he had done when he first saw her, that she had unusual beauty. Only her eyes looked desperately hurt. He did not like to see that.

99

When she had finished the meal, he let her talk. And she was only too glad to tell him everything. It was so much better than bottling it up. So it tumbled out, the rather sordid, tragic little tale of Vicky running away from home with Paul Dallas—not for the sake of love—but in order to make a career as a dancer. An action doomed to failure from the start, although she had been so sure of herself and so certain that Paul was genuine.

Digby said:

'I could have told you the moment I saw him that that young man was not genuine. Neither, if I may say so, is he quite the famous person which he liked to make himself out to be. He's just a third-rate exhibition dancer, and he appears to me to have third-rate morals as well.'

Vicky gave a heart-rending sigh.

'It seems like that now. Somehow it was quite different at home. Oh, you must think me an awful little fool to have been so taken in.'

'I don't at all. You've lived most of your life in a fairly sheltered way. As far as I can see you haven't in your life before come up against anything approaching this. Naturally you weren't able to deal with that young man as he should have been dealt with.'

'But the fact remains,' said Vicky, 'that I trusted him and let him bring me here. I know that was my real mistake—in letting him pay for my fare.'

'It wasn't very wise.'

She coloured hotly.

'Hopeless! I see it now. But it was the only way to get a start. My people wouldn't help me. They didn't approve of my becoming a dancer.'

Digby smoked in silence a moment and thought things over. He could imagine Vicky's people. She had told him enough to bring before him a very fair picture of the Waides and the atmosphere at Norman Park where Vicky had been born and bred. Just simple, rather 'sticky' people without much vision, and without any understanding of this rather queer member of their family. They were content with the normal routine of life. She wasn't. Digby didn't blame her for that. She had a temperament and she was one hundred per cent *alive*. He had never seen anything more vital than those blue, vivid eyes of Vicky, which even the tears had not been able to dim. Nor anything more intense than her lips and her husky young voice. There was something compelling about her. She was so responsive to the urge of life. She did not want to sit down in the heart of suburbia and 'vegetate'. Poor little Victoria Waide! The bird beating its wings against the cage. The old story of the starling: '*I can't get out!*'

And now that she had got out, her wings were bruised and she was battered and half-broken and dazed by the strangeness and enormity of the world into which she had escaped. Yet still she seemed reluctant to go back to her cage.

'It's pathetic,' he thought, 'and I don't know what the devil to do with the child.'

She had come to him for help, and he felt almost responsible for her. His right hand ached to land a good straight blow on Mr. Paul Dallas's jaw. He burned with indignation at the story which Vicky told him of her arrival at the hotel in Paris and the frightening insinuations that Dallas had made. He tried to make love to her in the train, too. Obviously the fellow had never meant to place her under the protection of a respectable dancing teacher. He had had other ideas. And just what they were, even Vicky hardly dared voice.

'Is your luggage still at the hotel?' he asked.

'My suitcase, yes. Oh! goodness—and I don't know where the hotel is,' she said, and sat upright, dismayed, as this thought suddenly struck her.

Digby shook his head.

'My dear child, you *have*——'

'Been idiotic,' she finished for him. 'I know! Oh, I know.'

'Well, if you don't know where the hotel is, it looks as though the suitcase is lost. Was there much in it?'

'Quite enough,' she said mournfully.

And her heart sank at the memory of what she had lost. Her dressing-gown, her night things, an ivory brush that her aunt had given her last Christmas, the little travelling clock which her dad had bought for her birthday. Lots of other small articles. In fact, most of her treasured possessions. It was a good thing she was wearing her one and only decent brooch.

Digby felt infinitely sorry for her. He was swift to realise that her people were not well off and that she had no money. He looked at her gravely.

'Listen,' he said, 'you know what you've got to do, don't you?'

'What?'

'Go back home—at once.'

The colour rushed to her face again.

'I couldn't possibly.'

'But you must. What else can you do?'

'Get a job over here. I couldn't go back and admit that I've been such a failure. They never liked Paul. I'd never hear the end of it if I went home and told them what he was. You don't know what Freda's like. She would make my life absolutely unbearable.'

'Does it matter so much what this sister says and does?'

'Yes. She practically runs the home and everybody in it.'

Digby bit his lip. He didn't want to hurt Vicky. He hated to think of her being bullied. He supposed her people would have neither the intelligence, nor the insight into psychology, to leave her alone and let her get back her self-esteem, her whole equilibrium. They'd say: *'We told you so!'* and never stop saying it. And she'd be driven crazy.

'Besides,' Vicky was saying, 'they might refuse to believe that I only came away with Paul—because— because of the dancing.'

'Surely they'd take your word.'

'I think Dad would, but I don't know about my mother

102

or sister. In fact I am sure Freda would be glad to think the worst.'

'That's nonsense,' said Digby briskly, 'the "worst" surely doesn't come into it.'

She felt a sudden rush of gratitude towards him.

'It's awfully nice of you to take my word for everything.'

'Why shouldn't I?' he smiled.

'Well, they mightn't, and I just daren't face it.'

'But, my dear child, when you talk about getting a job in Paris, you don't know what you're saying. You can't speak fluent French, and there aren't jobs knocking about for foreigners, anyhow. No—it's unthinkable. You are not at all the type to be left alone in Paris. You are under-age, anyhow. No, my dear, you'll have to go back home, no matter how much you dislike it.'

Vicky put a small clenched fist on the table.

'I won't!'

He thought that she looked quite amazing with that stormy colour in her cheeks, and those flashing, resentful eyes.

Lord! he'd like to photograph her in colour. He had just bought a new colour-camera. The latest process. He'd like to reproduce the blueness of this girl's eyes, the blackness of her hair, and the warm velvet whiteness of her throat. The artist in him reacted to her strongly. And the other side—the human one—that too reacted warmly to Vicky. He had seen and talked to a great many beautiful women, young and old. The artificial society type left him unmoved. The purely sporting, hearty girl did not interest him. But there was something unusual about this little girl from the suburbs. He could see just why that swine Dallas had taken her away. Any unscrupulous man would have made a shot at it. She was untutored, in a funny sort of way. But she would be responsive, swift to absorb anything that a man liked to teach her. Digby would have liked to have known her in different circumstances, to have become her companion. But that was impossible! Their lives lay apart. Besides, he felt that he was being

103

rather a fool to allow a young, unknown girl like this to captivate his fancy. Somewhat abruptly he said:

'You've got to go home, Vicky.'

It was the first time he had used her Christian name. It made her feel no longer so strange or awkward with him. Indeed, she felt that she knew him quite well. But she fought passionately against the idea of going back to England.

'There must be some way out of it,' she protested. 'I don't want to go back. You don't know what sort of a life I'd lead if I went back. Really—I couldn't stand it!'

'But what can you do here?'

'I'll have to try and find something,' she said stubbornly.

'Living on what, meanwhile?'

'I shall wire to my father for money. If he thinks I need it, he'll send it. I can give a post-office address so that they can't trace me.'

Digby leaned across the table, and looked at her with earnest eyes.

'Don't do that, I implore you. It'll never do for you to stay in Paris, my dear. Take my advice and give in. I know you don't want to. I admire your courage. But don't stay in Paris. It honestly isn't the place for you. I speak from experience. I have been round the world; I know. You *must* let me lend you the fare and get the afternoon boat back to England.'

'You're the kindest man in the world,' said Vicky in a muffled voice; 'but I can't accept any money from you. I have taken money from one man and never again!'

Digby threw her a quizzical smile.

'You don't think that I——'

'That you are like *him*? Oh, no, no!' she broke in quickly, anxious not to offend Digby. 'You are absolutely different.'

'You've no guarantee for it,' said Digby, 'but I do assure you that you *can* trust me. And if you'll let me give you your fare home, you shall pay it back bit by bit, in the future, so you need not feel embarrassment about taking it.'

She shook her head.

'I couldn't. I shall wire to my father.'

'Then, my dear,' said Digby gently, 'let him know where you are.'

She shook her head again.

Somehow he liked her for her obstinacy. She was brave. She wasn't going to crawl home, defeated. Yet he feared that she might have to face such a much greater defeat—if she stayed.

He made up his mind quickly what he must do. *He* must communicate with Vicky's father. Vicky would be furious. But he must do it. It was not safe to let her stay alone in Paris. And how could he look after her? He had come here with Jack Morgan for a week's holiday, and in order to see the Exhibition of Photography. What could two bachelors do for a young and pretty girl? Precisely nothing. No! Home she must go, even if he went to rather underhand methods to send her there.

So Digby Farnel temporised.

'All right,' he said, 'if you're going to be obstinate, send your wire. And meanwhile you'd better make yourself at home, and I'll look after you if you'll allow me to.'

'I can't stay here—a most expensive hotel.'

'And how safe do you think you'll be in a cheap and shoddy one?' asked Digby grimly. 'One experience of that kind has been enough for you, hasn't it?'

Vicky made no answer, but some of the colour left her cheeks at the memory of Paul and Madame Simone. So white, so desolate, did she look that Digby's heart ached for her. Poor, pretty thing! It had all been a horrible shock for her. She had been a little fool and she knew it, but that didn't make matters any better.

He had had many experiences in life, but never one like this—finding himself responsible for a lovely girl who was still 'an infant' in the eyes of the law. A runaway from his own country, abandoned in Paris.

'Now, don't worry for the moment,' he advised her. 'Just take off your coat and hat and go and sit in a comfortable chair in the lounge and rest. You look as though you could do with some sleep.'

Vicky admitted that she was dead tired. Her eyelids were heavy, and her head aching with exhaustion. She allowed her new and kind friend to take her to the lounge and settle her down in a chair with a cushion at her back.

'Just relax,' he said, 'you'll be quite quiet. There's no one about. I'll think things over and decide what's best to do. Then you shall meet my friend Morgan, who is a very good chap, and knows Paris better than I do. We'll see if he can suggest anything.'

Vicky looked up at him, the tears glistening on her lashes.

'You're very kind.'

He looked down at her. He wanted to say:

'And you're very beautiful!'

He longed to photograph her, just like that, with her graceful young limbs relaxed. She was exquisitely graceful. And she had charming, slender hands. She closed her eyes, and he allowed himself the privilege of looking at her a moment longer. Yes, he could photograph her like that, sinking into an exhausted sleep. Tired, disillusioned, yet with that touch of youth still burning brightly within her.

He sighed and walked away and stood a moment in the vestibule, pondering. He hated to go behind her back, but he must. He went to the concierge and talked for a few minutes. In less than half an hour he had traced the telephone number of the Waides at Norman Park. And while Vicky slept he talked with Vicky's father. Poor old man—he sounded quite stricken with anxiety, and obviously the whole family was appalled by what Vicky had done.

'She left yesterday without giving us any warning,' Mr. Waide told Digby. 'Her mother and sister and I haven't slept a wink. I am eternally grateful to you, Mr.—Mr.

Farnel. It was good of you to take pity on the girl and communicate with us. Will you please tell her that her sister Freda will come out at once and bring her home. She can catch the morning boat.'

'Wouldn't it be wiser for her to fly and get here quickly?' suggested Digby. 'Your daughter has some crazy scheme about going off on her own in Paris, and I can't very well force her to stay with me. The sooner Miss Freda gets here the better. I think I can persuade Vicky to stay with me until the afternoon, anyhow.'

Mr. Waide only hesitated an instant. He was not a rich man, but he was a thrifty one. He had a little 'nest-egg'. And this was an emergency—the worst that had ever befallen the Waide family. He hardly dared think what had happened last night. Vicky *alone* with that dancing fellow. Dreadful! It had broken her mother's heart. But they must get her home and take care of her and see that she didn't do anything like it again. What a mercy she had fallen into the hands of a gentleman.

Mrs. Waide, issuing instructions of an economic kind at her husband's elbow, was a little startled when that usually quiet and meek man took command of the situation in quite a dramatic fashion.

'Money is no object in a case like this!' he told Digby. 'Freda shall fly.'

Digby hung up the receiver. As he walked out from the telephone-box, he felt far from easy in his mind. Almost as though he had let that pretty child down. She didn't get on with her sister. Their meeting in Paris would not be a happy one.

Digby removed his glasses, cleaned them thoughtfully, and replaced them.

'I suppose I've done the right thing,' he thought gloomily.

He went back to the lounge to break the news. Vicky was still sound asleep. He sat down at her side and lit a cigarette. He thought:

'When she wakes—before I confess that I have sent for

her people—I must ask her to let me take her into the sunshine and photograph her. I should like just a memory of her——'

And he wondered, not for the first time since he had seen Vicky, why she attracted him so vastly, and why he felt such a queer tenderness for her.

He thought again:

'If I had been ten years younger, and ten times madder, I wonder if I wouldn't have done something really crazy—such as asking her to stay with me—marrying her—making what I know a man could make of her!'

Then he derided himself for a fool. While he sat there, Vicky's heavy lashes lifted. She opened her eyes and looked up at him. And he knew then, definitely, that not only did he hate telling her what he must tell, but that he positively disliked the thought that, after today, he might never see her again.

9

For the first time in his life, Digby Farnel was a coward. He shirked telling Vicky that he had sent word to her father. When she awoke from that sleep of exhaustion, she renewed her conversation about getting a job in Paris, and he discussed it all with her, feeling very guilty. He wanted to let her know what he had done, and yet he feared that if he did tell her, she might run away where none of them could find her. The mere idea of her being alone in Paris appalled him.

He wanted to keep her with him until her sister arrived. So he asked her to allow him to take come colour-photographs of her, out in the sunshine. Vicky complied with this request, not that she felt like posing for a photograph, but because she thought she would be ungracious to refuse. Mr. Farnel had been so kind to her.

She felt depressed and worried as she walked with him down the Bois de Boulogne. She took little interest in his technical explanations of his new and wonderful colour-camera, and spoke of the marvellous photographs he would take of her.

The morning was perfect. The sun shimmered through the green leaves of the famous chestnut trees with their creamy 'candle' buds. Paris was alive and gay and lovely. But Vicky felt flat and hopeless. She had boasted, once, that she could take care of herself. She was determined not to go back to England, but when she really thought about it, she wondered what on earth she could do, here, alone and with no prospect of a job. One couldn't exist without money, and suppose Dad refused to send any and forced her back home through sheer lack of funds?

Her sleep had brought her refreshment of body, but not of mind. She was lethargic and still wrapped in gloomy thought whilst Digby took various 'shots' of her. He, and all that was artist in him, was enchanted by the beauty of her sorrowful young face, but distressed by her depression. His attempts to cheer her up had little effect. And by the time they got back to the hotel, where he had persuaded her to lunch with him, he was feeling even more guilty for what he had done behind her back.

The first person Vicky saw when she stepped into the lounge was Freda!

The shock was so great that she could only stand still and stare at that familiar, angular figure and the anæmic face with 'disapproval' written all over it. A little breathless 'Oh!' came from Vicky's lips.

Digby looked from her to the other girl who came toward them.

'Who is it?' he asked uncomfortably.

'My sister, Freda. But how on *earth*——?' Then Vicky broke off and turned flashing angry eyes upon him. '*Oh*! You must have let them know at home. It was mean— *mean* of you!'

'Vicky, I'm sorry,' he said, and could not have felt more penitent than when he looked into those lovely reproachful eyes, 'but I had to do it. I couldn't let you stay alone in Paris. It was unthinkable. Do try to forgive me.'

Vicky said no more. She was past even being angry now. Her last hope of being independent, of making a new life for herself, of finding all the glory of life that she wanted, was quenched by the sight of her sister, here in Paris. Her spirits sank to zero. Drearily she greeted Freda.

'So you've come to fetch me, have you?'

'I have!' said Freda, in a voice as frozen as her face. 'A nice business this is. The misery you've brought Mum and Dad and——'

'Don't start nagging at me,' broke in Vicky with a flash

110

of her old spirit. 'Leave me alone for heaven's sake.'

'H'm!' snorted Freda. 'I wouldn't like to say what I *do* think.'

Digby, standing by, looking at the two girls, wouldn't have liked to have said what he thought, either. He took an instant dislike to Freda. He was amazed that two sisters could be so totally different. The one with her vital beauty. The other lifeless, and with a stupid, mulish lack of understanding written all over her face. Narrow-minded, narrow-chested, doomed to spinsterhood, thought Digby, and to an old maid's virtuous scorn of human failings.

He began to be almost sorry that he had brought her over here. Obviously Vicky was to be sympathised with, if she had to live in the atmosphere that Freda Waide exuded. But there had been no other course open to him.

Vicky, feeling utterly crushed, made the necessary introduction between her sister and Digby. Digby tried to say something graceful, but Freda cut him short.

'Very kind of you to let my father know about Vicky, I'm sure. Perhaps you'd tell us the best and quickest way we can get back to England, Mr. Farnel.'

'I haven't said that I'll go yet,' came from Vicky, sullenly.

Digby looked at her compassionately.

'My dear, you must,' he said gently.

Freda sniffed. Cheek, his calling Vicky 'My dear,' she thought. Still, he seemed a better type than that rotter Vicky had run away with. And how far had things gone between Vicky and the dancer? She'd like to know. She'd get the truth out of Vicky as soon as they were alone.

'You've caused trouble enough, Vicky,' she said, 'so don't start any more. You know perfectly well that you've got to go home with me.'

Vicky glanced bitterly past her sister to a chic, beautifully-dressed girl who had just come out of the lift, with a man. They were laughing and talking. The girl looked as though she had plenty of money. She was

111

soignée, attractive, obviously enjoying herself. And Vicky envied her, passionately and childishly. If only she was that girl! How intensely she wanted to be happy! How she dreaded going back to Norman Park, to the endless reproaches which awaited her. But she was defeated. Defeated by lack of money and the trick Digby Farnel had played in bringing one of her family over here. She *must* go back now.

Freda said:

'It cost my father a lot of money sending me over by air, Mr. Farnel, and I can't say I liked it very much. I thought flying very unpleasant. We shall go back by the next boat, if you can tell me when that will be.'

'You'd better have some food with me and a little breathing space now you're here, Miss Waide,' said Digby, trying to be pleasant for Vicky's sake. 'You'll have missed the day-boat. But you can go by night via Calais or Dieppe.'

'Whichever is the cheapest,' said Freda.

'Dieppe, in that case.'

Vicky came to life and put in her spoke.

'I'd just as soon get back straight away now. I don't want to stay here and prolong the agony,' she muttered.

'Try not to feel that way,' said Digby. 'And why not let my friend Mr. Morgan and me take you both out somewhere? You might as well enjoy yourselves now you *are* in Paris.'

Freda replied to that sharply:

'No, thank you, Mr. Farnel. This isn't a time for enjoyment. Vicky and I will go at once.'

'Perhaps it's as well,' thought Digby, 'otherwise I should be very rude to this young woman.'

Vicky was indifferent. It mattered little to her now what she did. Freda announced that she was going to ask at the desk how soon they could get a train to Dieppe. They could wait there till the boat left. She seemed to regard Paris as an evil city from which she must remove her young sister as soon as possible.

Left alone with Vicky for an instant, Digby put out a hand and gripped one of hers.

'Was I a brute to go behind your back like that? I'm terribly sorry. But it was all so difficult——'

She shook her head dumbly. The tears were gathering in her eyes. She felt quite broken. He pressed her fingers an instant, then dropped them, curiously disturbed by her small tragedy. Not small to her. Infinite! He could guess how hardly she was taking her defeat.

'Perhaps things aren't as black as they seem,' he added. 'Something will turn up for you at home—eh?'

She drew a hand across her eyes and gave a hard little laugh.

'What do you think can turn up? You see what my sister feels about me, and I expect my parents will feel very much the same.'

'I wish I could do something for you.'

'You've been very kind. And I know you acted for the best when you told them at home.'

'You will forgive me?'

'Yes,' she said in a tired, flat voice.

'Can I come and call on you when I get back to England?'

'If you want to,' she said, with the same lack of spirit.

'Perhaps you'd rather I didn't.'

She sighed.

'I suppose perhaps it would be better if you didn't for a bit. They won't want to be reminded of my—sins——' She laughed again.

He hated the sound of her unhappy laugh, and the knowledge that all her amazing and beautiful vitality, her spirit of youth and adventure, were dead in her this morning. He felt that it would be a cruel waste, unless something happened to revive her again. He felt, too, in this moment an insane desire to snatch her into his arms and kiss her—kiss some of the colour back into her cheeks and the light into her eyes.

'Good God!' he thought, 'I'm a monstrous fool. I shall be falling in love with this child unless I take care.'

Freda returned. They could catch a train to Dieppe soon after lunch, she said. They would take it. No, it was kind of Mr. Farnel to suggest lunch, but they would not stay. They would go and find a café somewhere alone.

Digby felt uncommonly irritated by her attitude. Sententious, righteous young fool! God help Vicky with such company for the journey back. A journey which for her would be wretched and humiliating enough without any Fredas.

Vicky made no protest when Freda finally carted her off. She was in no mood to enjoy Paris nor the interesting companionship offered her by Digby Farnel. She went away with Freda, after shaking hands with Digby and proffering her thanks for all that he had done. He watched her go. Something ached in his heart at the sight of that childish, drooping young figure.

Lighting a cigarette, and feeling quite dispirited himself, he rejoined his friend.

'You look as though you've just come from a funeral, old chap,' began Jack Morgan cheerily, and was startled when his friend snapped at him for the first time in his life and told him to 'shut up.'

'Oh—ho!' Jack Morgan thought to himself. 'I think old Digby's really fallen for that young thing. Just as well she's departed.'

Digby also thought that it was just as well. But strangely enough he did not enjoy his lunch, nor the golden day in Paris, nor the Exhibition of colour-photographs to which he had looked forward, for some long time.

10

For poor Vicky there was a singular difference between
the journey back to England from France, and that other
one which had seemed so full of promise which she had
taken, hopefully, with Paul Dallas. Twenty-four hours
ago. It seemed like a year. The intervening time like a
nightmare, with the exception, perhaps, of a few almost
happy moments in Digby Farnel's company.

There are nearly always discomforts attached to any
long journey, and the traveller's physical condition
depends so much upon how he or she is feeling mentally.
Vicky had not exactly enjoyed the journey with Paul. She
had been a little restless in her mind and anxious about the
future, and the Channel crossing had been a bad one. But
at least it had been exciting and a thrill. Going back with
Freda, she was so utterly miserable and disappointed that
it affected her physically. She began to feel really ill. The
day was perfect. The sea like glass. Vicky could not be
sea-sick, this time. But she collapsed.

Freda had nagged all the way from Paris to Dieppe. At
first Vicky had lashed out, then relapsed into stony
silence. Freda could continue her caustic and unsympathetic attack remorselessly—and she did!

To begin with she was annoyed because she could not
get Vicky to admit that she had 'gone wrong', as she put it,
with Mr. Paul Dallas. Freda had that side to her, common
to so many repressed, under-sexed women, which craves
for scandal and erotic detail. She hoped to extract some
'juicy information' from her young sister. But Vicky had
none to give. She informed Freda repeatedly that there

115

had been nothing 'like that' between herself and Paul Dallas. No amount of questioning could divert her from that truth. So Freda had to fall back on her own theories and let Vicky know quite bluntly that she did not believe her, and that their parents would not believe her, either.

'I bet he made love to you,' she kept saying; 'travelling all night with him like that. And I daresay you were scared in the end, and that's why you ran away from the hotel. Mum said there has never been anything so scandalous in our family before. Dad's simply horrified.'

Vicky had reached the stage where she refused to answer the gibes. She sat opposite her sister, staring hopelessly out of the window, wondering what she was going to do with life, now that her little world was smashed in pieces around her. It did not seem possible that she could ever put it together again.

Freda talked on. The whole thing was a terrible expense for Dad and they could ill afford it. And then there was Vicky's suitcase. Fancy her running off like that without it, and not even knowing the name of the hotel where it had been left. Disgraceful! All those good things left behind. That horrible young man would probably sell them and keep the proceeds.

A dreary little smile came to Vicky's lips when Freda made that remark. As if the suitcase or its contents mattered. As if anything so paltry could matter in the face of this disaster. Freda would never understand what a disaster it was to her, Vicky. Things had been bad enough before Paul came into her life. Now they would be ten times worse. Having tasted some excitement and seen a glimmer of the light of adventure on the horizon, the monotony at Norman Park would seem intolerable. Alas, the light of adventure was blacked out for her now. Nobody would trust her. She would be an object of contempt in her own home, for the thing she had done. She would never be able to get out for a moment alone, without cross-questioning or suspicion. Her sister could say, *ad infinitum*:

'Vicky can't be trusted.'

It was all awful. And not the least of the awfulness was the sense of personal failure. She had been so sure of herself and her ability to make her way in the world, and so certain that she was right in her judgment of people. She had thought Paul wonderful. She saw him now as he really was, a cad, an ignoble, commonplace young dancer, who had attempted an ordinary and not at all glamorous seduction of her.

Her thoughts were befogged in what seemed impenetrable gloom. Just now and again when she thought of Digby Farnel, that gloom lifted. Long ago, she had forgiven him for communicating with her family. She knew he was right. She could not have stayed over in Paris by herself, without funds. And it showed that he was a decent sort—so very much more decent than Paul Dallas could ever be. Besides, he had been infinitely kind. Depressed though she had felt, he had managed to make her laugh when they had walked together in the sunshine under the chestnuts along the Bois. He had an easy, charming way of talking, and she liked the way his clever, bright eyes gleamed through the horn-rimmed glasses when he smiled at her. Why had he been so nice? Why had he bothered with her? Perhaps because he liked her a little. He must like her. He had said that he wanted 'to call' when he came back to England. The idea that such a man as Digby Farnel should wish to trouble further with her restored, in some measure, her self-respect. But she saw no real chance of furthering a friendship with Digby Farnel—or with any man, once she got home. She would be chained to the family circle. By her own folly and indiscretion she had helped to forge those chains.

It was frightful to be young, not yet twenty-one, to know that men found her lovely, to feel vital and intense about life, and have to do nothing. Absolutely nothing but exist; utterly dependent upon her parents, forbidden even to take a job.

Once or twice, shutting her eyes to the ceaseless drone

of Freda's reproaches, Vicky contemplated running away from Norman Park a second time, even if it meant going out and taking a job as a housemaid. Then her depression and weariness overcame even that faint hope and she let it slide. She could do nothing. Nothing.

Freda mentioned Tom after a while. It wouldn't do to let Tom know what she had done. They'd have to keep it quiet, otherwise he wouldn't come to the house again. Tom was straight and had ideals. Just fancy Vicky doing what she'd done, knowing how devoted old Tom was to her!

That roused Vicky to retort:

'It's none of your business, Freda. And anybody listening to you would think I'd committed a crime. And if Tom doesn't want to see me any more, he won't. Or he'll take you out instead. That's what you've always wanted, isn't it?'

That stung Freda. She flushed and glowered at Vicky. Now it was her turn to maintain a haughty silence. So the sisters continued their unhappy journey. And there were hours of dreary waiting at Dieppe until the night-boat left for England. But on the boat Vicky came near to fainting and had to be helped down to the dormitory by Freda and a stewardess. Freda softened a little after that, and saw to it that Vicky was covered with a rug, had some eau-de-Cologne for her forehead, and was left in peace until the boat reached Newhaven.

But Vicky did not sleep. She lay with her face buried in the pillow, the tears rolling down her cheeks, feeling that her heart would break with the whole humiliating misery of the affair.

Perhaps Tom would find out about Paris and wouldn't want to see her any more. And he was the only friend she had. Well, what did she care? Nothing mattered now.

Then she remembered the strong kind pressure of Digby Farnel's hands about hers, and his charming voice saying:

'*Perhaps things aren't as black as they seem—something*

will turn up for you.'

She had told him that nothing would turn up. And that's what she believed in this black hour. The blackest of Vicky's young life.

The boat docked at Newhaven in the middle of the night. The passengers were allowed to sleep on board until morning. Vicky came off that boat looking and feeling a wreck. White as death and with large, red-rimmed eyes. So bad did she look that even Freda was scared. During the journey to London she forebore to nag or reproach her any further.

'I'm sorry you don't feel well, Vicky,' she said; but could not help adding, 'but I must say it's your own fault.'

And that was what Mrs. Waide said when she first saw her daughter.

Never would Vicky forget that drive from Norman Park station to the little house which had been her home most of her life. Under normal circumstances, of course, they would have walked. But she felt too sick and weak to attempt it, so reluctantly Freda ordered a taxi. When Vicky first saw the house—Dad's roses in full bloom today in the front garden under the warm June sunshine—she felt half glad that she was home after that nightmare in Paris, yet wholly reluctant to step out of the car and walk through the familiar front door. It was just as though imprisonment awaited her. The bird was being forced back into its cage.

Her mother welcomed her in the hall. A frozen unsmiling welcome, Mrs. Waide's thin, pale face expressive of all the virtuous indignation which she felt. It was a personal ignominy for her that any child brought up by herself should have behaved as Vicky had done. She knew all about the modern world, the independence of young girls today and all that, but the lax morals were for others—not for her girls. And she thought she had brought Vicky up to conduct herself decently. To think that she could have gone off in the night like that, with a young man whom she hardly knew!

However, the sight of Vicky's drooping figure and

ghastly pallor aroused the maternal instinct in Mrs. Waide, who took her arm and bade her be seated in the drawing-room. Edith should make her a cup of coffee at once.

'You look dreadful,' she announced. 'But I must say it's your own fault.'

With a tired gesture, Vicky drew off her hat and ran her slender, nervous fingers through her black curls.

'So I've been told already,' she said, 'and if you all keep on saying that it's my fault, I shall go mad.'

'Well,' exclaimed Freda, 'I don't think there's any need for you to be sharp with Mum, or surprised if we do say things to you. You've——'

'Never mind now, Freda,' interrupted Mrs. Waide. 'I'll see to Vicky. You look very tired, Free, dear. I'm sorry you had to make that long journey. Was the flying very bad? I was so nervous. I hardly knew how to let you go, but Dad insisted. And perhaps it's just as well. We couldn't have left Vicky alone in Paris.'

'Lucky for her that she found someone who seemed to behave like a gentleman,' said Freda.

Vicky leaned back in the armchair and shut her eyes. If only they'd let her go to her room and be in peace. But, of course, now that Freda had finished with her, it was Mum's turn. Edith brought the cup of coffee. Vicky's mother allowed her to drink it and then started cross-questioning.

What made her go off like that without even warning them? How could she have been so wicked, causing them all that terrible anxiety? What had Paul Dallas done to her? What had he said? Where did he take her? Dad said if he came back to England he'd set the police on him. Taking away a girl like that was a criminal offence. Was Vicky *all right*? etc., etc., until Vicky's nerve broke and she burst into floods of tears and demanded to be left alone.

'I'm perfectly all right. He didn't touch me. We were travelling all the time. Yes, he did try to kiss me, but I wouldn't let him. Oh, don't be so silly, Mum. You're talking like a bit out of a newspaper. I can take care of myself. I did. Do stop talking as though I'd been away a year—and come home with a baby in a shawl!'

'*Vicky*!' expostulated her mother, scarlet.

Vicky sobbed:

'Well, you keep on at me, and I tell you nothing like that happened.'

Mrs. Waide allowed her to quieten down. Forlornly Vicky sat there, wiping her eyes and blowing her small reddened nose. Then Mrs. Waide resumed the attack.

Who was this man who rang up then? What had *he* done? What had *he* said? Where did she meet *him*?

Vicky's replies satisfied the mother. Obviously Mr. Farnel was a good man. Lucky for her. Dad had said he sounded very nice over the phone. Then, having convinced herself that Vicky had come to no physical harm, she started on a new line of attack. The whole thing was disgraceful and a scandal, and had cost Dad the earth. Whereupon Vicky reminded her that there could be no scandal since nobody knew about it except themselves, and nobody need know—not even Tom.

'Tom!' exclaimed Mrs. Waide. 'Why, it makes my blood boil to think of how you treat that splendid fellow who wants to marry you. The best thing you can do is accept him and settle down, my girl, the very next time he asks you. We don't want any more trouble at home like *this*.'

'You won't have any,' said Vicky wearily. 'Please may I go to my room now, Mum?'

Somewhat reluctantly Mrs. Waide allowed her to go upstairs. There were still a great many things she wanted to know. She was still not quite sure of her young daughter, not positive that everything had been as proper as Vicky made out. But she supposed that she could not make Vicky say any more, today, anyhow.

'Better to go to bed if you feel ill,' she suggested.

'I'd like to,' said Vicky meekly.

'I am fed up about you losing your suitcase and all your things,' Mrs. Waide grumbled, following her up the stairs.

'I'm sorry,' said Vicky.

Mrs. Waide would have entered the bedroom with her, but Vicky protested at that.

'Mum, leave me alone, *please*. I do want to be let alone, really. Can't you see I'm all in?'

Mrs. Waide had no understanding, and was hurt.

'At a time like this I should have thought you would have wanted your mother. You are lucky to have a home to come back to. Some people wouldn't have welcomed you after your behaviour.'

Vicky's hands clenched. She looked dumbly a moment at her mother. She wondered if Mrs. Waide had ever committed any indiscretion in her life? If she had any personal experience of the frailty of human nature or the ignominy of defeat? But no—of course she had never been wild or impulsive or capable of a really rash action. She must have been like Freda when she was young.

At this moment Vicky would have been glad to fling herself into the arms of somebody who understood, and could talk things over, without prejudice. But her mother was a mass of prejudices and conventional theories and did not invite warmth or confidence from Vicky. Yet in that moment Vicky had some understanding of the older woman. She could realise what a shock and disappointment this had been to her. For an instant she forgot her own unhappiness. She said:

'I'm terribly sorry, Mum. I really am, for upsetting you and Dad.'

That should have called for sympathetic response and established some contact between mother and daughter. Instead it brought forth a fresh torrent of reproach from Mrs. Waide. Vicky might well be sorry. She had given them all a bad fright. Dad had gone off to the shop this morning feeling quite rotten. And heaven alone knew what they were going to do with Vicky now, unless she'd settle down to life at home like Freda. Look at the advantages she had over other girls! Others who were forced to go and earn their living and live in miserable digs. Dad had a good business, and here she was with plenty to eat, good clothes, no need to work. She could join the Norman Park Tennis Club, like she had done last year, and go to local whist drives, etc., and meet nice friends. Then there was Tom, and so on and so on, whilst Vicky sat on the edge of her bed listening to her mother's lachrymose voice, her slender shoulders hunched in an attitude of despair.

Oh yes, she had plenty to eat and drink and no need to work, and there was the local tennis club, and whist drives, *and* Tom! Perhaps she was wicked not to feel that her lot was a blessed one. Yet how much rather would she have gone to work every day and had her *freedom*. Known that she could do what she liked, when and as she liked, instead of living exactly as her mother and sister wished her to live.

She looked round the little room and saw in a corner the trunk which she had packed and had intended to send for as soon as she got settled in Paris. Sick and disconsolate, she remembered the wonderful schemes she had built up as she packed that trunk. The dreams she had dreamed of becoming a great dancer, of returning one day in triumph to mother and home, surrounded by that thrilling, glamorous atmosphere which can only be conjured up by success.

And within twenty-four hours she had been forced back, with life stripped of its thrills, revealed in all its real significance.

Vicky put her face in her hands and began to cry again.

Then Mrs. Waide condescended to pat her head, kiss her on the brow, and tell her 'to dry her eyes and be a good girl, and slip into bed.'

'You'll feel better after a nice rest, and we must all try to forget about this,' she said magnanimously. 'I'm sure you've learned for yourself that it doesn't do to go behind your parents' backs and fill your mind with all this stuff and nonsense about dancing. It's these films, I know! They give girls ideas and they ought to be stopped.'

With this world-shaking announcement, Mrs. Waide walked from the room and closed the door.

Now that she was alone, Vicky gave way to an abandonment of misery. She undressed, crawled into bed, and cried until she could cry no more. And she had the ridiculous feeling that it was an exact repetition of an incident, years ago, when as a small child she had been to a party, led the other children into some escapade (the spirit of romance and adventure had been bubbling in her even then!), and had been sent home in disgrace. After a long lecture from her mother, she had come up here to this same bedroom and wept in this same manner, feeling that the world was against her and nobody understood.

But it was so much worse today. She was no longer a child. She was a woman. She wanted her life to *mean* something. What could it ever mean here in Norman Park? How could she ever meet interesting, intelligent people—like Digby Farnel for instance? How would she ever meet a man with whom she could fall in love? She had thought herself attracted by Paul Dallas for a brief while. But when in the train he had first taken her in his arms, she had known that she loathed him. Where, then, was love? Where was her lover? Where was the passionate beauty of existence with all its fulfilment, which she *knew* awaited her somewhere in the world?

It was a bad home-coming for Vicky. And there was the meeting with her father to be got through yet. That, however, passed off not too badly. Mr. Waide, alone of the family, had some comprehension of the emotional conflict that was going on in his young daughter, and of that wild Irish streak which had led her to run away from home in a moment of madness. When he came up to her room to see her, he did not reproach her, or bother her with many questions. He just said:

'Well, dear, I expect it's been a lesson to you. I must say I'm glad to see you back again safe and sound. You must just try to be good and more settled, in future.'

Vicky flung her arms around his neck and kissed him with real warmth.

'I do love you, Dad. You always were an angel to me!'

He felt her wet tears against his cheek and grieved for her, his younger, and favourite daughter. Looking into the stormy beauty of her tear-filled eyes, he thought how lovely she was, and how sad it seemed that she should be so unhappy. Things weren't going to be easy for little Vicky in life. He had always known that, and that's why he so frequently got himself into trouble with Gracie by taking her part. Gracie and Freda were good women. But they didn't understand human nature. *He* knew that all right! And Vicky was only human, poor child. He felt uneasy about her future. Unconsciously he echoed his wife's words when he said:

'The best thing you could do, Vicky, would be to settle down and marry Tom. He's very keen on you and he's a fine fellow with a good farm, and you'd live in a nice country house. Why don't you turn your thoughts to him, instead of worrying about this dancing business?'

Vicky smiled at her father through her tears and made some non-committal reply. After he'd done, she lay with her arms behind her head, staring up at the ceiling and thinking:

'I suppose that's how it'll end. I'll be nagged into marrying Tom. At least, then, I'd have a home of my own, and I would be more my own mistress. Tom's always kind to me. He'll probably let me do what I want. It'll be pretty grim living here, being made to feel a naughty child by my mother and sister, for goodness knows how long!'

Then back came the thought of Digby Farnel. The flashing recollection of an instant in the Bois de Boulogne when he had posed her for one of his photographs. Quite simply, she had stood with her back to a tree, her hands behind her, her face lifted to the sun. And he had said:

'That's lovely! You look like some classic Greek, child! You should be wearing a long flowing robe, and have flowers in your hair.'

That had appealed to her sense of beauty and imagination. And then he had come forward and brushed a curl away from her cheek because it shadowed her eyes. His touch was delicate and she had recognised the fact that there was much of the sensitive artist in Digby. That was how she liked a man. But Tom could never be sensitive or an artist in a thousand years. He wouldn't know much about the Greek classics, anyhow!

She would like to see Digby Farnel again. But of course she wouldn't. He wouldn't come. He had promised to send her a copy of the colour photographs. He might do that. And perhaps he would write. . . .

Vicky wondered why she thought of this man so persistently. She supposed that it was because he had entered her life and befriended her at a very crucial moment. Queer, but she didn't think about Paul Dallas at all. She had wiped him right off the slate. But Digby Farnel had left an impression which would not easily be effaced.

11

There was nothing to liven those next few weeks for Vicky. Nothing and nobody—except Tom. And that of course was exactly why Mr. Collinson eventually won his heart's desire. For on Vicky's twenty-first birthday she changed her mind and promised to marry him.

All through June she had felt restless and unhappy. Regularly, at weekends, Tom came to see her. She had to admit that his devotion was quite touching. The way he motored all those miles in his old car just to have a meal with her and take her for a walk or a ride, or to the local pictures. At least he made her feel that he *wanted* her. And he looked upon her without the mistrust and suspicion with which she knew she was now regarded by her own family. For Tom did not know about Paris, and need never know. Tom had no idea that she had ever seen that exhibition dancer again after the night on which he and Vicky had attended the local dance.

. The only thing he did know was that Vicky seemed more than usually dissatisfied with life and had grown so thin that he could see hollows in her cheeks and her young throat, which disturbed him. He did not think it right that Vicky should be so thin. He made special efforts to please her. And on her birthday, which was at the end of June, he gave her the nicest present she had ever had, either from him or anybody else. A blue leather travelling vanity-case full of little blue enamel stoppered bottles and pots. The case had her initials, V. W., stamped upon it in gilt letters.

Tom presented the case to her with a sheepish smile.

'I don't know much about these things,' he told her; 'but the girl at the shop told me that was what young women liked these days.'

Vicky certainly did like it. It was not only beautiful and expensive, but had that feeling of glamour attached to it which never failed to thrill her. A make-up box—and from dear old Tom! How really pathetic. But what was there to make-up for these days? She never went anywhere or did anything except with Freda or Mum. Half-heartedly, she played tennis. Half-heartedly accompanied the family on their occasional outings. The crushing adventure of Paul Dallas and Paris had stolen the vividness out of Vicky's life and out of her heart, for the time being.

She had always looked forward to her twenty-first birthday. Had always thought it would mean something to become 'of age'. It meant, anyhow, that she was no longer an infant in the eyes of the law, and that she could marry whom she chose. But there was no choice. And she couldn't do what she wanted any more now than when she had been in her teens. She was tied to the family day and night.

Since her return from Paris, her mother had graciously elected to refrain from mentioning the episode, but little chance remarks from her now and again showed that she had far from forgotten it, and that she was keeping an eye on her wayward young daughter. Dad was as nice as he could be. Freda remained her caustic and unattractive self. It was little wonder that Vicky, feeling an intense loneliness in her warm young heart, should turn to someone for consolation. And equally natural that that someone should be Tom, who adored her.

She had never meant to marry him. He wasn't her 'type'. But he had shown up in particularly nice colours just lately, and the birthday party which he helped to make a success, held at the little house in Acacia Road, decided things.

Vicky was enchanted with her vanity-case. The family

were being especially friendly. Her mother had given her a new dinner dress which she had long wanted, and her father slipped a pound into her fingers and told her to choose something that she liked. Even Freda had come forward with something unusually generous from her. Two pairs of good silk stockings. One wasn't twenty-one every day, and on such an occasion Vicky couldn't remain 'sunk' or unmindful of the kindnesses accorded her. So during the party, she sparkled with some of her old gay lustre, and looked so lovely in her new peach-coloured taffeta dress, that Tom Collinson's steady heart missed a beat every time he glanced at her.

They had one or two neighbours in after dinner. Played card games, and later, when the dance band came over the radio, Dad pushed all the chairs and furniture back so that they could dance.

Only then, with Tom clumsily steering her round the little room, did Vicky shut her eyes and remember what dancing once had meant to her—what she had intended it to mean for her future. Then the brilliance faded from her eyes, and her lips took that hopeless curve which they so often wore these days.

Where was Digby Farnel? She had never heard from him. And it was only of Digby that she thought, when she remembered her one mad adventure. Albeit Paul Dallas had proved himself not quite so much the villain of the piece as her mother made him out to be. He had actually seen to it that her suitcase, with all its contents intact, was returned to her. A fortnight ago it arrived by Carter Paterson, with a letter—written by Paul from an hotel in Piccadilly—telling Vicky that he had brought her case over on his return to London, and that he wished to say he was sorry he had frightened her away that morning, and that he hoped she would not think too badly of him.

Vicky had only one answer to that note. With help from her father, she scraped together enough money to send Paul the fare which he had spent on her journey. And after that she had felt better, no longer under any obligation to him. No, she did not think too badly of him. In fact, she did not think of him at all. He wasn't worth a thought. But Digby Farnel she would like to have seen. And where were those colour-photographs he had promised her?

Later that birthday night, when the party broke up, the family tactfully retired and left Vicky alone with Tom. They were always hoping something would come of that— and on Vicky's birthday night, their hopes were fulfilled.

Tom made yet another proposal, couched, perhaps, in slightly more ardent terms than usual.

'Why not say "Yes" to me, Vicky? I'm terribly in love with you, you know that. I may be a bit clumsy in my ways, but I think I could make you happy if you'd give me a chance. Won't you marry me, won't you, dear?'

Vicky was sitting by the open window with the curtains drawn back. The summer night was calm and warm and there were stars in the sky. She was looking at those stars, her eyes half-sad, half-appreciative of the loveliness of the night. She was unconscious of the infinitely attractive picture that she made. Her figure slim and a little languorous, tiredly drooping with that 'after the party' feeling of fatigue. Her black silky curls ruffled by the night wind that blew upon her. She had the feeling that everything in the world tonight was lovely and yet sad. Beauty and sorrow seemed to walk hand in hand. If only one could be happy! Sometimes she dreamed that she was happy, but when she woke there was always a tear on her cheek, and an ache in her throat with which to begin a new day.

Then she heard Tom's voice.

He was terribly in love with her, he said. Well, it was nice to have someone in love with you. Good to be loved. Mum and Dad and Freda all cared for her in their way— but it was not a way which gave out any warmth or understanding. She couldn't go on living in this house month after month, year after year. She would only run away in the end and cause them fresh distress. It was so

130

wicked of them not to let her take a job. It was so out-of-date. If she ever had children, she would never chain them down. It could never rouse the best, only the worst, to chain one and give one this awful feeling of frustration which was hers.

Tom came up behind her and she felt his hand upon her shoulder.

'Won't you think it over, Vicky . . . sweetheart?'

It was that endearment, tenderly and boyishly uttered, that decided Vicky. And although she had never meant to do it, suddenly without warning she turned and threw herself into his arms. In tears, she wept against his shoulder:

'Yes, yes, marry me if you want to, Tom. Take me away.'

He was a little staggered and wholly enchanted by her sudden surrender. He held her close, patted her curls, and whispered a lot of foolish things into her ear. The sort of things he had not really thought himself capable of saying. He told her she was the sweetest and prettiest little thing in the world, and that she mustn't cry, because he wanted so much to make her happy and spend the whole of his life trying to give her that peace of mind which she was seeking.

'I know you're not happy at home, darling. And lately you've been terribly depressed, haven't you?'

'Yes,' she said, her voice muffled, her eyes still hidden, whilst her small hot hands encircled his neck, 'terribly.'

'Anything happened I don't know about?'

'Nothing that would interest you, Tom.'

'I'm awfully fond of your mother and father, and old Freda,' he said. 'She's a real good sort. But you—you're such a glamorous girl—'

'Don't!' she interrupted, '*please* don't call me that.'

'Why not?'

'There's nothing glamorous about me. I'm just a fool and I've made a mess of everything.'

He laughed and hugged her.

'You're certainly a little fool if you say things like that. How can you have made a mess of things at your age? Why, you're only a baby still, in spite of this twenty-first birthday.'

He found a handkerchief in his pocket and gave it to her. She wiped her eyes with it. And there flashed across her recollection the memory of herself in the Paris express, and of another man who had given her his handkerchief—Digby Farnel. And she had to laugh at the memory:

'I really can't become the sort of girl who goes round snivelling into men's handkerchiefs. I must pull myself together. And perhaps this is my destiny—to become a farmer's wife and get a thrill out of "Nature in the raw."'

Tom kissed the top of the silky head which enchanted him so.

'Do you really mean you'll marry me, Vicky?'

'Yes,' she said, and sealed her fate with that single word.

'Darling!' he said, quite rapturously for Tom.

Vicky wished that she herself could be altogether carried away by that rapture. Wished that she didn't just sit outside the circle, like an imp, deriding herself and everybody else. Now, in the midst of the proposal, she ought to be intoxicated with bliss. Wasn't that what happened in books and on the films? Where was the Vicky who impersonated Dolores Del Rio; who used to stick a rose in her hair and a shawl over her shoulder, and act the seductive siren of the day?

Poor Dolores! Here was no siren—but just a disappointed, rather bewildered girl, right out of her *milieu*, who lifted her lips for the first kiss of her accepted lover, and tried to be ecstatic about it all.

Vicky did not dislike that kiss. Did not feel the same repulsion or fear that she had felt in Paul Dallas's embrace, in the Paris train. There was something essentially nice about Tom. Nice and healthy and masculine. He covered her face with kisses, and eventually roused

132

some physical response from her. She kissed him back, shyly. Then with some warmth. Gradually those volatile spirits that were Victoria Waide's soared upward again, and she felt almost contented. After all, it was rather grand to have a lover and be engaged, and Tom was murmuring something about the ring that they would choose tomorrow. He had got a lot to do on the farm, but he'd let his man see to it. He'd stay another day in order to take her up to town to the jewellers. Yes, it was a thrill. A blessed relief after the awful monotony and hopelessness of this last month. In the circle of Tom's arms, Vicky began to make a dozen resolutions about being a good wife, and making Tom happy and forgetting that she had ever wanted to do anything else but marry him.

'Are you quite certain I won't disappoint you, Tom?' she asked him finally.

'Why should you?' he asked. 'There isn't anybody else, is there?'

'Nobody.'

'I think you'll get to like the farm. It's a lovely old place. When will you marry me, sweetheart?'

She drew away from his arms and smoothed the crushed fold of her pink taffeta dress. Marriage! Another thrill. And a mighty big step for any girl to take. But if she was going to take it, why not at once? She wanted to get away from home and the family. At least, when she was Mrs. Collinson, she would be her own mistress and not at the parents' beck and call, or coming in for one of Freda's spiteful taunts of which she was so heartily sick.

Vicky put her cheek against Tom's brown one and murmured:

'When you like. What's it matter?'

He picked up one of her hands and looked almost reverently at the smallness and whiteness of it. He had never seen such nails. They were a marvellous shape. Not exactly the hands of a farmer's wife! But he didn't want her to look any the less chic just because she was going to live on a poultry farm, bless her. She was so like an excited child, now that she had agreed to marry him. What a little creature of moods! No doubt she'd give him one or two difficult moments, but he'd cope with them. He could manage her. And, by jove! she could set a fellow's heart racing! Never before had she been so yielding, so sweet.

'We'll talk to your mother and father about it in the good old-fashioned way,' he said.

But Vicky tossed her curls and said:

'I'm twenty-one today and I shall do as I like. I'll marry you tomorrow if you like.'

'You're a rash child,' he said.

'Quite mad,' said Vicky; 'but then I always have been.'

'You'll soon settle down,' he said a bit tactlessly.

That dimmed her spirits a trifle. She didn't want him to say that. She didn't particularly want to 'settle down'. She would have liked him to catch her up in his arms and tell her that he was mad, too; that they could be mad together. But she mustn't expect too much. And Tom had really shown himself quite a good lover, tonight. More so than she had anticipated. He had said one or two quite wonderful things to her.

She seized his hand and dragged him to the door.

'We'll wake everybody up and tell them.'

Tom reddened, thrust his fingers through his thick fair hair.

'I say, ought we to——' he began.

Vicky interrupted him with one of her lovely, bubbling laughs—a sound rarely heard in this house these days—and opened the door.

'Of course! Isn't it an *occasion*? And they won't be asleep yet.'

So a moment later the whole house knew. Mr. and Mrs. Waide appeared in dressing-gowns, leant over the banisters and called down their good wishes, and if there was any woman in England more heartily relieved than Mrs. Waide, she would have been difficult to find.

A very real warmth and pleasure animated Grace

Waide's face when she said:

'Well, now, how *nice*. I *am* pleased, my dears!'

Mr. Waide rubbed the back of his grey scanty hair and added his greetings, not perhaps as heartily as his wife. He had more imagination. He wondered whether Tom would make that queer, madcap daughter of his really happy.

The one person to withhold congratulations was Freda. She pretended to be asleep and stay asleep. She lay in the darkness in her room, her teeth clenched, her pale, expressionless eyes brimming with tears. Tears which she could not restrain. She hated Vicky! *Hated* her for getting Tom. She felt degraded and humiliated because she had been so overlooked. Tom was a damned fool! Vicky would never make him happy in the way that she, Freda, could have done! Tomorrow, of course, she must control herself, and offer good wishes and all that. But not to-night. Not with the thought of those two down there in each other's arms.

Vicky didn't deserve it—after that affair in Paris. And if it hadn't been bad enough her going away with that Dallas fellow, there had been something up between herself and that Mr. Farnel. Mrs. Waide and Freda were both certain of that. For a fortnight ago, while Vicky was at the tennis club, a large square envelope had arrived for Vicky, with the Paris postmark. Freda and her mother had consulted each other about it, and decided that if this was any communication from that blackguard Dallas, it would be best that it should not be delivered to Vicky. Mrs. Waide considered it her duty to open the packet.

To the surprise of both women, they had discovered two colour-photographs, of Vicky, obviously taken in Paris. One of her posed against a chestnut tree. One sitting on the side of what looked like a stone fountain. Exquisite colour and pose, although the artistry of the pictures was totally lost on both Mrs. Waide and Freda. But what had not been lost upon them was the significance of those photographs and the note accompanying them.

'*I am sending these for you to keep. My own copies will*

135

be framed and treasured. Be happy, my dear. Perhaps one day I shall see you again. I hope so. . . .'

And the initials D.F. had signed this note.

Harmless enough, but a great deal could be read into it—and was. They agreed that Vicky must have been shameless to allow the man to photograph her, directly after that affair with the other man. And why should he address her as '*My dear*,' or say that he 'treasured her photograph'? Just another flagrant example of Vicky's wild ways, and Mr. Farnel was no better than the rest.

The beautiful colour-photographs were flung ruthlessly into the Ideal boiler and the note accompanied them. And so Vicky wondered from day to day why the promised photographs never came from her friend in Paris.

But that night, celebrating her birthday and engagement, she was not thinking of Digby. Her thoughts were only of Tom and the new thrilling state of being engaged. She *knew* she would have happy dreams that night. But she didn't! For curiously enough—and to her secret shame—it was Digby Farnel, not her fiancé, of whom she dreamed. It was he who, all over again, handed her his handkerchief and dried her eyes. He who kissed her lips like a lover and called her sweetheart. She was immensely, breathlessly stirred. She gave back to him something of her real self—something of the soul in her—something that she had not given Tom at all.

Then he was gone. And she woke up to find the sunlight streaming into her room, and the tears drenching her pillow. She realised that it had just been a stupid dream, and that this was the day on which she would be going with Tom up to town to buy her engagement ring.

12

There began from that time onward a spell which might be termed a happy one for Victoria Waide. But it was a happiness with a curiously false value. An excitement which she deliberately built up about herself. Her engagement to Tom Collinson brought no real inner excitement—no real sensation that she was fulfilling herself, or her proper mission in life. However, things were certainly brighter and better at home.

The engagement ring was bought. Tom spent more probably than he could afford, and it was the sort of ring that Vicky had always wanted. Not a stereotyped diamond. But a beautiful clear aquamarine which, she declared to Tom, looked like blue ice-water, as clear as a Norwegian lake. It brought Tom no visions of a Norwegian lake. He had never seen one, and he didn't think Vicky had, but she was a funny, fanciful little thing, and the point that concerned him was that the jeweller had assured him that it was a good stone and good value.

The aquamarine looked very charming on Vicky's slender finger, and she was naturally proud of her status as an engaged girl. Certainly it gave her an importance and dignity, in the eyes of the family, which she had not possessed before. She was no longer the black sheep, the despair of the household. Both mother and father beamed upon her and Freda made an attempt, even if a half-hearted one, to be nice, and take some interest in the purchase of Vicky's trousseau.

It was that trousseau which kept Vicky busy until the middle of July. For hers was not to be a long engagement.

She was going to marry Tom at the end of the month. She was 'of age'. The parents saw no reason why she should not get married at once if she wanted to. Indeed, Grace Waide, without inquiring too deeply as to whether her young daughter was making a match that would really suit her, encouraged an early wedding. As she told Freda, she would not feel really happy until she saw Tom walk up the aisle with Vicky. Then she would breathe again. Vicky's husband would have the responsibility of the girl and all her strange ways.

Mr. Waide was not ungenerous about the trousseau. Vicky and her mother were kept busy in the shops, and Freda helped make some of the lingerie. She was good at needlework and did some beautiful stitching and embroidery. What she actually felt about this wedding, she did not betray. She was always reticent. But to her mother, she let fall occasional remarks to the effect that she could not see Vicky settling down as Tom's wife, and that she hoped Vicky would not disappoint him.

The days rushed by now—filled with shopping and preparations. Tom came up one Sunday and drove Vicky down to Sussex to see the farm. He wanted her to redecorate and furnish the best bedroom and the sitting-room, if she so wished. He felt it a little unfair that she should be made to accept as her future home a place which had been lived in so long by a bachelor.

Vicky's first impression of Tom's house was good. Her sense of beauty was fully enchanted by the first glimpse.

Tye Farm nestled at the foot of the Downs, about ten miles out of Brighton and not far from the famous Dyke. A typical Sussex farm-house, long, low, half hung with weathered tiles which the centuries had tinted to lovely faded colours, and with a Horsham slab roof, yellow with lichen, and tall Elizabethan chimneys. The massive oak beams were weathered to an exquisite grey.

That was the farm-house, flanked by tall trees, and with one immense oak in the front which was in the full beauty of its foliage when Vicky first saw it. Away to the left were the tumbledown timbered out-buildings. In front, a small garden. The garden was disappointing. It had only a few straggling, unpruned roses, and a few equally uncared-for, unkempt herbaceous plants. Tom had no time for gardening, he pointed out to Vicky rather shamefacedly, but he would get one of the men to clear up a bit and mow the lawn before she came to live at Tye Farm.

The disappointing and ugly part was at the back. Vicky loathed at sight those unending rows of poultry houses and the runs full of the White Leghorns which were Tom's pride and delight. She always knew she would dislike those chickens. Senseless, unattractive creatures.

On this, her first visit to the place, she would have liked a lover who would, for instance, have stood with her before that oak and shared her raptures over the symmetry of bough and rich green leaf, or her delight in the old grace and beauty of the house itself.

But to Tom these things were just part of the landscape and meant nothing individually. All his raptures were for the fowls and their houses. He was so proud of those new runs; of the fine roosters, of the fact that the output of eggs was increasing under the present system, etc., etc.

He expected her to take a delight in the whitewashed cold little room in which there were nothing but empty packing-cases and a long table bearing scales, and baskets and baskets of eggs. Eggs which had to be weighed and packed, day after day.

After a few moments of standing there looking at them, Vicky realised that she would soon grow to hate the sight of an egg, and would possibly never want to eat one again. But she dutifully admired everything. Poor old Tom! After all, she thought, it was his job, and naturally he was proud of it, but he was horribly practical! He so rarely paused to say a romantic word. There were kisses and embraces, yes. And he was very much in love with her. But he was not a man to sit down and analyse emotion, which she liked to do at times. He left her to take it for granted that he was in love with her, and that was *that*!

She had a faint and perhaps forlorn hope that his passion for her, or at least the outward expression of it, might alter and increase after their marriage. And perhaps her own feelings toward him would intensify, too. She hoped that it would not always be quite so 'ordinary' as it was now. She wanted something more unique and thrilling to evolve from their union.

If the outside of Tye Farm had enchanted her, the interior failed to do so. There was loveliness in the great beams and the huge open fireplaces, and the big tiled kitchen. But in general the place was rambling and seemed to Vicky full of ghosts. When she first entered the hall, her arm through Tom's, Tye Farm struck a chill in her heart. She was sensitive to atmospheres. Romance might be here—romance of the ages. But there was something lost and lonely about the place. And it would be frightfully cold in the winter. (She shuddered to think of the winter at Tye Farm.) Very different from the cosy little modern house in which she now lived. Although Tom's house was much more artistic, it was certainly not as comfortable. No central heating. Not even main drainage. All the water had to be pumped up, and the hot-water system was twenty years old and inadequate.

The place was furnished as she had imagined it would be, with the things which Tom had inherited from his father. None of it attractive or fitting in with the place. Massive Victorian carved mahogany. Good stuff, but hideous. Atrocious paintings in gilt frames which no doubt had cost money when they were bought, and that was why Tom stuck to them. He did not know the first thing about painting. But it made Vicky wonder exactly what a man like Digby Farnel would have thought of them.

She was cheered by the thought that she would be allowed to refurnish the sitting-room and the big bedroom which looked out over the Downs, and was to be *their* room. Tom suggested with a rather foolish grin (which annoyed her), that they might stick to that big Victorian bed; but Vicky was out to have everything new up there.

And *two* beds, she told Tom definitely. It was modern and hygienic. He agreed. He generally let her have her way. But afterwards, when she thought over that incident she was depressed by it. Wouldn't a girl, romantically and desperately in love, have felt otherwise about that sleeping accommodation? Perhaps so. But then she didn't think she was either romantically or desperately in love with Tom. She was beginning to think that she was not in love with him at all—just frightfully fond, and looking upon her marriage as a way out from the awful monotony of life at home.

She returned from that trip to Sussex in a mood by no means elated, although she described everything gaily enough to the family, and enjoyed herself planning what she would do to modernise and cheer the place up a little bit, on the money which Tom was prepared to expend.

That next morning she went up to London by herself. Freda was busy, and her mother had an attack of neuralgia. Vicky was going to look at curtain patterns. Something in green and white chintz, she thought, for the sitting-room at Tye Farm. And they would have a green carpet in place of that terrible old patterned one with roses on it, which was there at the moment. She would amuse herself trying to find some bits of old oak and do away with that appalling cabinet of china and the depressing leather chairs which had belonged to Tom's father. She must get a couple of good easy-chairs and cover them in chintz to match the curtains.

Just before midday she found herself walking down Bond Street. Not that she meant to shop in that expensive district, but she liked to look in at some of the lovely things and 'get ideas' for her home. It was interesting and fun to have some money to spend and her own home to think about. She felt quite cheerful and it was a gorgeous day. She liked the heat and could stand even the sultriness of London. She looked fresh and young in her green linen dress with a short coat, a tiny straw hat perched on the side of her dark curls, and a spray of yellow roses pinned

141

to her shoulder. More than one man looked twice at her as she passed. And one man coming toward her did more than look. He stopped and stared. She was unconscious of his scrutiny until he was right in front of her, sweeping the hat from his head.

'Why, it's you—Vicky!' he exclaimed.

She found herself looking up at Digby Farnel. Her heart began beating fast at the unexpected pleasure of seeing him. The same Digby, his clever, attractive eyes shining through their glasses. A very elegant Digby, in beautifully-cut grey flannels, and carrying yellow chamois gloves.

'*Oh!* Mr. Farnel! What a surprise!' was all she could say.

He gripped her small hand.

'What a very lucky meeting. And how small the world is. After which cliché: how are you, my dear? Where have you sprung from this summer morning?'

'From home.'

'Norman Park?'

'Yes.'

'Just doing some shopping?'

'Yes.'

'And I was on my way to my tailor. The last person I expected to meet was your charming self.'

He might have added that the one person he most wanted to see was Victoria Waide. He had been greatly disappointed because she had not answered his note, nor even troubled to thank him for his photographs. He was a busy man with plenty to do and a large circle of friends, but somehow he had been haunted by the memory of that Paris episode. Of Vicky, herself. At this very moment, on his mantelpiece in his flat, was his best colour-photograph of her.

When he was alone he often looked at the pure beauty of her remembered face, and her exquisite colouring, and thought of the wistfulness in her eyes and how reluctant he had been to let her go out of his life. Something about this child appealed to him vastly. He felt it even more keenly now that he saw her today. But she was not the distraught, desperate young woman who had fled to him for protection in Paris. She looked radiant and remarkably pretty.

He said:

'What did you think of your photographs?'

She stared at him.

'My photographs? You didn't send me any.'

His brows drew together.

'I certainly did. Two enlargements—with a letter.'

She shook her head.

'You must have sent them to the wrong address.'

He frowned and tapped his forehead.

'Surely not, or I would have got them back from the Dead Letter Office. I posted them from Paris a fortnight after they were taken. But I put my own address on the letter. Let me think . . . I sent them to Miss V. Waide, 14 Acacia Road, Norman Park.'

'That's quite right.'

'Then I wonder why you didn't get them.'

Vicky was silent a moment. Her face was grave. She began to wonder if those photographs had come and if the family had intercepted them. If they had . . . how furious she'd be . . . She'd ask Mum and Freda as soon as she got back. They had no right . . .

'I shouldn't be surprised if they didn't arrive when I was out, and were kept from me,' she said with a short laugh. 'You've no idea what a frightful fuss there was about everything when I got back. I daresay if there was a French postmark on the envelope, they might have thought it best to keep it from me.'

'Well, I'm damned,' said Digby Farnel, feeling and looking cross.

'Of course, it mayn't be so, but I'll soon find out,' said Vicky.

'I'm very pleased to see you again,' he said. Then, with a quick glance at his wrist-watch: 'Look here, it's a quarter to one. How about having some lunch with me?'

She hesitated, but only for an instant. It would be grand to have lunch with him—to talk to him. There was an immense fascination for her in listening to Digby Farnel talk. And she was so glad to see him again, and to know that he *had* written and *had* remembered, though it made her blush a little to remember all those absurd dreams which she had had about him.

She did not pause to wonder whether or not she ought to lunch with him. Why shouldn't she—just because she was engaged to Tom? So she said:

'I'd simply love to, if you really mean it.'

'I certainly do. Let's think . . . where would you like to lunch?'

'Anywhere,' she said.

He looked into those great intense blue eyes of hers and felt his heart leap absurdly. She hadn't altered. She was just as peculiarly alluring to him now as she had been in Paris. It was so rarely that he met any girl who affected him that way. Why waste the precious moments? Why waste such feeling? If he wanted to see Vicky and go on seeing her, he had every right to do so, so far as he knew.

'Let's go to the Berkeley Grill,' he suggested.

Vicky nodded. Excitement was bubbling up in her now. An excitement such as she hadn't felt for months. She had never been to the Berkeley in her life. She had always wanted to.

There was something so facile and charming about Digby. He made her feel as though she had known him all her life. That was how she had felt about him when they had first met.

And then she found herself in the restaurant, facing him, watching while he ordered the lunch. She left it entirely to him. The waiters seemed to know him. He was very much the 'man about town'. She liked the way he did everything. He ordered melon and trout, and quail, and a bottle of hock. It sounded the grandest lunch to her. And there was a glamour attached to it all which she had felt

144

with Paul Dallas, only that had been spurious and this was real. There was nothing cheap or false about Digby Farnel. She honestly felt that she could believe every word that he said.

When he leaned across the table and told her that she was looking as beautiful as ever, she could believe that he meant that, too. But it did not enchant her so much as it depressed. Her spirits went down to zero suddenly. For she remembered Tom and that forthcoming marriage which was only ten days ahead. Why they should sink at the thought of Tom, she hardly knew, and had no time to analyse. But they did.

'What's the matter?' Digby asked, lighting a cigarette, while he drank his sherry, smiling across the table at her. 'You're looking sad. Your whole expression's changed. You were quite happy just now.'

Vicky laughed and made a non-committal reply. It gave her a warm sort of feeling that he should notice her change of expression. That was how a woman liked a man to be. It would never enter Tom's head in a thousand years to notice whether her eyes were sad or gay.

Then suddenly, as though defying herself, she took off her gloves and held her left hand out toward Digby Farnel.

'Look what's happened to me.'

He looked and his brows went up. For no real reason he was disappointed. So she was engaged! *That* was what had happened to her.

'Well, well!' he said, 'my congratulations. Who's it to?'

'Tom Collinson.'

'Collinson? Is that your friend who runs the poultry farm in Sussex?'

'Yes.'

'When are you going to be married?'

'In less than a fortnight.'

'I hope you'll be very happy,' he said gravely.

She made no answer. But with a sudden sense of hopelessness, she knew that she wouldn't be happy and that it was all futile—utterly futile! She ought never to have agreed to marry Tom. He couldn't make her happy. She didn't want to be his wife and live down in that ghost-ridden old farm-house. She didn't want to spend her life gazing upon thousands of chickens and listening to ceaseless conversations about eggs. She must have been mad. But she'd done it. It was much too late. She couldn't put it off now. And if she did put it off, what would she gain? Precisely nothing but a return to imprisonment and boredom at home.

Anyhow, she was a little fool to allow this meeting with Digby Farnel to upset her whole apple-cart. Why should she be so disturbed because he said that he 'hoped she'd be happy'?

Digby, watching her through the curling smoke of his cigarette, knew precisely what was going on in her mind. And he too was struck by the futility of things. The tragic child! Must she always make some hopeless mistake in her life? She wasn't in love with this fellow. She didn't utter one rapturous word. Besides . . . what a ghastly waste of all her youth and beauty, to be put down in a poultry farm in the wilds of the country for the rest of her young life.

He imagined what had happened. She was taking this way out after her disaster in Paris. It was wrong. And it was utterly unfair that she shouldn't have more chance in life.

Of course he was half in love with her himself. He knew that now. And it wouldn't take him much to fall headlong in love. A pity he was so cautious and sceptical—and a bit cynical about love and sex and marriage. Otherwise he might have swept her away, himself. He was quite sure he could have made her happy, and he was sure that he would not have grown tired of her beauty and that sensitive nature of hers.

Still, she was going to be married to her poultry farmer and there it was.

The first part of that lunch was not particularly happy.

Digby and Vicky carried on rather a strained conversation about nothing in particular. But later they forgot themselves a little and talked more intimately.

During coffee, Digby said:

'Is this marriage going to keep you locked away in the country for ever, I wonder?'

'I suppose so,' she said.

Her cheeks were a little flushed and her eyes sparkling again after the food and wine and the warmth of the friendly conversation with him. Digby always seemed able to get to the root of things with her. She felt that she could talk to him. She added:

'I don't know whether I shall be a success as Tom's wife. I don't think I'm doomed to be very successful.'

'Oh, yes, you are. You must be. You have so many gifts.'

'A great gift for being a little idiot,' she laughed.

'Aren't we all idiots, my dear,' he said, and sighed.

'I shan't ask you to my wedding,' she said, with another laugh; 'it wouldn't amuse you.'

'No, I don't think it would,' he said abruptly.

She was not sure what he meant by that. But he looked at her suddenly in a way which made her heart hammer against her ribs. And then she thought:

'I should be mad if I ever saw this man again. He affects me in a way nobody else has ever done. I'd better remember that I'm going to marry Tom, and go and buy my curtains.'

And Digby thought:

'I wonder what the hell that marriage will do to her? She may settle down to it or it may make her intolerably unhappy. The whole thing's monstrous. Why do people get driven to do things just because they're unhappy? And why, in God's name, must they jump out of one difficulty into another?'

He called for the bill and paid it. A moment later he stood out in the sunshine with Vicky. And he saw no radiance in her young face now. Only a brooding sadness which upset him vastly, for there was an echo of it in his own spirits which he had never felt there before.

Always in distress, this child came across his path. And he never seemed able to help her. If only she hadn't got herself engaged to that fellow . . . things might have been different . . . or was he just a sentimental fool who wanted shaking?

'Where are you going now?' he asked.

'John Lewis, I think,' she said.

Digby hailed a passing taxi.

'I'll take you there.'

'Don't trouble——' she began.

But the taxi was there at the kerb, and she jumped in and Digby took his place beside her.

They moved through the traffic, stopping now and then when the red lights warned. And Vicky felt, with every moment that passed, that fate could not have been more unkind than to bring her into contact with this man again. She had built up a romance for herself with Tom. And Digby had unconsciously shattered it by a glance and a smile, and a touch of his hand.

This was the man whom she might have loved with all her soul. Might . . . if only . . . but what in heaven's name was the use of thinking that way now?

Something impelled him to take her small gloved fingers in his.

'I'm glad I saw you again. I want you to be very happy. Will you try?'

'Of course,' she said with a forced brightness.

'Send me your new address, and perhaps I may call and see your lovely farm-house. I'd like to photograph it.'

She knew she ought not to say 'yes', but everything in her snatched at the hope of seeing him again even after she was married to Tom.

'I'll send you the address,' she said.

He looked at her. She looked back. And suddenly before Digby realised what he was doing, he had drawn her into his arms.

148

'May I wish you happiness—like this——?'

The sunlit world and the traffic and the people reeled around Vicky for a single instant as she felt his lips touch her mouth. *Her dream* . . . her dream come true. . . . Digby holding her in his arms, kissing her, and everything in her that was real and vital rushing to the surface with his kiss.

She felt so choked when he released her, that she could not speak. Hardly knowing what she did, she stepped out of that taxi, when the commissionaire opened the door. She heard Digby's voice following her:

'Good-bye! Good luck!'

In the big store, against a crush of people, she was horrified to find her eyes blinded with tears.

The taxi-driver pushed back the little glass sliding-door and spoke to Digby.

'Where to now, sir?'

Digby didn't know. And he didn't much care. His eyes sought to follow that slight, graceful figure in the green linen dress threading its way through the crowd, until it was lost to view. He was astonished to find how the touch of her lips had set his heart racing. And he was furiously angry with himself for having kissed her and precipitated such unexpected feeling in himself. She was going to marry her poultry farmer and settle down. He had no right to give her a second thought.

'Where to, sir?' repeated the driver.

Gloomily Digby gave him the address of his Club. Sitting back in a corner of the taxi, where a moment ago Vicky, with all her sweet, appealing youth, had sat beside him, he removed his glasses, wiped them carefully with a silk handkerchief, and put them back with a gesture of intense annoyance. He was annoyed with himself and with the world in general. He wanted Vicky here again—back in his arms. He wanted to tell her that she couldn't marry that other fellow because she was going to marry him. That was good! From a confirmed bachelor. That would make old Jack Morgan smile!

149

He'd better get out of England. Take a cruise. Go to the West Indies, anywhere to get away from this fantastic feeling that he was in love with a girl whom he had only seen once or twice in his life—he, who had never been in love.

If he thought she was going to be happy, he wouldn't mind. But his intuition told him that she would not. When he had kissed her, her lips had clung to his and one of her small hands had crept around his neck. As though she had wanted that kiss—needed his love.

'Fool!' said Digby Farnel to himself, and changed his mind about going to the Club, and told the taxi-driver to take him to Dean & Dawson, in Piccadilly, where he would see what boats were due to sail, and where he might take himself with his colour-camera, for a complete change.

13

One morning, about the beginning of September, Vicky got out of bed, walked to the window, pulled back the curtains, found that it was one of those superb golden days when summer is barely tinged with the autumnal chill, and forthwith sighed.

She should not have sighed on such a perfect morning. The fair Sussex countryside surrounding Tye Farm was at its best. The Downs were wreathed in an opalescent mist, the sun just breaking through a rift of cloud, showing a chink of heavenly blue. The great oak, too, was half veiled by the curling vapours of the dawn, and the lawn looked as though in the night a million cobwebs had been spun across the grass from blade to blade, gossamer and glittering. From the eaves came the excited piping of awaking birds, and in the two tall trees to the left of the house a family of rooks, which nested there, quarrelled and screamed at each other.

A lovely autumn day. But the loveliness was spoiled for Vicky by so many things. By the incessant crowing of those roosters, for instance, reminding her of the thousands of chickens on Tom's farm. By the thought that today was a Saturday—and that meant shooting. Every weekend since the first of September, shooting had been organised, which meant that Vicky had to get a big lunch ready and entertain all the farmers for miles around, and very often their wives.

Of course, there were one or two nice people, like the Richardsons who had a dairy farm a few miles away. Richardson had been in the Navy, was retired, and his wife was a very pleasant woman, and somebody of intelligence with whom Vicky liked to talk. But the average local 'wives' at the shooting parties bored Vicky beyond belief. Besides, she hated having to walk round with the guns, as Tom liked her to do. She had long since come to the conclusion that she was not a country girl and that she hated country life, and particularly loathed to see anything killed.

On her first day out Tom, who prided himself on being a good shot, had brought a partridge down almost at her feet. The sickening thud as the soft little body fell had filled her with horror. She had picked up the dying bird, her tears flowing. Tom had laughed and told her not to be so tender-hearted. She had hated him for laughing, and never quite got over that episode. It might be stupid. There were plenty of women who were fond of shooting, and no doubt the others thought her a sloppy little idiot. But she didn't like it, and that was that.

There were so many things she didn't like.

She stood there in her pyjamas, looking gloomily down at the garden. She resembled a sleepy boy with her tousled curls, her bare arms and throat tanned to a rich brown by the summer sun. And she looked extremely well.

It was a healthy enough life at Tye Farm. There was always plenty of good Sussex meat, home-made butter, fresh cream from the Richardsons' dairy, and their own eggs. (She had reached that pitch which she had anticipated, when she really hated the sight of an egg on her breakfast table.) And she was always out of doors. Yes, a healthy life. Last Sunday when the family had come down from Norman Park, they had congratulated Tom because his wife was looking so fit. But of course they never did see farther than outward appearances. Neither did Tom. And none of them bothered to inquire how Vicky was feeling *inside*.

To herself, Vicky made no bones about her inner feelings. They were awful. She wasn't a bit happy in Tye

Farm, and from no point of view could she say that her marriage had been a success. Except perhaps from Tom's. He was so delightfully blind to what was going on around him, so lacking in imagination that she verily believed he was happy. And never happier than when he had his arms around her. Which was the one thing now that she would have run a mile from if she could.

No, taking all things into consideration, and looking back on the two months of her marriage, Vicky was quite certain that she had jumped from the frying-pan into the fire. She had been better off at Norman Park, even under the tyranny of Mum and Freda. She had been free there. She had thought herself a prisoner. But in reality she had been free. She had fondly imagined that marriage would give her independence. It had given her none, and taken away what she had had before.

True, she was Mrs. Collinson. She could order the servant about and have what food she liked, and do what she wanted in the small ways. But there was always Tom now—a much more formidable jailer than Mum or Freda. She had to do what *he* wanted. Not because he made unreasonable demands or bullied or tyrannised. He was easy-going and, in his fashion, anxious to please her. But he was her *husband*. And a husband expected things of his wife . . . expected her always to be there at meals, and every evening . . . expected her to take a perpetual interest in his job. Tom, for instance, never understood why she, Vicky, could not feel as hilarious as himself when the price of eggs went up, or his wretched hens laid more than usual . . . or why she wasn't as annoyed as he, if a fox got away with a few chickens or one of the farm-hands gave trouble.

And then there were the nights. Those nights were purgatory for Vicky. At least in her own home she had been alone. But here she must always share a room with Tom.

He was not the type to approve of husbands and wives having separate bedrooms. He would have been hurt to the bone had she even suggested it. So there, always, in the twin bed beside her own, he slept—and snored. She was sure he had adenoids. And sometimes when her nerves were bad and she couldn't sleep well, she would lie awake listening to that stertorous breathing till it drove her almost to a frenzy of fury. She would switch on the light and hurl a pillow at him. That would wake him. Quite good-humouredly he would apologise and turn over on his other side. But very soon the snoring would begin again. And Vicky would lie with her hands pressed to her throbbing temples, asking herself why girls were crazy enough to imagine that marriage necessarily spelled 'romance'.

She supposed it was all her fault. If she had loved Tom enough, she wouldn't have minded anything, and being alone with him, like this, on the farm might have been heaven. She wouldn't have felt bored. There would have been that subtle difference . . . the presence of a man whom one adored. She could have put up with so many hardships or disappointments if the sound of *his* footsteps had made her heart beat a fraction faster; if the thought of a passionate embrace had thrilled her instead of seeming a menace.

It was terrible to think that in such a short time Tom's physical presence should have become the very antithesis of delight. But it was so. She had realised that during their honeymoon.

She had tried hard to fall in love with him on that honeymoon, which they had spent over in Ireland. Tom was fond of fishing and had an uncle living near Killarney. He had lent them a cottage on a beautiful piece of water.

The scenery enchanted Vicky. There was a spell in Ireland which she could not resist. It had as much glamour in it as any romantic girl could desire. But the tragedy, which had so soon manifested itself, lay within herself. Inevitably she awakened to the fact that it doesn't matter where you are, it's a question of *whom you're with*. And she had been bored, bored, *bored*, sitting beside Tom watching him fish, by the hour. Watching him eat. (He was a hearty eater and always enjoyed his food.) Watching him sleep. (He could sleep at any odd interval in the day when he was tired.) He had a wonderful gift for closing his eyes and 'dropping off', which annoyed her.

As for love . . . Vicky had learned that to Tom, love was rather like food. To be taken at intervals, when so required. It was not a beautiful spontaneous fever for him, as it would have been for her under different circumstances. The sudden ecstatic union of lovers wholly in love and unable to resist their torrent of feeling. It was prosaic. Like everything else about Tom. So maddeningly practical and level-headed was he that it became an acute irritation to her. She felt she could beat her clenched fists upon him sometimes, and ask why he didn't wake up and *feel* about life and beauty and books and music and art as she did. But he didn't. He didn't understand any of those things. And she could never change him. He was far too set in his ways.

She had never told him she was bored. It would only have offended him and he would see no reason for it. In his opinion she had as much as, if not more than, many wives. A beautiful old farm-house to live in. A husband. A car. He had taught her to drive so that she could go into Brighton to do her shopping. And once a week he took her to a cinema. They had a couple of dogs—a spaniel bitch which he used to shoot over and a Labrador puppy. And there was always something doing on the farm. When they were short-handed, there were hundreds and thousands of eggs to be washed and weighed. She could never complain that there was nothing to do.

Vicky knew all that, and did what was expected of her. For days on end she would stand in that depressing outhouse, washing eggs until her fingers grew red and cold and all shrivelled up from being dipped so constantly in water. But her brain worked busily all the time, which was the trouble. It would have been so much better if it hadn't worked; if she had no feelings. At least no feelings against

155

this sort of life, nor inclinations toward another.

But sometimes her thoughts would wing far away from Tye Farm to Paris . . . to the Bois de Boulogne where she had walked beside a man who talked to her of a dozen interesting things, and who saw and felt about the beauty and glamour of life just as she did herself. Or she would find her mind reverting to London . . . to a lunch at the Berkeley . . . to an exchange of ideas, essentially thrilling. And finally to a farewell kiss which had burnt her lips, and since burnt unforgettably into her memory.

Where was Digby now? God alone knew. Possibly he had forgotten her. But she had never forgotten him. And she would never forget that one embrace until she died. The thought of it, exquisite bliss and anguish, had blunted the edge of her inward happiness until finally it had worn all real happiness away.

She had grown to hate Tom's kisses because she remembered that other one. And she was even more bored with Tom than she might have been, because she knew that with Digby Farnel she would never have been bored. It was not his money or position that attracted her. It was the man, himself. For she could imagine that had he been forced to live in a place like Tye Farm and keep poultry, he would still have been that quick-thinking, intelligent, amusing person that he was. And they would have laughed together. Oh, she and Tom never laughed! Never had any of those little intimate jokes which lovers ought to share together.

There was nothing *alive* about this existence with Tom at Tye Farm. And her dread of the approaching winter was growing, day by day. It appalled her to think of the long dark nights when she would be cooped up in the farm-house, unable to get out; when there would be nobody to talk to but Tom.

Furthermore, she was only twenty-one last June. That was very young. And there was the whole of her life in front of her. Presumably it would be spent on this poultry farm with Tom.

It was in such an attitude of mind that Victoria Collinson gazed upon the waking world, this September morning. Therefore, there was not much joy in her heart when the beauty of nature unfolded itself before her.

With a long-drawn sigh she turned back to the room. Annie, the general maid who had replaced Tom's bachelor cook when he married Vicky, was just coming into the room with their early morning tea.

Tom groaned and grunted, sat up, ran his fingers through his stiff, tow-coloured hair, and blinked at the figure of his young wife standing there in the sunshine.

'Hullo! You're up very early.'

She walked to her bed and sat on the edge of it.

'It's going to be a hot day. There's a mist over the Downs.'

'Too hot for shooting, really.'

'Then why not cancel it?' said Vicky hopefully.

He poured out a cup of tea and handed it to her.

'My dear Vick, you know I couldn't do that.'

'You wouldn't miss your day's shooting for the world, would you?'

'Not if I could help it.'

'Well, I don't think I'll come,' she said abruptly.

More wide awake now, Tom looked at his wife and decided that she was a bit off colour.

'What's the matter?'

She avoided his gaze and stirred her tea.

'Nothing. But you know I loathe these shoots.'

'What, haven't you got over *that* yet?'

'No, and I never shall.'

He laughed quite good-naturedly.

'You are a funny little thing.'

'I'm a town girl and always shall be.'

'Don't say that. You've got to live here for the rest of your life, my dear.'

To hear that secret dread of hers spoken so openly and crudely shook Vicky's nerve and made her less careful than usual of what she said to her husband.

157

'I don't know that I *will* stay here for the rest of my life. Why should I?'

He stared, and stopped in the act of lighting his cigarette.

'My *dear* Vicky!'

His round blue eyes looked so amazed that she would have laughed if she hadn't felt so miserable. His hair was standing up on end like tow. He really looked like a foolish farmer's boy before he was spruced up a bit, and there were times when he had such a *stupid* expression.

'Well, why should I?' she repeated crossly. 'Just because you enjoy life on a poultry farm, that doesn't say that I've got to put up with it for the rest of *my* life.'

'Aren't you enjoying it, then?'

She hesitated a moment. His obvious surprise was so pathetic, so indicative of the lack of vision in Tom. It never entered his head to find these things out for himself. And after all, what good would it do, making him unnecessarily unhappy? She had married him and she must abide by her bargain, and if Tye Farm was her husband's home, no doubt she would have to remain in it—'for the rest of her life', as he had just reminded her.

'Don't you like it down here?' Tom was questioning her in a troubled voice.

She gave a short laugh.

'Oh, yes, I'm only fooling.'

Relieved, he lit his cigarette and lay back on the pillow and held out a hand.

'I thought you really meant it for a moment. Come and kiss me.'

That was the last thing she wanted to do. And so like Tom! Kisses could cure anything—for him. Any time she had shown irritability or become quarrelsome, or they argued, he took it for granted that the final kiss would put everything right. And it did for him. But, oh God, it didn't for her! It just made things worse.

She forced herself to go and sit beside him and take his hand.

158

'What would you do if I really meant that I didn't want to live here for the rest of my life?' she asked him.

'Well, it would be a bit awkward. After all, this is my house, and I'm building up the business, and all that.'

'But a lifetime's a long time.'

'Not long enough when you're happy,' said Tom in a cheerful voice.

Vicky's dark curly head drooped a little. That was true. But how much too long it could be if one was unhappy! If only Tom was the type of man into whose arms she could throw herself and say:

'Don't let's stay here and build up a business. Let's go away somewhere and learn more about life and the world . . . and ourselves. . . .'

But Tom would just tell her she was talking rubbish. Perhaps she was. Once or twice since their marriage, he had told her she was over-romantic and that the only thing that mattered was earning one's living and being a decent citizen. No doubt he was correct. But sometimes it would be grand to go a little mad and not be so correct.

'I daresay country life's a bit strange to you still, dear,' Tom was saying, squeezing her fingers; 'but I know you're going to love it. And if it's a bit lonely when I'm working, well, let's hope the day will come . . .'

He stopped and gave her a meaning look.

Vicky blushed scarlet and snatched her hand away. Of course, Tom hoped they would have a child. She knew that. And he was quite right about it. But she didn't want one. And that was, perhaps, all wrong of her, again. But she didn't want one, only because she didn't love Tom as she should. It would be a wonderful thing to bear a child to a man one loved. But not unless . . . oh, not unless, for it could only be born in *his* likeness and mean a fresh burden. . . .

She got up and put a hand to one flaming cheek, telling herself that she must be careful not to let her feelings get the better of her. She *must* settle down at Tye Farm, and if, eventually, she had a baby, she must welcome it.

Tom stared at her again.

'You're being very funny. What's up?'

'Nothing. But I don't think I'll walk round with the guns, if you don't mind.'

He scratched his head.

'Well, if you're really not fit—but the others will think it funny. I told them we'd have lunch in the barn down by Warren Corner.'

'Oh, I'll come down with the lunch,' she said drearily.

Tom got out of bed and approached her.

'You're not being like yourself to-day, Vick.'

'Don't call me that. It sounds like a cold cure!' she said with an hysterical laugh.

'You are a rum child.'

'Well, leave it at that. I'm rum.'

He eyed her doubtfully.

He had always known Vicky was temperamental, and congratulated himself that he could get over her moods. But there certainly were times when he did not understand this wife he had chosen. Physically she was ravishing, and he knew that he couldn't have had a more attractive wife. Whenever they had friends in, she was always the sparkling one. She put other girls in the shade. But there were drawbacks about life on a farm with Vicky. She wasn't very domesticated. She seemed to hate mending and sewing, and asked for money to have a woman in to do it, which seemed to him gross extravagance. A wife ought to sew on a chap's buttons. Vicky seemed for ever with her nose in a book—always curled up in an armchair reading. Or listening to some radio programme. He had bought a radiogramophone to please her, although he didn't care for music, himself. She spent a lot of her cash on records. He didn't understand those sentimental things, but she seemed to go all 'moony' about them, and of course she was, and always had been, crazy on anything to do with dancing or films.

Freda had recently spent a weekend with them, and although she wasn't a patch on Vicky for looks or fascination, he had to admit she was damned useful in or outside the house. She'd put on an overall and spent a whole afternoon helping him because they'd got an epidemic of gapes amongst the fowls, and had to catch all the young chickens and stick feathers, dipped in tar, down their throats. And she got through a whole lot of mending, too, that Vicky had neglected. A jolly good, conscientious girl, Freda. But Vicky seemed to quarrel a lot with her. They never stopped bickering, and he had been quite glad when Freda left and there was peace in the farm-house again.

A bit dolefully Tom regarded his wife. She looked back at him, her large blue eyes almost defiant. He couldn't think why. Then suddenly he noticed the exquisite grace of her slender limbs, poised there in thin silk pyjamas, revealing so much of her loveliness. Fired, he drew her against him.

'Say good morning nicely.'

'Why don't you leave me alone!' was her reply with a violence which completely mystified him, and she turned and ran out of the bedroom. He heard the bathroom door slam and the water being turned on. Thoroughly hurt, he went back to the bed-table and poured himself out another cup of tea.

In the bathroom, Vicky, with her face hidden in her hands, was shaken by weeping.

She felt that Tom had every right to complain and to feel hurt and that she was an ungrateful, bad, discontented person. And she had meant, when she married him, to be so good, so dutiful. And she had wanted to be so happy! But it was all going wrong.

She would just *have* to crush down her sensation of revolt and of disappointment and face up to life. It was no good behaving like a rotten little coward, or being a cad to Tom just because he bored her.

A few moments of such self-condemnation and remorse, and Vicky was out of the bathroom again, back in the bedroom, and in her husband's arms.

161

'I'm sorry I was such a little beast! You're always so nice to me, Tom.'

That was the moment for him to give her a cigarette and tell her a funny story. Instead of which he kissed her eagerly and accepted her surrender as his due.

14

Another month of life at Tye Farm, and Vicky had almost schooled herself to sit on her emotions and ignore the memory of what she had really wanted out of life. Almost, but not quite. There were occasions when she broke, and became to Tom an incomprehensible 'stormy petrel' whom he made no real effort to understand. He could not see why she should not be content with him and the life they led together.

Now the days were shortening and the longer nights, which Vicky had dreaded, were setting in. It was autumn with a vengeance. The early mornings were freezing cold. Winter was well on the way. The berries were red in the hedges. The big oak was shedding its leaves and the dismal funeral procession of summer passed by, remorselessly dealing out death and decay in its wake.

To Vicky that autumn was nothing short of a nightmare. It had been bad enough at Tye Farm when the days were sunny and the farm-house cool and pleasant to live in. But now it was the reverse. It was not only a cold October, but a wet one, accompanied by frequent gales. And Vicky's mental distress was increased by the physical hardships to which she was exposed. As anticipated, the draughts in Tye Farm were wicked. Vicky seemed to be able to do nothing to keep out the cold when the north wind blew and found its way through those plastered, timbered walls.

There was plenty of wood for fires, but unless one was sitting right inside the old open fireplace, the rest of the living-room was very cold.

The bedroom was a torture. Tom was not mean, but he was certainly not extravagant, and he, himself, seemed not to feel the cold. He was always hearty, ruddy, buoyant with health. He disapproved of fires in bedrooms, and insisted on all the windows being wide open. He even tried to tease Vicky out of having a hot-water bottle, but she clung to that fiercely, hating Tom for his heartiness. It had been cold at Norman Park in the winter, but at least they had had gas-fires, and anyhow, there was nothing like an old Tudor farm-house for sheer discomfort, unless properly modernised.

When Annie went sick with the 'flu, there was nobody to do the cooking or housework except Vicky, with occasional help from one of the boys off the farm, if and when Tom could spare him. Vicky had to struggle with a big antiquated range, and cooking had never been her strong point. Tom grumbled at the food, and she resented his lack of gratitude for what she managed to do. She began to get colds and felt far from well.

By the beginning of November, husband and wife were quarrelling frequently. Although Tom's good nature invariably held out, he was beginning to lose patience with Vicky because she was not turning out the housewife or helpmeet that he had expected—that his mother, for instance, had been to his father, before them.

And Vicky knew that she was a failure, and despised herself for it. Nevertheless, Tom made no effort, as far as she could see, to look at things from her point of view. It never once entered his head that *he* was failing *her*. He was much too self-righteous for that.

There was an awful time when, after a heavy frost, the pipes froze and the boiler burst, which meant no hot water for days, except what they boiled up in kettles. There followed incessant grumbles from Tom because he had to put in a new boiler.

Vicky finally lost her temper, one evening. Tom hadn't had a bath for days and didn't seem to mind. But Vicky could not bear being without hers.

'You don't seem to mind about anything!' she stormed at him. 'You're an absolute boor. All you mind is having to pay the bills. You don't care how uncomfortable I am, and I'm absolutely sick of this hateful old house!'

'You ought to have married a wealthy man and lived in a castle!' he flung back.

It was on the tip of her tongue to say:

'I certainly ought not to have married *you*!'

But she desisted. One thing she had learned in these four months of her marriage was not to tell Tom exactly what she thought. But she decided that if something did not happen soon to break this awful monotony and bring back some sort of colour and warmth into her existence, she would go mad.

For the next two days men were busy in the house putting in the new boiler and pipes. Heavy boots clanged on the stone floors and left a trail of mud everywhere right through the house. The days were filled with incessant clanging of hammers upon iron. A noise that reverberated through Vicky's head. And it rained. Rained pitilessly, lashing the casement windows of Tye Farm with a violence that seemed to wake up all that was most passionate and rebellious in Vicky.

She did not go out. While Tom worked on the farm, she wandered disconsolately round the house, feeling one with its ghosts; a mere wraith of the old Vicky who had once so eagerly held out her arms for life and love and happiness.

Annie followed the workmen round, mopping up the footmarks, muttering that she would 'give in her notice'. Vicky tried to help, but soon retired. Annie said she could work better alone; Vicky was only too thankful to leave her to it.

Wherever she looked there was mud. The garden was bedraggled and ruined. There wasn't a leaf left on the trees now, and the Downs were dark and sinister, lowering behind the farm. They seemed to close in upon Vicky like menacing giants.

She was in a nervy state, losing her appetite and losing weight. And she spent her time wondering how she could get away from Tom and Tye Farm without being asked a dozen questions or starting another quarrel. But where could she go? If she went home they would merely tell her to go back to her husband and not be 'so silly'. Freda was for ever reminding her that Tom was marvellous and the farm was wonderful. Her mother would be the last person on earth to understand the bitter frustration of her marriage; the agony it was to see all one's hopes and dreams trampled underfoot.

Mud and rain! Rain and mud! Thousands of chickens scratching in it. Vicky began to feel quite sorry for the senseless creatures, although even they had houses fitted out with artificial sunlight. They needed it, Tom told her. That she needed sunlight or that inner happiness which is so much more valuable than ultra-violet rays, he never bothered to think. That was so like Tom.

One day, in the middle of November, Tom went to Horsham to see a man on business. He asked Vicky to go with him, but she refused. She had no wish to drive in the old Ford through the rain and sit for hours alone while Tom discussed eggs with somebody.

After he had gone, she wished she had remembered to ask him to bring back some flowers for the house. There wasn't a single plant or flower in the place. It looked so cheerless. And he wouldn't remember to bring her flowers, she thought. He wasn't that sort of man. He was much more likely to buy a new incubator or something for his blessed farm.

Vicky wandered forlornly through the house. Her cupboards wanted turning out. She took out all her dresses, shook and brushed them and put them back. With a slight ironic curve of her lip she looked at the two pretty evening dresses which had been bought for her trousseau. One, she had never worn. And those lovely little silver sandals—just made for dancing—what on earth had been the good of buying them? They never changed into evening-dress at Tye Farm. Never went to shows at which one wore such clothes.

Would she ever dance again?

She remembered Paul Dallas. What a little fool she had been in those days! Well, that type of temptation would never come her way again! But swift upon that remembrance, came the thought of Digby Farnel, and that brought a deeper pink to her thinning cheeks.

How heavenly that lunch at the Berkeley had been with him! Yet sometimes she wondered if their meeting that day had not also been something of a calamity. For somehow the very next time that she had lifted her lips for Tom's kiss, she had felt something within her recoil. And it had gone on recoiling. . . .

She had tackled her mother and sister about those colour-photographs, that same evening. And they had confessed to the interception and burning of her letter. There had been a brief, violent row, which had only ended in sarcastic reminders from both Mum and Freda that she had no right to be interested in Mr. Farnel or his photography. She was engaged to Tom. That had ended it.

It was only too true. Vicky knew that she had no right to be interested in Digby. Not that the family had any right to destroy her correspondence. Still, what was the use of rowing about it? Sometimes she wondered had she received that letter, and known that Digby Farnel had remembered her, and wanted to see her again, whether she would have accepted Tom's proposal.

She shut her wardrobe, turned back into the room, cast a brief glance at Tom's clean shirt and collars which had just come back from the wash and had been laid on his bed, and told herself not to be a fool. She was very much Tom's wife now, and she must walk down the path she had chosen, with as good a grace as possible.

The sound of a car—not the familiar harshness of the old Ford, or the Richardsons' milk lorry, which were about the only two motor vehicles which came regularly to

Tye Farm—brought her to the window. She peered down through the rain, and suddenly her eyes widened with interest. A peculiar sensation of excitement caught at her heart-strings. What a marvellous car! A long, low, blue and silver thing—a sports saloon—just turning into the muddy drive. Such an awful road it was, up to Tye Farm— all cart-ruts, and inches deep in mud. The beautiful car would be spattered and ruined. Who was driving it? She couldn't see from here. Now she could! Now the driver had turned his face. Through the rain she discerned his features—horn-rimmed glasses. It was *Digby*. Digby, himself! The very person of whom she had been thinking. After all these months!

Everything in Vicky came alive. She turned, dashed down the staircase, slipped a little on the polished oak, grazed her knee, but went on without feeling the pain. And the next moment she had flung open the door of the farm-house like an excited child.

'Hel-*lo*!'

Digby stepped out of the car. He made a dive through the drenching rain, and reached the cover of the doorway.

'Vicky! So this is your place. I've had the devil's own business finding it. Been directed by the most amazing number of half-wits. The first person I asked said he was 'a stranger here', and the second was deaf-and-dumb. My God, what a day!'

His charming, gay voice gave her the old thrilling feeling. Flushed and bright-eyed, she found herself holding out both hands, and he took them and wrung them warmly.

'It's terribly nice to see you,' she said.

And so simply and sincerely did she say it, that he believed in the warmth of her welcome, and was touched by it. He took off his coat and hung it in the hall. Laughing and talking, they walked together into the sitting-room. Annie, the maid, was on her knees before the fire with a pair of bellows, trying to blow some life into the logs.

'It's so cold!' Vicky grumbled. 'I'm afraid you'll be

168

frozen. Annie, put on another log or two, and get some tea quickly for Mr. Farnel.'

Annie departed, muttering that it wasn't really teatime, and she had some washing to do. But Vicky paid little attention to the mutters. She was too used to them. She stood in front of the big open fireplace with Digby. He looked round and congratulated her on the beauty of the place. She told him quickly that she hadn't been able to afford to buy what she really wanted, although she thought the chintzes would please him. And they did. He at once remarked on the lovely green.

'It's a very subtle colour,' he said, with a gesture of the hand.

She had heard him say that many times. He was very fond of that word 'subtle'. And colour always fascinated him. He told her that he liked the irregular shape of the room and the beams, and the deep cream of the old plaster on the walls. The exterior of the place was grand. The light was fast fading, but he had seen enough to judge.

'I could take a superb colour-photograph of it in sunlight,' he said.

She nodded silently. It seemed strange that Tom never noticed any of the beauties in the way that this man did. But then Tom was so horribly practical. It would be all the same to him if the curtains were pink or blue, or the farm-house seventeenth-century, or an Edwardian stucco villa, so long as it was cheap to run.

Digby commented on the floor.

'Yew, eh! Glorious—and you could dance in here easily.'

'Could, but we don't!' she said with a little laugh.

Digby took the cigarette which she offered, lit it, and gave her a penetrating look over the rim of his glasses. He had been wondering for months what marriage had done for this child; whether she was happy, and had found something in life at last. But he gauged from the timbre of her voice and of that little, discontented laugh, that it was not so.

His first impression of her when he had seen her framed in the doorway of the farm-house had been that she was lovelier than ever. There was an exquisite colour in her face then, and she was still golden from the summer's tan. But now the flush had died. He could see that she was thinner, graver, and definitely older. Of course, that was to be expected. Marriage must mature a young girl. But he would like to have found peace in her eyes. Instead, he read nothing but unrest.

Was it dastardly of him to feel just the slightest pleasure in the thought that she was not entirely happy with the man she had married? It would be a damnably selfish emotion. He was ashamed of it.

But the truth was that Digby himself had lost what peace he used to have. The summer had not been a success. He had gone to the West Indies, done some beautiful photographic work, met one or two attractive women, even tried to have a mild affair with one girl who had seemed inclined towards him. But he had soon run away from her.

He had come back to England knowing that that kiss which he had exchanged with Vicky had cast a spell upon him which he would not have thought possible. He had wanted her from that day onward. And he wanted her now that he saw her again.

He had tried to forget her. And he had not deliberately set out in search of her. He had gone down to Brighton this morning to see an aged uncle who was in a convalescent-home. It was only a few miles from Brighton to this place. And he had a new fast car. He couldn't pass the Dyke without remembering that Vicky had told him Tye Farm lay under the shadow of those Downs. So here he was. Preposterously content to see her again, and with a 'divine discontent' at the sight of her. He had never known any girl to move so exquisitely. And that sad, red mouth of hers—so ripe for kissing—God! what sort of a man was the husband who hadn't been able to waken her to the ecstasy of womanhood which was her heritage?

All these things Digby thought, but for a while he talked about the farm and about her life down here and asked dutifully about the chickens. Then, seeing that Vicky was as disinterested in poultry as himself, desisted.

Vicky, too, tried to be dutiful. She said how nice Sussex was. How beautiful it had been here all the summer, when she had lived out of doors. How hard-working Tom was. How pleasant it was to have a home of her own. That sort of thing. Whilst all the time her lips and eyes were saying:

'I'm bored, bored, *miserably* bored!'

She questioned Digby about his travels. He showed her one or two photographs, which he had in his pocket. One in particular of a brown beach. A sea of lapis lazuli. A green vivid palm, spiky and queer against the hot blue of the sky.

'Nassau,' he said. 'You'd love that. Do you remember that photograph I took of you in the Bois de Boulogne? I'd like to have taken one of you on this beach. You'd fit in with it all out there. You're like one of those slender young palm trees.'

She caught her breath and laughed a little and joked with him. And she would have given her soul to be out there on the burning beach, feeling and *living* beauty as he felt and lived it. While she looked at more photographs, she wondered what women he had met and if there was one in particular in his life. How lucky she would be, that woman! How divine it must be to live with somebody as sensitive as this man—with all that fine appreciation.

Tom thought of life only in terms of money; how much things cost, and what he could make and put by. He and Vicky had reached a pitch, indeed, when they rarely discussed anything but work, income-tax and—the chickens! Always the chickens!

She lit a cigarette. Tom never cared to see her smoke, but occasionally she had her cigarette. She sat on a hassock before the fire which was leaping brightly now around the big dry logs which Annie had brought in. With elbows on her knees and chin cupped in her hands, she looked at Digby with her earnest, interested eyes, and listened to him. He went on talking, all the while very conscious of the beauty—and of the sadness—in those eyes.

When she asked him where he would be going next, he told her that he did not know. Possibly he might stay in town for the winter. His friend Morgan had gone abroad again. Digby was a little bored—unusual for him. In reality he liked a job. But now he was so disgustingly well off, he had no need to work. But he was thinking about going in for cinema-stuff, he said—colour-photography for the screen. Indeed, he found himself talking quite a lot about himself to this girl. She had become like an old friend. Then, feeling that he had been egotistical enough, brought the conversation back to her.

'You are going to be here the whole winter?'

'Yes.'

He looked round the room thoughtfully, and listened to the sound of the rain which was still beating against the casements. Every now and then an extra squall of wind brought a wild splash against the glass. The room was warm and comfortable here close to the fire. But beyond, there were shadows. And it was cold. The house had an eerie feeling about it. He had just begun to sense that. And he imagined that out in those big stone passages the rambling old place would seem even colder and lonelier.

In between the squalls of wind, could be heard the faint chug . . . chug . . . of the electric-lighting plant working close to the house.

Digby frowned. Vicky wouldn't be happy here. How could she be? It was a dreary old place, and she was young and full of life. What was that husband of hers thinking of, keeping so young and lovely a wife here, shut away from the world?

'What do you do, Vicky?' he asked. 'How do you spend your days?'

'Doing nothing.'

'But right through the winter——?'

172

'Yes, and right through all the winters for the rest of my life, as far as I can see,' she said, with a sudden little burst of feeling.

He shook his head. It was monstrous. But what the devil was the use of him coming here and saying so, unsettling her; even suggesting that she had been made for a different kind of life? He would be worse than a cad if he did so.

He heard her say:

'Will you come and see me again?'

'Of course I will—if you'd like me to.'

Suddenly she threw her cigarette into the fire and put her hand against her lips.

'Oh, lord! I was forgetting.'

'What?'

She looked up into his eyes which smiled at her so kindly.

'I don't know what on earth I'm going to say to my—to Tom. I mean, *who* are you? Where am I supposed to have met you? You see, he doesn't know anything about Paris.'

'Ah!' said Digby with understanding.

'He'd never understand in a thousand years about that episode,' added Vicky.

Digby thought, privately, that the man must either be a fool, or just lacking in ordinary understanding—or both. That was the pity of it, that this girl with her warm romantic heart, and her intense appreciation of all things beautiful, should be tied to a man without sensitivity or understanding.

Why had the little fool married him? The poor, sweet little fool. As an escape, of course. If only she had realised how much better had been her other prison. In her suburban home it had been dull for her, but there had also been hope. Now there was none. And, of course, she knew it. That was why that trapped look lay in her big bewildered eyes. She was not a clever, shrewd young woman of the world, like so many of the smart modern girls one met these days. She resembled that old-

173

fashioned name of hers. Poor little Victoria! Fate had given her a highly emotional impressionable nature, and then punished her for it.

While he was turning over these things in his mind, a new sound came through the stormy night. And it brought Vicky to her feet, flushed and apprehensive.

'That's Tom, now. That's our car.'

Digby began to feel that he had no right here, and was putting this girl in a tight corner. Yet he wouldn't have missed seeing her again, and quite inordinately he wanted to take that hunted look away from her. Good God! anybody would think she was afraid of her husband.

Vicky divined his thoughts. She said rapidly:

'Tom's awfully nice. You'll like him, I'm sure. But he just isn't like you—I mean he would never understand about Paris; and my people thought it was better he shouldn't know. So, if only I could introduce you as——'

'Somebody who had lost his way in the Dyke and called in order to be directed,' finished Digby. 'Anything you like. I'll carry it off.'

Her cheeks burnt. Her heart beat quickly and painfully. If only Tom hadn't come back! It was rotten to feel that way, but she did. She didn't want these lovely moments interrupted. They had been lovely—with Digby. She could never get tired of hearing him talk. And she had grown also to like watching him. Handsome he was not, in the strict sense of the word; but she admired that slim, debonair figure of his, and the vital way in which the dark hair sprang back from his forehead, and the intelligence of his hazel eyes. He *was* vital, utterly different from any other man she had ever met.

Perhaps it would be silly to lie to Tom about Digby. Yet what was the use of dragging up that Paris episode? It had meant nothing. Just a piece of childish idiocy. She never thought about Paul Dallas these days. But Tom might imagine a dozen things—like Freda and Mum had imagined. He had their way of thinking.

Vicky was no good at intrigue, but desperation came to

174

her aid. There flashed across her mind a story which she could tell.

Only the other day somebody had dropped in here and asked if the poultry farm was for sale. They had been told that it wasn't. Couldn't Digby say the same thing? Then she laughed. As if Digby, driving that beautiful racing car, looked like a man who wanted to buy a small poultry farm!

She could hear Tom putting the Ford away in the garage. In another moment he would be here. A little hysterically, she said:

'Oh, say you lost your way. I suppose that's best, but I honestly don't think you'd better tell Tom about Paris.'

'Won't that mean that I can't come to see you again?' Digby asked her regretfully.

She hesitated. That would be awful. Never to see Digby again. He had brought her more happiness in this last hour than she had known since her marriage. Because of that very feeling in her, perhaps she ought not to let him come again. But she found herself saying:

'Oh dear! Then say that I met you at some party in town, before I left Norman Park. I needn't explain in detail. Only let's say you know me, so that I can ask you down again, in front of Tom.'

For a moment their gaze met. And they both knew perfectly well at that instant that it would be so much better for them not to meet again. But such is the weakness of human nature that they both denied it to themselves, and made their plans to do otherwise.

'Don't worry, I'll say something suitable,' murmured Digby, and then turned away from her, feeling that had he done the right thing and told her that he wouldn't come again, he would have hurt her. That knowledge both pleased and disturbed him.

Into the drawing-room came Tom Collinson.

He was very wet. The side curtains on the old Ford were torn. The rain had drenched him during that journey back from Horsham. He hadn't pulled off the business deal

175

which had taken him to the market, so he was cross as well as tired. He was also late for work. In five minutes he would have to go off and join Jones, his head-man, who always helped him with the last 'feed'.

'Of all the filthy nights——!' he began.

Then he stopped, astonished. Who the deuce was this fellow, with his horn-rimmed spectacles, in the grey elegantly-cut suit? Tom had not noticed the Bentley. He had come round the back in from the garage and through the kitchen.

Vicky, a little flustered, came forward and made the introductions.

'Oh, Tom, this is Mr. Farnel. Mr. Farnel, this is my husband.'

The two men nodded to each other. Digby's keen gaze summed up Vicky's husband with his usual swift perception. He looked an ordinary nice chap, a bit uncouth perhaps; the farmer-type with his breeches, gaiters, and clumsy boots. His wet tow-coloured hair was standing up on end—it made Tom appear rather comic.

Tom looked back at the stranger doubtfully.

Farnel? He had never heard of him.

Vicky was saying:

'I met Mr. Farnel some time ago at a party. He heard I was married and as—as—he was on his way from Brighton to London—he called in on us.'

'Oh!' said Tom. 'Quite so!'

Digby cleared his throat.

'I'm afraid I must be going. It's rather a long run to town.'

'I wish we could ask you to supper,' said Vicky, trying to speak naturally, 'but——'

'Thanks all the same, but I must get back,' cut in Digby.

'Can I offer you a drink?' asked Tom.

Digby had never really felt more in need of a whisky and soda, and he said so. It was really quite an absurd position to find himself in, he thought angrily. The sort of position he had told himself he would never get in with a

176

married woman. On the other hand, why feel so guilty? He hadn't been making love to the fellow's wife.

He might have wanted to. But that was different. Damn the whole thing! The sooner he got away from here, the better.

Tom poured out a whisky and soda and brought it to Farnel. Then he excused himself. He must go and feed the chickens, he said. He told Vicky to offer Mr. Farnel a cigarette, and departed hastily. He never allowed anything to interfere with his chickens, and when the boy was off duty, old Jones couldn't do the feeds alone.

Left alone, Digby and Vicky looked at each other. Digby gulped down his drink and said:

'Well, that wasn't very difficult.'

'No,' said Vicky miserably.

He knew that she was miserable. Heavens! but the evenings alone with Collinson must be long for her. Poor child! Why had she done it?

Vicky walked with Digby to the front door, asking herself that same question, and with a sense of futility and despair that she had never known in her life before.

Seeing and talking to Digby again, comparing him with Tom, had brought home her mistake so forcibly that it was almost past enduring.

She opened the door. The wind shook through the big rambling passage and struck ice-cold against her. The big oak tree opposite the house was creaking and groaning, bringing down showers of raindrops with every sway.

Oh, the darkness and dreariness of the November night! Oh, the isolation of Tye Farm and the far more bitter isolation that was in her very soul!

'Don't come out, you'll catch cold,' Digby began.

But she interrupted:

'I don't care!'

Without coat or hat, she insisted upon walking with him to the car. He switched on the lights. She stood, an instant, looking with wistful eyes at the graceful lines and the luxury of the saloon. It was so very 'Digby', this car.

He looked down at her upturned face. How pale it was in the darkness. He was filled suddenly with sadness for her and for himself. He knew now that he would give half his life to be able to go back to that day at the Berkeley, when she had only been engaged to Tom. It was then that he should have told her that he would take her away if she cared enough; and asked her to marry *him*. But he had failed her and himself, because, then, he hadn't been sure. He really should not see her again.

He heard her small desolate voice:

'Thanks awfully for coming to see me. And you will come down again, won't you?'

He took her hand and, on the spur of the moment, carried it to his lips and kissed it twice in the palm.

'Yes, if you want me to. And if you're in town at any time, you know my Club. Good-bye, my dear.'

His lips against her hand brought mingled pain and delight. She was shaken with an uncontrollable longing to be held a moment against his heart. That was impossible. Then he was gone. The car moved off into the drenching rain and the shadows.

She stood alone, her small figure swaying a little in the tempest like the trees. But she was unmindful of the cold or the rain. She only knew that she loved that man who was driving away from her, loved him more than she had ever loved anybody in her life. She was wildly and hopelessly in love with him. And she didn't know how she was going to carry on.

She turned and walked slowly back into the house. She stood shivering a moment in the passage. In a few moments Tom would come in from feeding the chickens and she would have to sit down and do some darning and listen to his account of the trip to Horsham. No doubt, she would be questioned a bit more thoroughly about Digby Farnel! She was quite sure that Tom had not been too pleased to find a perfectly strange man, of whom he had never heard, here alone with her.

Slowly she went up the oak staircase. With every step

she took, her heart seemed to sink lower. Digby had gone and taken all the vitality and significance of life with him. Again and again she lived through that instant when he had raised her hand to his lips and kissed it. She thought:

'Digby—my *darling*!'

The old oak boards under her lagging footsteps creaked and groaned. She felt as though they were laughing derisively at her as she went.

15

'Where the dickens did you meet that chap?' Tom Collinson asked his wife as they sat at their supper, that same evening.

Vicky helped herself to a tiny portion of cheese. She had already refused the cold meat and pickles. She was not hungry. In fact she had seldom felt less inclined for food.

The dining-room, which was one of the biggest rooms in the farm-house, was always perishingly cold. Tom considered it extravagant to light a fire in the big open fireplace, because it burnt too much fuel, so the heat was supplied by an inadequate anthracite stove. There were some beautiful massive beams in here, and possibly the best oak floor in the place. But the furniture was unattractive. Much as Vicky disliked it, Tom had insisted upon keeping this huge reddish mahogany table; the Victorian chairs with their shiny black seats; that hideous inlaid sideboard with its ornate mirror which hurt Vicky every time she looked at it. Added to which the lighting was poor. The whole room had a melancholy gloom at night which never failed to depress her. Tonight that depression was acute. Reaction, after seeing Digby again, of course. And she was weighed down by the awful prospect of the long days ahead. Not only the days, but the *years*.

Tom was at his most unattractive this evening. His good humour had not returned, since that fruitless journey to Horsham. And since Vicky was not in talking mood, most of the meal was conducted in silence until Tom shot his question about Digby.

She kept her eyes on her plate as she answered:

'Oh, some place or other.'

'Your people know him?'

'Yes.' (That was true in a way.)

'Looks as though he was stiff with cash.'

'I think he's very well off.'

'Whatever made him look you up all of a sudden?'

'I don't really know, except that he was passing this way.'

Tom, his mouth full, ceased to pay attention to his food and looked at his wife for a moment. She had changed from her tweeds into a blue woollen dress with a spotted scarf. She was so cold at Tye Farm that she could never bear to change at night into anything thinner. She had tied a blue ribbon around her head which gave her a 'little girl' look. Her eyes were large and sad. But Tom saw nothing sad in them. Neither was he touched by any beauty in her at that instant. He was resentful because she was so uncommunicative. He didn't talk much himself, but when Vicky kept silent, even he noticed it.

'What's the matter with you tonight?'

'Nothing.'

'What had that fellow got to say to you?'

Then Vicky, whose nerves were under a strain, momentarily lost her head. She flung her knife down on the plate and rose from the table.

'Do stop nagging at me.'

He put down his own knife and fork and stared at her, round-eyed and deeply hurt.

'We—ell! I like that, to say I'm nagging! I've only asked you a few questions. What are you so touchy about? Your friend's visit doesn't seem to have had a very good effect upon you. An old flame, perhaps!'

She was scarlet now, trembling a little.

'Oh, don't be so stupid!'

Then Tom grew irritated and thrust his plate away.

'You're being the stupid one, I think. For goodness'

sake sit down and finish your supper.'

'I have finished.'

Tom was never irritable for long. Indeed, as a rule, he was maddeningly placid. It was one of Vicky's complaints that nothing seemed to affect him. He broke into a smile.

'Oh, come on, silly. What are we quarrelling about? You haven't eaten anything. Buck up, old dear.'

Vicky set her teeth. It drove the devil into her when Tom called her 'old dear'. But she tried hard to recover her equilibrium. It was no good letting her nerves get the better of her just because she was unhappy and wanted Digby Farnel back again.

She must try to remember that Tom was what the world would call 'an excellent husband', and she, no doubt, was a poor kind of wife.

She sat down again, and in suffering silence ate one more small portion of cheese. Annie came in with some tea. Tom preferred it to coffee. Following Annie came a bouncing Labrador puppy. He immediately leapt upon Vicky. Heartened, she gathered him up in her arms and stroked his silky ears.

'Darling Sooty,' she murmured.

Tom cast an eye at the retriever and grunted.

'Your infernal puppy was chasing chickens this afternoon. Jones said he got into the run. If he does it again, he'll get a dose of lead.'

At another time Vicky might have taken this threat with composure. But tonight it had a volcanic effect. She laid her cheek against the puppy's head and flashed a look of withering scorn at her husband.

'You *would,* wouldn't you? Kill my pet dog if it touched one of your beastly chickens!'

'I didn't say I'd kill him, but I'd give him a lesson.'

'Don't you think of anything but your chickens? If you knew how sick to death I was of the very sound of them . . .'

She stopped, choking. It was the first time she had

actually voiced such sentiments. Tom's blue eyes froze. He said, coldly:

'That's too bad! I must say you're being your nicest, this evening.'

Vicky put the Labrador pup on the floor, rose, and walked out of the room.

Tom finished his meal. Nothing short of an earthquake would have prevented him from doing that. He drank his tea, smoked a cigarette, then sauntered into the sitting-room. The thought of Vicky and her moods had not concerned him much while he sat alone. It was the chickens he had been thinking of, and the fact that there had been a shortage in eggs to-day.

He found his wife, rather white and tight-lipped, hunched on a hassock in front of the fire, darning stockings. She did not look up as he approached her. But the sound of the heavy, clopping boots over the polished floor aroused in her a feeling akin to hatred. A feeling which frightened her. She did not want to hate Tom. It would be too appalling to hate someone she had to live with for the rest of her life.

If he had let her alone that night, the black moment might have passed over. Or if he had even talked to her gently and with insight; seen that she was unnerved and troubled and tried to help her, she might have turned to him in relief, anxious to be comforted; wishful to chase those dark shadows away from her.

But Tom Collinson, most unimaginative of men, understood nothing of women and certainly did not try to understand Vicky. The four months of their marriage had not lessened his regard for her. He was still devoted. But he was the type of man who considers that there is, and must be, a difference between the days of courtship and matrimony. One couldn't go on saying nice, flattering things. One made love in the proper place at the proper moment, but everything else must be taken for granted.

It was not in his make-up to sit and talk with Vicky in a way that would draw her closer to him. The moment he took his place by the fire, he harped back upon their quarrel during supper.

'You *were* in a silly state. What got into you?'

She made no reply.

Aggrieved, he went on:

'I don't see why you should hate the chickens, anyhow. Your husband runs a poultry farm, so that's where your bread-and-butter comes from, which you might remember.'

Still no reply from Vicky. She continued darning.

'Anyhow, you knew I didn't mean to kill Sooty, but you've darned well got to train him not to get into the runs.'

Then Vicky spoke:

'I'll try.'

He pulled his pipe from his pocket and knocked the bowl against the stone hearth.

'How long was that fellow here this afternoon?'

She dug her needle into her hand, gave a little exclamation, and stopped to suck the tiny trickle of blood which oozed from the slender finger.

'Not long.'

'What was his interest in coming?'

The blood rushed to her face.

'Aren't I supposed to have any friends, now that I'm married?'

'I don't see what you want with wealthy young men who've got nothing better to do than to hang round ladies' tea-cups.'

'And who said that's what he was like? What do *you* know about him?'

Tom lit his pipe and puffed at it slowly.

'Oh, I know his type.'

'Then you're wrong, because you don't know it at all. And he doesn't just hang round ladies' tea-cups! He takes marvellous photographs.'

'Oh, ho! Ladies' photographer, is he?'

Vicky jammed the needle into the stocking and dropped

her workbasket off her lap. She was in no fit mental state to stand Tom's irritating banter to-night.

'No, he's *not*! And you're just trying to be clever, and to upset me!'

He took the pipe from his mouth, half-closed one eye, and looked at her stormy face. A sudden mistrust filled him. A mistrust of Vicky and that fellow who had been here this afternoon.

'What's he to you, anyhow, that you should get so upset by the mention of him?'

She clenched her teeth and did not answer.

'I must tackle the family,' added Tom, 'and find out a bit more about your photographer.'

Vicky stood there, exasperated beyond bearing. It would be fatal if Tom started to question the family about Digby Farnel. Absolutely fatal. She *must* pull herself together. This sort of atmosphere between Tom and herself would never do. Where was it leading? Only to unpleasantness and misunderstanding.

Somehow or other, she forced herself to smile.

'We're both just being silly,' she said. 'Let's have the wireless on.'

Tom was easily mollified. He turned on the wireless, picked up a copy of *Poultry World* and glanced through it. It was the only type of literature he ever favoured. Vicky continued her darning, feeling anguished. Feeling that life would be intolerable unless she could kill this new acute longing for Digby, and her even more acute distaste for Tom.

Very much out of harmony with her thoughts was the gay dance tune which now filled the sitting-room, and echoed through the old farm-house. She wondered if she would ever dance again. If, indeed, she would ever put on those little silver shoes which lay in her cupboard, upstairs.

Through the dance music she seemed to hear a gay charming voice which said to her:

'You're like one of those slender young palm trees. . . .'

185

And she could see herself, head close to his, looking at that coloured photograph of the West Indian beach, and feel again that thrill which his words had brought to her. . . .

How wonderful it would have been out there in Nassau with him! Was she just a sentimental little fool, building up a romance which did not exist? Or did he care a little what happened to her? Those kisses on her hand had told her that he did. They had been warm and sweet against her palm.

The wild tears sprang to her eyes, but she forced them back because she dared not cry. She could have no explanation of such tears.

Over the radio a man was singing:

> '*I've got you under my skin.*
> *I've got you deep in the heart of me . . .*'

Tom looked up from his paper and grunted.

'Tripe!'

Vicky gave him a withering look. Abruptly, she said:

'I'm tired. I'm going up.'

He put down his pipe and held out his hand.

'Come and be nice to me for a minute.'

She shut her eyes. If Tom was going to start love-making, it would be the last straw. She would never be able to control herself. She tried to joke him off. But he was now in a comfortable mood, having enjoyed his food. The fire was warm, and he had forgotten his jealousy. But he wanted a kiss from Vicky. And what Tom wanted, he generally took regardless of anybody else's feelings.

Vicky was pulled down on to his knee. She started to shiver uncontrollably. His eyes took on that hazy, rather stupid look which meant that he was feeling lover-like.

She thought:

'I don't want him to touch me! I want to be left alone. *I want to be left alone!*'

Tom said:

'Was my little Vick in a horrid temper during supper?

186

Never mind. Give your old Tom a nice kiss.'

His lips came down upon her mouth. Something in her recoiled . . . and snapped. She pushed his face away and struggled off his lap. Maddened, hardly knowing what she was doing or saying, a stream of hysterical words, none of them very complimentary to Tom, broke from her. They left no room for doubt in his mind that Vicky did not want him to embrace her.

He stood up trying to look dignified, without much success. It was not a very dignified position for a man to find himself in. And he was not only astonished, but shocked by this revelation of her distaste. Things had seemed all right between him and Vicky up till now. What the devil had changed her like this? What the *devil* . . . ? His mind went floundering, seeking an explanation.

Vicky, in floods of tears, rushed up to her room, flung herself across the bed and cried desperately.

It was not long before Tom was up there with her, switching on all the lights, determined that she should not have her grief to herself. He was not only hurt, but angry now. There seemed to him no possible reason why his kisses should not be welcome to Vicky at all times.

Resentfully he looked at the blue, huddled figure on the bed.

'So that's how you feel about me, is it?'

Only her weeping answered him. He went on:

'Oh, well, I think I understand what's the matter. You're keen on this fellow who came this afternoon. That's it, isn't it?'

She choked down her sobs, sat up and faced him. Her face was distorted and pitiful. And the state of her mind was pitiful. For she knew that she had been crazy to let her feelings get the better of her. She had sown the seeds of jealousy in Tom tonight, and whatever happened, she could not undo that rash action. She knew, too, that he was right and justified in his accusations against her. What was the use of fostering his suspicions? It would only ruin

187

his peace of mind, and it was bad enough that her own should have been destroyed.

She had made a terrible mistake in marrying Tom. But she could see that not only was it her personal tragedy, but that it would also be his, if she allowed it. He had been so content. All the misery was on her side. Much better to do her utmost to forget Digby Farnel for ever, accept the existence here with her husband, and settle down to it.

The dreadful part was that Digby's coming today had shown her so conclusively what she felt for him, and what, indeed, he might have felt for her.

It wouldn't be so easy to settle down now.

But in this hour Vicky made a very gallant effort to put things right between herself and Tom. And she made it exclusively for Tom's sake. Her outburst over, it left her in a state of physical and mental lethargy which was helpful, under the circumstances. She wiped the drenching tears from her face and put out her hand to her husband.

'I was mad, Tom. I didn't mean what I said.'

He sat down on the edge of the bed. He looked miserable, but his anger evaporated. And when Vicky gave him her hand, he took it eagerly.

'I must say you were the limit, Vicky. You said some pretty unkind things. Don't you love me any more? What have I done?'

She hid her tormented face against his shoulder.

'You've done nothing. It's all me.'

'Is it true that you're keen on that chap?'

'No, no,' she cried wildly, and felt that it was a good lie, well told.

He looked relieved.

'Well, then what put you into that mood?'

'I can't explain. Perhaps I'm not well.'

'Then you'd better have a doctor.'

'I don't want a doctor. But perhaps I need a change.'

Content now that he had her in his arms, he stroked her

hair. He was always quick to forgive a slight. But he remained completely mystified by Vicky and her hysteria, and no more ready or willing than he had ever been to get to the root of things with her.

'Well, we'll put it down to health,' he said; 'but I don't see why you need a change. You've only lived at Tye Farm for four months.'

She kept silent. He would never understand how those months had dragged, or how much more they were going to drag in the future. He would never understand anything. But she could plainly see that unless she could sit on top of all her emotions and crush them down, wipe Digby Farnel from her memory, and say goodbye to all that meant romance to her, life with Tom would be a very wretched thing.

'I don't know how I'm going to do it,' she thought, 'but I suppose I must try.'

With a twisted smile, she wondered what Digby would have said if he could have known the result of his visit! She felt sure he would have hated it, for her sake alone.

'I'm like that, Tom,' she said. 'I need changes now and again.'

'But I don't see how I can take you away now,' he said in a worried tone, 'there's much too much work to be done.'

She shook her head mutely. He wouldn't take her away. He wouldn't see that it meant spiritual life or death to her to get away from *herself* just at the moment. Yet, what good would it do, going away with Tom? She wanted to be alone. Like Greta Garbo. She began to laugh hysterically.

'What's the matter with you now?' asked Tom.

'I was just thinking . . . how funny . . . it's all been!'

He didn't see anything funny in it. He said:

'Oh, well, I'd rather you laughed than cried.'

She patted his shoulder.

'Don't be cross with me any more, Tom. I'm sorry about it.'

'We'll forget it,' he said.

'Thank you,' she said humbly.

'And now what about my kiss?'

She raised her face obediently. She wondered if the whole of the rest of life with Tom would be a martyrdom.

16

It was, perhaps, a stroke of luck for Vicky that she came down to breakfast that next morning late, and missed the doubtful pleasure of having to open her letters at the table opposite Tom.

She never had a big correspondence. Sometimes she heard from old school-friends. More regular news came from her mother, telling her odds and ends of family gossip; how life was going on at Norman Park. But the mail was always welcome. Anything to break the monotony of life at Tye Farm.

Today she found two letters awaiting her. One, in a blue envelope, was from Freda, written in her precise, rather mean little handwriting. Unusual! Freda rarely wrote to her sister. But it was the other letter which claimed Vicky's immediate attention. She picked it up, saw on the flap the crest of a Club, and the postmark 'Piccadilly', and knew at once that this was from Digby Farnel. The first letter she had ever received from him. The last had been intercepted. Well, this one, at least, had reached her safely. What an unexpected thrill!

For a moment Vicky stood holding the envelope unopened, her heart beating so that it seemed to shake her slight body. All the colour drained from her cheeks. Such was the emotional effect of hearing from the man who mattered so profoundly, and who should not have mattered at all.

He must have written and posted this late last night. Late, while she had sobbed herself to sleep; hushing the sobs for fear that Tom might hear her.

In the early hours of the morning she had wakened, and been unable to get to sleep again, suffering from that miserable and particular depression which attacks one in the very early hours when there is any trouble.

Hour after hour in the grey November dawn she had lain wide-eyed, watching the room grow lighter, listening to the unceasing crowing of the cocks, hearing the milk-lorry drive up, and then Annie moving about in her clumsy fashion in the room below, crashing fire-irons as she cleaned out the hearth. Realising that this was another day and that there would be so many others just the same.

Tom there in that bed beside her, blissfully, heavily asleep. Long hours, on the farm, and the long nights to be got through and nothing to look forward to but—this!

She had forlornly hugged to herself her thoughts of Digby Farnel. Futile, to try to banish them. Why should she not be allowed her dreams? They were all that were left to her. And surely her heart was a secret dwelling-place for *him*, where no man, not even Tom, might enter.

While she had dressed, Vicky had administered a lecture to herself. It was no use repining or making herself or Tom miserable. Today she would be more cheerful—much nicer than usual to Tom. Tonight the Richardsons were coming in for some supper. They would play cards. Tom had taught Vicky how to play bridge. It bored her, but it was better than doing nothing. And she did like Nora Richardson. They would probably have a talk together. This afternoon, she would drive into Brighton, and buy something special for dinner. She must remember, too, to take in that blue milk jug which Annie had broken. It was worth riveting.

But now, holding his note, every single thought in Vicky's mind disappeared—save the thought of Digby. She tore open the flap. Of course it wouldn't be a sentimental missive. Why should it be? Just because she was in love, it didn't mean the same applied to *him*! But it was marvellous of him to write at all. Comforting to feel that he had taken that trouble.

He said:

'This is just to say how pleased I was to discover your retreat yesterday, and to see you again. If I may, I shall run in and see you again next week as I have got to go down to my Uncle again. I am afraid the old man is on his last legs. This time I would like to see more of the farm in daylight. Don't forget to let me know when you are in town, and perhaps you will have some lunch with me.

'Best wishes.
'Yours,
'D.F.'

It was astonishing how that very simple and formal note pleased her. It proved so definitely that he *wanted* to see her again. Vicky was half-enchanted and half-despairing as she re-read every word.

She cursed herself for being a little fool, because she trembled so. And much though she would have liked to have kept it, she went straight into the sitting-room, and put the letter on the fire. It wouldn't do to let Tom see that Mr. Farnel had written! Not after last night. As for Digby coming again, of course he oughtn't to. She should write at once to his Club, and warn him that there had been trouble. But every instinct in her rebelled from doing so. It would be too degrading to let Digby think that Tom was so stupid; that she permitted such tyranny. Digby wasn't used to the kind of woman who, Victorian-like, sat well under her husband's thumb, and had no men friends after marriage. He was modern. He would think it ridiculous that she could not go up to town and lunch with him. Much though she yearned to do it, she dared not. It would be utterly impossible for her to get away from Tom and Tye Farm. He would have something very strong to say if she told him she was going to meet another man for lunch, and she couldn't deceive him. It wouldn't be worth while.

But if Digby chose to come here again on his way back

from Brighton, what was there to prevent it? Everything in her yearned to see him once more. Strange that she should want her peace so violently disturbed. What little peace there was left for her, now that she knew how much she loved him! Yes, shameful though it might be for a married woman to make such an admission to herself, Vicky made it. She loved Digby. She treasured every memory of him, from the first hour in the Paris hotel when he had dried her tears with his pocket handkerchief and been so sympathetic and understanding.

Annie's cross voice cut through her thoughts:

'Mrs. Collinson, ain't you eating your breakfast? It's getting late.'

Vicky pulled herself together and went back to the dining-room. While she ate her meal, she opened Freda's note.

Freda had written to say that she was not at all well, needed a change, and would like to spend a week at the Farm. Mum and Dad had both thought it would do her good. If Vicky and Tom would have her, perhaps they'd come up to Norman Park the day after tomorrow, which was Sunday, and fetch her.

After breakfast, Vicky sat down to answer her correspondence of this morning. She left the reply that she most wanted to write until the last. First of all she told Freda that she could come down and stay as long as she liked. She would ask Tom, she said, if they could drive home after lunch on Sunday and fetch her.

Vicky did not particularly want her sister. They never got on. But any company was better than none in this gloomy old house. She only hoped to goodness Tom would not think of mentioning Digby Farnel's name, in case Freda let the cat out of the bag.

And then Vicky wrote to Digby Farnel. Saying nothing that she wanted to say. How could she write one word of the intense feelings that were within her? But she extracted some miserable comfort in being able to send a few friendly lines. It was at least some form of communication with him.

'Dear Digby,
*'It was kind of you to write, and I was awfully glad to
see you again yesterday. I am afraid I can't possibly get up
to town, but I hope to see you again one day.*
'Ever yours,
'Vicky.'

What an inadequate letter from a girl madly in love! She
could have wept over it, but she sent it, conscious that
Tom, had he known even about those few simple lines,
would have been annoyed and suspicious.

All through that day Vicky kept telling herself that Tom
was right, that she was wrong and that it ought not to
matter to her whether she saw Digby Farnel again or not.
But unfortunately the ethics of right and wrong could in
no way crush down her need of him. The struggle that
went on in her young mind and heart, not only that day
but during the succeeding ones, was stiffer and more
difficult to bear than Tom would ever know.

He, never seeing anything until it was thrust under his
nose, continued life in his usual placid fashion, oblivious
of the emotional conflict taking place in his young wife.
He was much too busy to notice whether she looked
happy or unhappy. As long as she was in for meals, to talk
to him, and there at night, and was not actually weeping,
he took it for granted that she was all right.

One person noticed the strain which was written all over
Vicky's face. That was Nora Richardson, the wife of the
retired Naval Commander who ran the dairy farm half a
mile away. On the night when she and her husband dined
with the Collinsons, Nora talked for a few minutes alone
with her young hostess. The men were still chatting over
their business in the dining-room.

Nora Richardson was a woman of forty. She had a
daughter of her own, learning to speak French at a school
in Switzerland. A high-spirited and lovely girl of whom

Nora was reminded, in a dim fashion, by Mrs. Tom Collinson. Something in the way those big luminous eyes were set, in the length of the black lashes, and in her wide, sweet smile. Vicky was so much younger than Mrs. Richardson, she felt a motherly feeling toward her. And it hurt her to see a young wife of four months so obviously unhappy.

Mrs. Richardson had told her husband long ago, when she first met the Collinsons, that it was a *mésalliance*. Collinson was straight as a die, steady as a rock, but no husband for a pretty, imaginative child, like this one whom he had brought to Tye Farm. In previous talks with her young neighbour, Mrs Richardson had divined that Vicky's home life had not been congenial. So it was apparent, at least to Mrs. Richardson who had a shrewd eye and a very understanding nature, that Vicky had married in order to escape the boredom of one home, only to find the other a good deal more boring.

Nora was infinitely sorry for the child. It made her think a lot about Elspeth, her own pretty daughter abroad. It would be awful if Elspeth came back and rushed into marriage with the first man who asked her, because she was bored at home, only to find all the beauty and sweetness had gone out of her life because she was not really in love with her husband.

Mrs. Richardson prayed that it wouldn't be so for Elspeth. She condemned Mrs. Waide who had made life so intolerable for Vicky that she did this thing. And yet the problem was not easily solved. What could one do with a young daughter these days when one had no money? Charlie Richardson had been 'axed' at the wrong time of his life, and it was hard for a man over forty and out of the Service to begin again. Fortunately Nora's husband had had enough money to buy this Sussex farm, and they were doing well and liking it. But what sort of life would there be for Elspeth when she returned? And what sort of men would she meet—except Tom Collinson's kind!

Tonight, Nora Richardson was more than usually troubled about her young friend. There was nervous strain stamped on every feature of Vicky's face.

'How's life treating you, my dear?' Nora asked as she pulled out the tapestry work upon which she was engaged, and started to work.

Vicky, in her favourite position on the hassock in front of the fire, gave a laugh which had little humour in it, and answered:

'All right, I suppose.'

'Things been dull?'

'M'm.'

'It isn't a very thrilling existence for you, I must say. I'm a middle-aged woman and I don't want to gad about, but you wouldn't be human if you didn't.'

Vicky raised her haunting blue eyes and said:

'I don't really want to "gad", Mrs. Richardson, but——'

'But what?'

Vicky looked a moment at the other woman. She had always been passionately envious of Nora Richardson because she seemed so content. She adored her husband. Vicky was not surprised. She thought Charles Richardson a delightful person. He had a tremendous sense of humour, and created an atmosphere of goodwill wherever he went, and was full of enthusiasm about life. In his turn, he adored his wife. The love and sympathy that existed between them were obvious. And often Vicky thought:

'To be in close contact like that. . . . To be in love. . . . How miraculous! That's what marriage should be. And then one wouldn't mind being shut away in a farm. It would become Paradise!'

After a pause she said:

'I suppose I'm just a discontented little fool. I don't know what's good for me.'

'We none of us know that,' said Nora Richardson.

'But you always seem awfully happy.'

'I think I am. I've had a lot of illness, and Charlie has had a lot of financial trouble since he left the Navy, and

Elspeth is a big expense and responsibility. But we are happy.'

'That's because you're still in love!' said Vicky impulsively.

'Yes,' said Mrs. Richardson.

Then she stuck her needle in the canvas, bent forward, and touched Vicky's shoulder.

'My dear, I'm older than you are. I've seen a lot of life. I don't think you've seen very much; don't think me impertinent if I pry a little into your private life, but I would like to know what's getting you down so badly.'

'You couldn't be impertinent. You're frightfully kind. I love talking to you!' broke out Vicky all in a breath. Then she stopped and shook her head as though faced with an insoluble problem.

Nora Richardson saw the scarlet colour leap up under the girl's skin. Saw the quivering of her underlip, and her heart ached for Vicky Collinson. She thought, rather crossly, that that stolid young man talking to Charlie in the next room was a bit of a fool. This girl was no longer in love with him, and little wonder. Probably she never had been. Nora was very much afraid that that tell-tale colour meant that Vicky was in love with somebody else.

A moment later and she knew. For Vicky, desperately needing to unburden that young heart which was so surcharged with emotion and misery, blurted out a little of the true state of affairs.

'I suppose you think me awful, Mrs. Richardson. But there *is* someone else I used to know . . . and I've seen him again and I . . . Oh! you'll think me dreadful.'

'But I don't at all, my dear. Why should I? I've judged all the way along that this marriage wasn't right for you. It isn't surprising that there should be somebody else. You're very pretty, and I'm sure you appeal to men. But what a pity that you couldn't have married the right one.'

Vicky lowered her head.

'There was never any question of it. But, oh! if only one needn't *feel* things so badly.'

The elder woman drew closer and put an arm about the slim shoulders.

'Poor child! I'm so very sorry. But don't be ashamed of what you feel or begrudge it. To feel intensely is the essence of life. There can be no real beauty without suffering. And if you've seen beauty and truth even for a few moments, consider the pain worth while. Some people go right through their lives without that revelation.'

Vicky, her eyes full of tears, lifted her head and looked at Nora Richardson. Those words sank deep into her mind. And she felt a sudden easing of the anguish—a relaxation from that awful tightness of repression and misery.

'You talk like *he* does,' she whispered. 'He always spoke about beauty in that way. You do understand, so very well! I'm glad I told you.'

'I'm glad you did, dear.'

'Sometimes it's almost more than I can bear.'

'Yes. I've seen love and life in many phases and I've known many unhappy marriages. I realise how human beings can suffer, and how unutterably lonely each one of us can be within ourselves. I wish you could be happy, my dear. You remind me so often of my Elspeth. She is impulsive and passionate. I pray she'll make the right choice when the day comes.'

'I hope to God she does,' said Vicky, with a vehemence which hurt Mrs Richardson.

'Do you see *him* now?'

'I've only done so once.'

'You must just try your utmost to put it all out of your mind. At least, if you must think of him, think, as I say, gladly of those moments which you've had, and let them be a comfort and not a grief to you. Of course, you've made your mistake, and by that I know you must abide, my poor dear.'

The sound of men's voices coming through the hall reached Vicky's ears. Swiftly she wiped the tears from her lashes.

'I realise it only too well.'

Nora Richardson pressed her hand.

'Don't be too unhappy. And come over to the farm and see me any time you feel like it, and have a good talk.'

Vicky clung to that kind hand for a moment.

'Marvellous to know that I *can* talk to you.'

Then Tom Collinson and his guest joined them, and the conversation became general.

Going home that night Nora Richardson said to her husband:

'Charlie, that poor little thing's going through purgatory. She doesn't care a jot for that husband of hers.'

'He seems a good chap,' said Charles Richardson.

His wife snapped:

'Don't be dull and unimaginative, Charlie. I wouldn't love you just because you were a "good chap."'

'I trust,' he said, 'that *you* are a good woman, anyhow.'

'No other chance, my darling.'

'Well, don't mind me, if one comes your way.'

She put a hand on his knee.

'Stop fooling a moment. I'm worried about little Mrs. Collinson. She's in love with somebody else.'

'Good God, she's only been married a few minutes.'

'That doesn't matter. It might as well be years. She shouldn't have married that man at all. She's quite a unique sort of girl—full of temperament. And he's a stick. As far as I can see, she's in love with somebody she met before him, and things went wrong.'

'Well, what's going to happen?'

Nora Richardson thought of Vicky's tear-filled, tormented eyes and shook her head.

'I don't know. But I think something's bound to happen—or that child will break.'

'Who's the chap she's keen about?'

'I don't know. She didn't say.'

Charlie Richardson sensed that his wife was really concerned about their young neighbour. As he pulled the car up outside their farm he squeezed her hand, and said:

'When I see all these modern messes of marriages, it makes me thankful for you, Nora, sweet.'

She put her hand against his shoulder.

'When I think what that child is suffering it makes me thank God for you too, darling. I only wish she could be as happy as I've been. It makes me scared for Elspeth—I can tell you. Marriage becomes a grim institution when it makes a pretty child of twenty-one look like a soft, gentle little animal caught in a trap.'

'Well, we can't do anything about it, old lady.'

'Nothing. That's the worst of it. There's nothing to be done.'

Which was precisely what Vicky said to herself going to bed that night.

'There's nothing to be done!'

But before she slept, she repeated to herself many times those other words of Nora Richardson's, which had found such a poignant echo in her heart.

'Don't be ashamed of what you feel. To feel intensely is the essence of life. . . . And if you have seen beauty and truth even for a few moments, consider the pain worth while. . . .'

That was how she must try to think for the rest of time. She had seen beauty and truth with Digby Farnel as it should be—mere flashes—but she had seen them. She must be glad and remember the moments for what they were worth.

At the end of that week she had reached a stage in which she half hoped that Digby would not come again because it would be almost intolerable seeing him. Yet she had not the strength to sit down and write to tell him so. She had never really told him what she felt about him. Pride forbade that she should say to him now:

'Because I love you so much, I can't bear to see you again.'

So she did nothing.

On Sunday, she and Tom drove to Norman Park to pick

up Freda. Never a source of happiness for Vicky. But she did not bicker with Freda quite so badly as she had done when they had lived together. Possibly some of Vicky's old fighting spirit had been broken. At any rate, when Freda was caustic, Vicky retaliated in mild fashion compared with the old days.

They all had lunch together. Mrs. Waide, who was devoted to her son-in-law, gave her young daughter only a cursory glance, remarked that she looked 'quite well', and then talked exclusively to Tom. Mr. Waide, however, with something of real perception, saw full well that his young daughter, whom he missed sadly, was not a happily married woman. He had no chance to talk to her alone and it was not his way to interfere. But he grieved for her in his heart, and after she had gone remarked to his wife that he was not too happy about the child.

Mrs. Waide sniffed.

'Stuff and nonsense. She's perfectly all right. She's got a splendid husband.'

'She look so thin and pinched.'

'That's just the winter. It's probably a bit cold on the farm.'

'H'm,' said Mr. Waide, and kept the rest of his thoughts to himself.

Mrs. Waide added:

'If she doesn't appreciate Tom, then more's the shame. Poor Freda would have given her right hand to marry him.'

And 'poor Freda' was thinking exactly the same thing when she motored down to Tye Farm with her sister and brother-in-law. Vicky's marriage with Tom had in no way altered Freda's regard for the young man. She thought, with her mother, that Vicky had a splendid husband, and her private opinion was that Vicky didn't deserve him. She didn't know how to make a man happy. Freda thought her very inattentive to Tom. Always dreaming. She had got so very quiet and strange. What was the matter with her?

That very first night at the farm, Freda, as was her custom when she stayed with Vicky, set herself out to wait hand and foot on her brother-in-law. She fetched his slippers for him. She found his tobacco-pouch when he lost it. She discussed the chickens for an hour, exhibiting what Tom considered a most intelligent interest. (Freda had been reading up the subject!) And she was good at figures. She was able to talk over the financial side of the business. Vicky, on the other hand, was hopeless about money or any economic subject.

Tom smoked his pipe more thoughtfully than usual that night, and looked at the two sisters. How different they were! Vicky, so much the prettier, of course, huddled there over a book. She was for ever reading romantic nonsense, he thought. Filling her head with a lot of tripe instead of facing realities. Freda, in the soft shaded light, did not look too plain in spite of her pallid face and ashen, lustreless hair, but of course she was no beauty. On the other hand, there was something thoroughly *domestic* about her appearance tonight which won Tom's approbation. There she was, knitting socks which she said were for him. Darned good of her! It never entered Vicky's head to knit socks for a chap. Then he felt disloyal and switched his mind back to the chickens.

Freda said:

'Who've you seen lately, Vicky?'

'Seen?' asked Vicky in a vague voice.

'Yes. Any new callers?'

'Ah! ha!' put in Tom with a heavy attempt at humour. 'Your sister's had an old admirer down here lately, Freda.'

Freda lifted her head from her knitting. The needles went on clicking, but she looked sharply at her sister.

'And who was that, pray?'

The novel nearly fell from Vicky's fingers. Her heart had jumped. The crimson stung her cheeks. This was what she had dreaded. Now for trouble!

Tom yawned and said:

'Some fellow called Farnel. Vicky said you all knew him at home.'

Freda stopped knitting. She, too, reddened. With anger against Vicky, and disgust. Her mouth narrowed to a thin line. Then she said:

'Yes, I know him.'

Tom suddenly sprang to his feet.

'Listen! Did you girls hear that fox? I did. And I heard him yapping last night. I'm going out with my gun. I want to kill the brute before I lose any more chickens.'

He walked out. The sisters were left alone. Nervously Vicky returned Freda's gaze. She cleared her throat. Freda said:

'And what, may I ask, was Mr. Farnel doing here?'

'He—he happens to have relatives in Brighton and called here on his way driving back to town.'

'You've been seeing him, then, since Paris?'

'You know that. I told you and Mum that I saw him in London. And I told you, too, that you had no right to stop his letters to me.'

Freda snorted.

'So you're having an affair with that man! Not content with all the trouble you've caused with that other young swine, you——'

'Now look here, Freda,' broke in Vicky, with rising anger, 'you've no right to say I'm having an affair with Mr. Farnel just because he happens to call here. And it's none of your business, anyhow.'

'I'm older than you and——'

'You can't pull that stuff over me any more,' interrupted Vicky. 'I'm married now. That elder sister business is a farce, anyhow.'

'Then I might trouble you to remember you're married.'

'You don't need to remind me. And you don't need to come here and make mischief.'

'I consider you've no right to be seeing that man.'

'And why not?'

'Does Tom know the truth? Does he know Mr. Farnel was a stranger to you until he helped you in Paris?'

Vicky swallowed hard.

'No.'

'I bet he doesn't! said Freda tossing her head. 'Poor old Tom! Of all the nice, kind, trusting men——'

'Oh, be quiet!' interrupted Vicky again, her strained nerves on edge. She jumped to her feet and put the book under her arm. 'I'm not going to sit here and listen to lectures. I tell you it's none of your business, and if you are going to make mischief, you'd better go home.'

Freda started to make some acid reply, but Vicky had gone.

Freda sat knitting until Tom came back.

'I saw the brute, but couldn't get him,' he announced. 'You all alone? Vicky gone to bed?'

Freda laid aside her knitting and smiled at her brother-in-law.

'Yes. I waited to see if I could do anything for you. Would you like a cup of tea?'

'Well, now, that would be nice,' said Tom. 'We'd better just go and see if the range's out. This is not a town house, you know. No gas fires.'

'If you want some tea, I can soon light a fire,' said Freda.

He thought for the second time that night what a grand girl Freda was. There was plenty to be said for her even if she was on the thin and scraggy side, and had none of Vicky's voluptuous charm.

And Freda always shone in Tom's presence. Shone because she was secretly in love with him, and had been so for years. Inwardly she criticised bitterly Vicky's whole attitude and behaviour. It wasn't fair that Vicky should be here, as Tom's wife, mistress of Tye Farm—a position for which she, Freda, would have given her right hand. Vicky didn't deserve Tom. Why, if Tom knew about Paris . . .

A small fire was still burning in the kitchen. Freda made the tea, and she and Tom sat at the kitchen table drinking it and chatting. After a while Freda brought up the subject of Digby Farnel.

'If I were you, I wouldn't have that man hanging round Vicky,' she said, feeling it was time she made a little mischief.

Tom looked at her sharply.

'Why do you say that?'

'I just don't like him,' said Freda.

'H'm,' said Tom. 'Where did she meet him?'

'Oh, never mind,' said Freda, 'but I'd just keep an eye on him if I were you.'

That was enough to reawaken Tom's former jealousy of the London stranger whom he had found down here with Vicky. But he was not the man to ask many questions. Rather, he brooded over things in his mind and kept his feelings to himself. He did not resent what Freda had said. He saw that she had warned him for his own sake. It was obvious that she was fond of him. He was rather touched. And before they went to bed he patted her shoulder and told her that she was a 'good kid'.

Freda went to bed in ecstasy. She thought him marvellous. And she felt no remorse for going behind Vicky's back and making insinuations. Indeed, she told herself that if need be she would tell Tom about Paris. She wasn't going to let Vicky play fast and loose with his affections.

17

That very next morning, Vicky decided that on no account must Digby be allowed to come to Tye Farm whilst Freda was here. It would be fatal. Freda was no real sister. And she had a very decided penchant for Tom. She would not hesitate to make trouble.

Vicky had started the day off with a good lie. Immediately after breakfast she told her husband and her sister that she was taking Sooty, the Labrador pup, for a walk as far as Poynings, which was their nearest village, about a mile from the farm. She wanted to go to the Post Office, she said. She knew quite well that Freda loathed walking and would not offer to accompany her, and Tom was busy helping Jones collect eggs.

She must telephone to Digby. She only knew his Club address. But she could leave a message for him. She could say: 'Don't come down until you hear from me again.' Then she would write and explain that Freda was on the warpath.

As she anticipated, Freda made no offer to walk with her, so Vicky went out alone with her puppy.

After the recent storms, the countryside squelched with mud. Many of the fields were under water. The morning papers had said that there were floods all over England.

But Vicky thought how beautiful Sussex looked today. The wind had changed. It was much colder, and there was frost in the air. But the pale November sun was shining as bravely as it could, over ploughed fields and sombre woods, and the sky behind the green rim of

Downs was a clear, soft blue.

The Labrador puppy, his silky ears flopping, bounded about the road in front of Vicky. She tried to keep him to heel, her heart jumping every time a car came by. It was no fun walking in the country these days. How one hated motor-cars when one wasn't in them!

There were a lot of things one hated in life! This sort of thing. . . . Having to lie, for instance, and to send a message to a man which was contrary to everything in one's heart!

No doubt if she once stopped Digby from coming, he would never come. He would think it best. But, oh! how hard that would be!

By the time Vicky had reached the Post Office, the exercise in the brisk wind had whipped the rich colour to her cheeks. She had seldom looked lovelier or felt more downcast than when she put through that telephone call to Digby's Club.

The result of the call was unexpected. The man who answered told her that Mr. Farnel had already been in for his letters and would not be returning that day. When she asked if they could give her his home address, they said that they were not permitted to do so without members' permission.

With that she was forced to be content. But she walked back to the farm with a curious tight little feeling inside, the peculiar sensation that something was going to happen. Digby might even be on his way to Brighton to-day. He had said that his old uncle was gravely ill. Just supposing he turned up to-day! Vicky's heart almost stopped beating at the thought.

But there was nothing to be done about it. She must just trust to luck. More than anything on earth, she wanted to see Digby. Yet under the circumstances, it would be madness to foster that wish.

The rest of the day went badly for her. Time dragged. Freda was more than ordinarily unkind and spiteful.

Tom was visible only at meal-times. And after lunch Freda volunteered to help him wash eggs, and went off with him, obviously relishing the prospect of being allowed to work with her hero.

Left to herself, Vicky sat down before the fire with a newly-laddered stocking. She seemed to spend her time mending stockings. Tom said she ought to wear woollen ones, but she could never bear to. She supposed she wasn't sensible about such things.

At mid-afternoon, when the November day was beginning to wane, and the sun had gone in and everything was grey and chill, there came a sound for which Vicky had almost been waiting all day. *Something* had warned her that she would hear it. With a fatalistic sensation, she dropped her mending and tore to the window, that young heart of hers beating wildly as she heard the full-throated roar of a racing engine. And she saw a beautiful sports saloon—Digby's car—turn into the drive and roll up to the house.

So he had come! He had come, and Freda was here. Vicky could not think straight. But she found herself out in the cold, stammering a greeting to Digby as he stepped from the car and drew off his guantlets.

For a moment they held each other's gaze. It was a tense moment, unlike any other between them. From the eyes of both ran the silent message which conveyed each to the other the intense pleasure of that meeting. So intense was it, that Digby Farnel had to shake himself mentally. He had no right to be so glad to see the child! Heavens! How pretty she was with that glow on her face and the luminosity of her remarkable eyes.

'Well, my dear,' he said, lamely.

'Oh, Digby——' she said in a breathless way.

'You didn't expect me to turn up!'

'I tried to stop you. I phoned your Club.'

'But why?'

'Freda, my sister, is here.'

209

He looked at her gravely.

'I see. And you think she might make trouble with your husband?'

'She might! Oh—I don't know!'

Digby took a case from his pocket and lit a cigarette. She watched him, almost childishly anguished by the sight of that thin gold case which she remembered. And those fine, sensitive fingers, still brown from the West Indian sun . . . so utterly unlike Tom's muscular, rather coarse hands. A dry, hot sensation caught her throat. She heard him say:

'It's the devil. I wanted to see you, my dear, but I suppose, under the circumstances, I'd better go away again.'

Then rebellion flared in Vicky. The old feeling of flaming revolt which had been hers at home. She flung back her head, her large eyes flashing.

'No! Why should you? Why shouldn't I have my friends? I won't be kept a prisoner just to please Tom and Freda. And I won't have you drive away again, without coming in for some tea.'

He saw full well how much his visit meant to her. He saw, too, that she was a bundle of nerves. How pathetically unhappy she was in this place. He could not have been more sorry. And he was sorry for himself, too, because he wanted immensely to comfort her—to smooth that beaten look away from her small face.

'If you think I should come in, I will,' he said. 'but I don't think——'

'Yes, please do!' she said, in a choked voice.

At that moment Tom and Freda, having walked from the back of the house round to the front garden, appeared on the scene. Freda, in an overall and wool cardigan, and Tom, as usual, in knee-breeches, gaiters, and old coat. He had a dead chicken hanging from one hand. He rarely lost his temper, but he had lost it now. The boy had just brought him this chicken. Sooty had killed it. And it was one of his prize Leghorns.

But Vicky did not even notice what he was holding. She was conscious only of the feeling that she would not be bullied and subjected entirely to Tom's wishes. Digby was her friend. He had come to see her, and she was going to welcome him, whatever her husband or sister had to say. As they approached, she saw the righteous indignation on Freda's pale face, and Tom's ill-humoured expression. She ignored both. She said, in a rather high-pitched voice:

'Oh, Tom, Mr. Farnel has been to Brighton to see his uncle, and is just on his way back. He wants to take a look at Tye Farm in daylight.'

'Oh!' said Tom, shortly.

Freda nudged his arm and muttered:

'Take a look at Vicky, *I* should say. Cheek! him turning up again like this.'

Digby, thoroughly uncomfortable, had every inclination to be short and sharp in his greeting of Freda, whom he had thought in Paris to be the most unattractive girl he had ever met.

Perforce, Tom said:

'Come along in, Mr. Farnel.'

'I haven't much time——' began Digby.

'Oh, do,' broke in Vicky.

Tom, without waiting to hear what the other man replied to his curt invitation, now turned to Vicky and flung the limp, still bleeding chicken on the ground at her feet.

'That's one of my best birds, and it's your darned dog again!' he said.

Digby saw Vicky's face turn from red to white.

'Are you sure Sooty did it?'

'He did, and I shall thrash him within an inch of his life, and you'd better get rid of him as soon as you can.'

He spoke more roughly than he had ever done to her. The chickens were an obsession, and at the moment his mind was much more taken up with this minor tragedy than with Vicky's visitor. Not that the sight of Farnel improved his humour.

Digby stood by, silently smoking, his pulses jumping with peculiar irritation against Vicky's husband. He sensed that this was an old grievance, and that the dog was a great favourite with Vicky. What the deuce did Collinson want to upset her for like this, even if he had lost a chicken.

He heard Vicky give a cry.

'You're not to thrash Sooty!'

'I shall, and I'll tie the chicken round his neck for the rest of the day, and that'll teach him.'

Vicky had no wish for a scene to take place in front of Digby, but the thought of her warm-hearted, loving little retriever puppy being thrashed—and then tortured by Tom—was too much for her. White to the lips, hands clenched, she said:

'Don't you touch Sooty. He's my dog, and if you tie that beastly bird round his neck, I'll untie it.'

'Don't be ridiculous, Vicky,' put in Freda. 'Tom's quite right.'

Digby looked at Freda with secret loathing. The miserable young woman! Always out to make trouble. God! But he could see what sort of a life Vicky led here, quietly bullied. It wrenched his heart-strings to see that hunted look in her eyes. Hell! Why couldn't they even let her have a pet dog in peace.

Tom picked up the chicken, then turned on his heel and started to walk away.

Vicky called after him:

'You're not to beat Sooty. I'll pay for the chicken! I'll pay out of my own money. You're *not* to punish him.'

Tom made no reply. He disappeared round the back of the house.

Vicky stood irresolute. She wanted to rush after him and save her dog. She wanted to stay with Digby. Her already overstrained nerves were breaking. Digby took a quick look at her, pitched his cigarette into a bush, and took her arm.

'Steady, my dear. Don't let it upset you. I don't suppose he'll hurt the pup.'

'I love Sooty,' said Vicky under her breath, her lower lip trembling. 'He's the only thing I *do* love in this place, and if they take him away from me——'

'Ssh!' Digby pressed her arm against his side. He hated to feel her trembling so. Poor little Vicky! Driven to hysteria by two perfectly good, respectable people, who purported to care for her.

Then Freda, with a dark look at her sister, said:

'I don't think that's a very nice thing for you to say—the only thing you've got to love in this place, indeed! And what about Tom? If you had any decency, you wouldn't allow this Mr. Farnel to come and see you.'

Vicky began to speak, but Digby silenced her.

He could stand some things, but not being called 'this Mr. Farnel', quite so contemptuously by Miss Waide. Retaining Vicky's arm, he looked Freda straight in the eyes, and said, in a frozen voice:

'Might I ask if it is by any chance your business whether or not I call upon Vicky?'

'I consider it is. I'm her sister, and I'm very fond of Tom. And I might ask, in my turn, if he knows about Paris. No! he doesn't! And if he did know that Vicky just picked you up in a train, then ran from one man in one hotel, to another, *to you*, he might have something to say. It was a disgrace—the whole of that show. You may not have been doing anything wrong like the other man, but I shouldn't think Tom would want anyone connected with the affair in his house.'

After which speech, Freda turned, marched away, and disappeared indoors.

Vicky breathed hard and fast. Her eyes were enormous, feverish, in her white face. Under her breath, she said:

'That was pretty insulting! As if you had been anything but terribly kind to me! It's all because she hates me, and wanted to marry Tom herself. Oh! I wish to God

213

she had! *I wish to God she had!*'

Digby took her other hand.

'Hush, my dear. Please! Don't upset yourself like this.'

She tore the hand away, and put it against her quivering lips.

'I wish I were dead!'

His heart was wrenched.

'Vicky, my *dear* . . .'

He realised that the whole of this scene had taken place out in the cold. He had on a coat, but Vicky had come straight from the house without a wrap. She was shaking, not only with nerves. She was frozen.

He sought desperately in his mind for a solution to her problem. It never entered his head that, when he came to see her today, he would find himself plunged into this sort of crisis. Yet he was not sorry he had come. She needed somebody to stand by her, and needed it pretty badly. She was right on the verge of breaking. What in heaven's name could he do? He was more than half in love with her, and he knew it. He could barely tolerate the thought of driving away and leaving her like this. He would never have a moment's rest, haunted by the memory of her unhappiness.

While he stood there, trying to warm her cold little fingers with his warm ones, and Vicky fought against the hysterical desire to break down and cry, the frosty silence was broken by a loud yelp, followed by a series of howls.

Digby felt the girl shudder right through her body. She cried:

'He's hurting Sooty. I knew he would. He's beastly about Sooty. Just because I love him. Just because he likes his horrible chickens better than anything. Oh, poor Sooty——'

'Darling, don't worry—I don't suppose he's really hurt. You know what puppies are.'

She shook her head dumbly. She was past even noticing

214

that he had involuntarily used that term of endearment. She leaned so heavily against his arm that he thought for a moment she had fainted.

'Look here,' he said, 'you can't stand here like this, and I'm not going into the house, so you jump into the car for a moment. You'll catch a frightful cold.'

She did not care. Neither had she any fight left in her. Freda and Tom could do what they wanted, think what they wanted——

She put her hands up to her ears to shut out the sound of Sooty's mournful howling. Digby, with an arm about her, led her to the car, and made her sit in it. Then he took his place beside her, and tucked a rug over her knees. Her dark curls were dishevelled, falling about her pale, distraught young face.

Digby, looking at her, felt an unaccustomed madness. A feeling that he would like to switch on the engine and drive this child away to the warmth and beauty and happiness which she needed, and of which she was so shamefully starved. And he needed her, too. All her youth and sweetness. That childish appeal which found such an echo of tenderness in his heart, and awoke all his protective instincts. He had known for some long time that he wanted to go on protecting her for the rest of his life.

The brief winter afternoon was declining. The grey-blue shadows of twilight were creeping around the old farmhouse. There was going to be a heavy frost. Already it was dusk. One or two orange lights gleamed palely through the casements. In this car, they could not be seen from the house. Quite still they sat a moment, their fingers locked. Then he spoke.

'I can see that it is hopeless for me to come and see you any more. I'll have to go away, and stay away this time.'

He hated saying it, both for his sake and hers. It seemed so brutal on top of her misery. For he knew that by leaving her, he consigned her to a fate which he would not have been able to endure in her place. A death in life on this lonely farm, with that clod of a man, or one of her unsympathetic family. And she was only twenty-one. She had all the rest of her life to face. He could scarcely bear it for her.

Her reaction to his words were swift and human. She gave a broken cry:

'Oh, no—oh, Digby, no!'

'I must,' he said. 'What else is there for me to do?'

'I don't know,' she whispered, and raised a convulsed young face to his. It was more than he could stand—that look in her eyes. He knew then that he loved her far too intensely for his own peace of mind. For a moment he forgot the man to whom she belonged, and the house outside which they were sitting. . . . Freda's malevolent gaze possibly spying on them through the windows. Nothing seemed to matter but the need to bring her comfort, and so console himself.

'Vicky, my darling . . . my poor sweet. . . .'

And then she was in his arms. He was holding her close, her hands were clasped about his neck, and at last his lips were against her mouth. In a wild, straining embrace, they sat there. All the pent-up emotion in Vicky was let loose. It was an embrace almost too anguished for delight, and yet, delight it was to be in his arms again, and this time to know that he held her as a lover and as a lover stooped to kiss not only her lips, but her hair, her shut eyelids, and the aching pulse in her throat.

They were both a little crazy during those moments that followed. And they said all the things they had never meant to say:

From her:

'I love you so! I love you! I always have!'

From him:

'Darling, how sweet you are! I love you, too, and I can't bear you to be hurt like this.'

She put her cheek against his, holding him close to her,

216

wishing she could, indeed, die before the passionate ecstasy of that embrace should end. Before she would have to tear herself out of the warm sweetness of his arms and go out into the cold, alone again.

'You don't love me, Digby. How can you?'

He smoothed the dark curls back from her face. Taking off his glasses, he laid them aside, and looked long and closely into her eyes. There was a warmth and radiance on her young face now which completely transfigured it. And for her, he was a boy again. Not the serious-minded Farnel whom his friends thought a confirmed bachelor. But a foolish young man in love for the first time, and for the first time tasting the sweetness of his beloved's kiss.

'I'm afraid I do love you, my dear,' he said, 'that's the devil of it. And I'd give anything to go back to the summer. I ought to have run away with you then. I know it. When I kissed you in the taxi that day, you knew it.'

'Yes.' She gave a long sigh, her fingers twining feverishly about his hand. Her mind was in conflict. On the one hand, she was enraptured by the thought that her love was no one-sided affair, that she did not give it unrequited—and he loved her in return. On the other hand, it seemed too awful that they should feel like this and that she should be married to Tom——

'Oh, Digby,' she added, 'why did I marry Tom? Why? Why?'

'One makes these mistakes.'

'And pays for them the rest of one's life!'

'That's the monstrous part of it. No child of your age should be allowed to marry—particularly if she is unhappy at home. Ten chances to one she'll marry the wrong man. And in a way, I feel the responsibility for this. I ought to have carried you off, myself. I think I might have made you happy, mightn't I?'

She turned her face and hid it against his shoulder.

'It would have been heaven with you.'

217

'My poor sweet! What the devil do we do now?'

She shook her head dumbly. She felt his fingers smoothing her hair, tender and sensitive as she had always known they would be. And when she thought of Tom, everything seemed to go black in front of her. Ecstasy fled from her, leaving a sick, desperate sensation.

'I've got to be firm. We both have,' said Digby. 'I ought never to have come down and disturbed you like this. The sooner I go away again, the better.'

She had to smile to herself. That was so like a man! The harm is done, then away rides the lover! But in the same breath she reproached herself, for she knew she was as much responsible for this crisis as he was—if not more so. For surely she had loved him long before he had loved her.

'I've got to remember that you are married,' said Digby. 'It's obvious that we can't meet again, darling, isn't it?'

'I suppose so.'

'We must both just try to get over it, Vicky.'

That brought a bitter cry from her:

'I never will, never till I die. You know that! You may be able to get over it. I expect you will. I don't think it will ever mean as much to you as it does to me. You're sorry for me, that's all.'

He protested hotly:

'I won't let you say that. I love you, my dear.'

She caught hold of his hand and carried it up to her lips.

'I adore you with every breath of my body, and I'll remember you as long as I live. But things are different for you, you're a man. You can go away and do lots of things that will help you forget. I have nothing—nothing.'

He caught her close again, and kissed her lips, not once but many times.

'My poor sweet little Vicky. Darling child!'

She returned his caresses with all the fervour of her being. She knew full well that she had never before realised what it might be to love a man and be loved. To go back to Tom, after this, would be like death.

'Oh, Digby, how can I say good-bye to you and never see you again!'

'God knows, I don't want to leave you. Queer though it may seem to you, my child, this is the first time in my own life that I've ever felt this way. I always thought I should never fall in love, and certainly not with some other fellow's wife.'

'I can't think of myself as that. I belong to you.'

'Unfortunately, my darling, you belong to your husband, and I've no right to be sitting here making love to you.'

It was on the tip of her tongue to cry:

'Don't leave me. Take me away.'

But she curbed that. There are some things that must not be said. Some things that must not be done. She had got to go back to Tom and make the best of a bad job.

For a long while they sat silent, very close together. Now it was quite dark. They could scarcely see each other's faces.

Then Digby felt for his glasses, put them on, and gently drew away from her.

'I can't keep you out here any longer. It'll look so bad. I feel I have behaved badly enough as it is. But I'm not going to be sorry that I have told you I love you, my dear, and I shall remember the things you've said to me, all my life.'

She felt that if she stayed there with him another moment, she would never have the strength to get out of the car. Sooty was still howling. She started to shiver again. The haunted look came back into her eyes, but it was too dark for Digby to see it. She said:

'I'd better go. Good-bye.'

He took her hand and kissed it.

'God be good to you, my dear. I'll think of you often.'

'I'll never stop thinking of you,' she said despairingly.

'And I have only one more thing to say to you, Vicky. If things get too bad, you must let me know—and come to me.'

That was a temptation which illuminated the darkness for a moment. Her heart leapt wildly. But she shook her head.

'I can't do that. I can't ask you to pay for my mistake in marrying Tom. I've just got to put up with it.'

From the house came Freda's voice:

'Vick—y, Vick—y! Come in at once! Tom wants you.'

She shuddered, opened the door of the car, and jumped out.

'Good-bye, darling, darling Digby!' she said in a choked voice, slammed the door again, and disappeared from his sight.

For an instant he sat there staring through the blue darkness at the farm-house which had swallowed her up. He had never in his life been more conscious of misery, or of the feeling that one woman in the world held his happiness in her small hand, as Vicky did in hers. The one woman! And she belonged to that fellow in there. He was leaving her to a wretched sort of fate which he scarcely dared visualise.

He lit another cigarette and switched on the engine. It cost him a tremendous effort to drive away from Tye Farm and leave Vicky there, knowing that he must never see her again.

18

Tom Collinson and Freda were both in the sitting-room waiting for Vicky when she entered the house. She tried to escape up the stairs, but Tom called her. Almost sullenly, Vicky answered that summons. And now for the peroration! She didn't care. She didn't care about anything, since she knew that Digby Farnel loved her. She could not even feel a sense of guilt when she walked into that sitting-room, her lips still burning from his kisses. She could not even think for the moment that their good-bye had been final. That would be too terrible. Coming straight from his arms, she was in a state of exaltation, and momentarily all other feelings were temporarily submerged.

After the cold of the frosty night, the sitting-room struck warm. She could feel her cheeks flaming. She knew that her hair was rough. She did not care. With something like defiance, she looked at her husband and her sister.

They stood together, their backs to the fire. Upon the faces of both was written accusation, shocked disapproval.

Tom's mouth was a thin line. Hands locked behind his back, he addressed his wife:

'What do you think you've been doing?'

Her breast rose and fell with the tumult of her emotions. Flinging back her head, she answered:

'Talking to my friend, who wouldn't come into this house after the reception he got from both of you.'

'I like that,' said Tom. 'I like that, indeed. Now that I know where you met that man, I wonder you ever had the impudence to let him set foot in my place.'

Vicky turned from him to Freda, who had the grace to

221

avoid her sister's scornful gaze.

'So you've sneaked, have you?'

'Since you insisted on seeing Mr. Farnel, I considered it my duty to warn Tom,' Freda mumbled.

Vicky's hands clenched.

'And how many lies have you told? What sort of a wrong impression have you given? You've always hated me. You've always been jealous. I suppose you think this was a good chance to get back on me——'

'Don't you start on Freda!' cut in Tom; 'and you're a fine one to talk about lies. You've told me a few.'

Vicky's heart thumped. Hysteria was rising in her again, but she tried to control herself. She wasn't going to let them beat her down. She had Digby's love to remember— Digby's embrace. That would give her courage, and protect her from any onslaught that was made against her.

'How have I lied to you, Tom?' she flashed.

Tom turned to his sister-in-law.

'Perhaps, Free, you had better give Vicky and myself a moment together. I'll soon settle this for good and all.'

'All right, Tom.'

Freda picked up her knitting and walked out of the room without another glance at her sister. She felt she had done Tom a good turn by telling him the truth. It was time he knew about Paris. And he had thanked her, too. He knew that she had his good at heart. He was such a fine, upright man. She couldn't imagine why Vicky didn't appreciate him.

Left alone with her husband, Vicky tried to quieten the nervous racing of her heart. The glorious colour which had been on her face when she entered the room had all gone. She was very pale. She went up to the fire and stretched her cold hands to the blaze.

'Well,' she said, in the same quiet voice, 'how are you going to settle it?'

'Look here,' he said, 'why didn't you tell me before where and how you first met that man?'

'I didn't see any reason to. What was the good of raking up an old story?'

'Not so old. It only happened last June.'

'Maybe it did, but I don't see what difference that makes.'

'You said he was a friend of your family's.'

'And what of that?'

'It was a lie. In fact, Freda told me that your mother stopped him writing to you.'

'On the other hand, my father thanked him for behaving in the gentlemanly way he did in Paris.'

'Gentlemanly way!' said Tom, sneering. 'A fine gentleman *he* is!'

'He is! He is!' said Vicky passionately.

'Fooling round with you in Paris, and taking you for walks to photograph you——'

'He didn't fool round; and what's wrong in being photographed? Oh, I daresay Freda's made a fine story. She'd do anything to get back at me. Nobody would think she is my sister. She's always loathed me——'

'Rot!' broke in Tom, roughly. 'She's a very nice sister, and thinks of your good, which is more than you do of your own!'

'Take her part, then!'

'She's a very good pal to me. She told me about Paris because she thought I ought to know. And I'm surprised at your parents not making you tell me before I married you!'

Vicky gave an hysterical laugh.

'What . . . that Mr. Farnel protected me in Paris, and rang up Dad and told him to send someone to fetch me! Is that what you wanted to know? Well, you know it now, and it ought to prove to you what he is.'

'He's proved what he is, all right, coming down here after you. And how about this other fellow? The dancing chap you went to Paris with. My God! You made a fool of me all right!'

Vicky faced her husband, stiffening in every limb.

223

'Look here, Tom, I don't know what Freda has been saying, but I think you'd better hear that story from me, hadn't you?'

'A bit late in the telling, aren't you?'

'Why should I have told you before? It wasn't your business. It all happened before I became engaged to you.'

'Maybe it did, but I don't consider it should have been kept from me.'

'Why? What good was it going to do telling you? I made a mistake in going to Paris with Paul Dallas, but what would have been the object in raking it all up for you?'

'Because I came to you with a decent record, and I expected you to come to me with one.'

She shrank back as though he had struck her, scarlet to the roots of her hair.

Then she said in a frozen little voice:

'What exactly do you mean by that?'

'Just what I said. I thought you were just about perfect.'

'Then you made a mistake,' she said, with a broken laugh. 'No one's perfect, and least of all me. But I don't think any man need have minded marrying a girl who had never done anything more than I did before I married you.'

'What more could you have done?'

'What are you insinuating? Just what has Freda been saying?'

'No more than I ought to know. You went to Paris with that dancing fellow.'

'I travelled as far as Paris with him, I admit.'

'Just for the trip, eh?' he sneered again.

'You're being simply hateful.'

He gave her an ugly look. She was aghast to know how really ugly Tom could become when he was roused. She could see him bristling with dark suspicions. Almost hating her. Filled with righteous indignation because he thought he had had something kept from him which he should have known. She could not begin to think of

Freda's awful treachery. She could only stand there, appalled by the thought that her husband was ready and willing to believe the worst. As ready as Freda herself.

Tom said:

'Don't you worry about me being hateful! It's what you are that matters.'

'And what do you think I am?'

'A little cheat!' he flung at her.

She went from red to white and white to red again. Then she gave an hysterical laugh.

'Tom, you're not trying to tell me that when I married you I wasn't a "good girl", are you?'

His own face flushed duskily.

'You went to Paris with a chap who was certainly no better than *he* ought to have been. You travelled with him all night. You were infatuated with him——'

'I deny that!' she broke in. 'If I was infatuated with anything, it was with the thought of dancing. I wanted to dance for my living. You know that. And Paul offered to train me.'

'I bet he did.'

'Don't stand there casting those horrible insinuations at me all the time!' she said, driven to a frenzy. 'If Freda has led you to believe the worst about Paris, she's wicked— *wicked*! And I think you're dreadful to believe her instead of me. You must be very ready to think the worst of me. You must have wanted to have something up against me.'

He looked a brief instant into her flashing eyes, then turned away.

'I was crazy about you when I married you, and you know it. I don't believe you ever cared a jot for me.'

'It isn't true. I was terribly fond of you, but I never pretended to be in love in the way that you were, and you knew that.'

'But I didn't know about Paris,' he said stubbornly.

She looked round her almost despairingly. She was at the end of her tether. She could not stand much more. She could barely think straight. Things were going round and round in her brain. Tom's beastliness, his suspicions, her sister's betrayal of her, all mixed up with Digby's love and her despair. She knew this mulish mood of Tom's. She knew that if he had got it into his head that he had been treated badly by her, nothing would ever get it out.

She made a desperate effort to put things right.

'Tom, listen. You've *got* to listen. Whatever you think, you must believe what I say. I went to Paris with Paul, but there was nothing in it. Nothing. It was absolutely innocent. And Mr. Farnel behaved marvellously to me—you can't accuse me of keeping anything from you that you should have known. It isn't fair. It isn't true!'

He thrust his hands in his pockets, and stood glowering at her out of the corners of his eyes.

'None of it sounds innocent to me.'

'But Tom, I'm telling you. I give you my word——'

She stopped. She saw no change in his expression, no softening. He seemed to have no doubt that she had behaved as badly as she could. It was horrible! He could not say after this that he loved her. Love was not like that. Love was kind. It believed the kindest things. Love was understanding and forgiving. If Tom, this night, had had one grain of human feeling and sympathy—had held out a hand and said:

'I take your word. Let's wipe it out. Don't see that fellow Farnel any more, but let me try to understand you better and make you happier. . . .'

If he had only spoken like that, acted like that, she might have been in his arms. She might have cried out her misery against his shoulder, and they could have started life all over again. She would have respected him for his attitude and felt that he was her friend, even if she could not feel passionate love for him.

But instead, backed by Freda, he stood there, disbelieving and condemning, insulting her in his slow, stubborn fashion.

The last ounce of her goodwill towards Tom vanished. And with it, the last shred of hope. With hunted eyes,

226

Vicky looked around the sitting-room. It was filled with flickering shadows from the fire. She felt that it was a prison—that the whole of this farm-house was a place of torture—that unless she could escape from it, she would go mad.

Tom said:

'I'm not so keen on taking your word as I used to be.'

She flinched. He added:

'And you won't be receiving any more gentleman friends. I shall see to it that you behave yourself in the future. It'll take me some time to get over what you've done, I'll tell you.'

She faced him again, breathing hard and fast.

'Then you believe the worst of me, do you?'

No answer. He took a pipe from his pocket, and set it between his teeth.

'I see!' she said. 'So my future with you will be jolly, won't it? You, thinking all the time that I cheated you when we got married—making up all sorts of horrible things about Paris which never happened. You, watching me as though I were a criminal—likely to break out at any time—putting me through the same sort of hell as I had with my family when I went home again. . . . And you're supposed to be my loving husband! My God. . . .'

She began to shake with laughter. Tears gushed into her eyes, and pelted down her cheeks.

'It's been bad enough down here as it was!' she went on, past caring now what she said. 'You've never worried about my happiness. You haven't cared for anything except whether the chickens were doing well. You even hurt my dog when I asked you not to. I hate you. I despise you. I wouldn't live with you again for anything on earth, and nobody's going to make me!'

He put his pipe in his pocket, marched up to her and seized her wrist.

'Oh yes, you will, and you'll do what you're told in future.'

Her eyes gleamed up at him from a deathly white face.

227

If he had had any sense, he would have seen that she was not in the state to be treated roughly. But he thought of nothing except his own grievance against her. He had only himself to blame that night for losing Vicky finally and absolutely.

What spirit that was left in her, refused to be broken. And the thought of Digby who did understand, and who had said, in Paris: 'Of course I believe you,' when she had told him about Paul, was a stimulus which nothing could destroy.

She whipped her wrist away from Tom's fingers, and sprang back from him.

'I'm not going to be bullied by you, and I'm not going to stay in your house. You can't make me. You can't lock me up. People don't do such things these days! I've tried my best to be a good wife. I may have failed. I daresay I have, and I may not be as righteous as my sister, Freda. But, thank God, I'm *not*, if that's what righteous people are like. I won't stay with you. You can divorce me. You can do what you like. *But I won't stay. . . .*'

She broke off, gasping, sobbing, and rushed out of the room.

He stood irresolute, pulling the lobe of his ear, scowling after her. Of course she was just being hysterical. She didn't mean what she said. She wouldn't run away—she wouldn't!

He heard the front door slam. He turned and ran out of the sitting-room into the hall. Freda met him. She looked pale and scared.

'Vicky's gone. She put on her coat and rushed by me like a lunatic. Where's she going, Tom? What's happened!'

His breath quickened.

'I don't know. Perhaps I'd better follow her. She was in such a state——'

'Oh, dear,' said Freda.

'Did she say anything to you?'

Freda lowered her gaze.

228

'As a matter of fact, she did, Tom. She said we all believed the worst, so she'd give us something to think about. She said she was going up to London to that man.'

Tom, who had been putting on his coat, stopped dead. His eyes narrowed.

'Oh, she said that, did she? Then she'd better go and get on with it. I've finished with her. I can see now that everything you've said is true.'

He took off his coat again, and hung it up. Freda watched him, her pale eyes brighter than usual. Vicky would be all right. She needn't worry about Vicky. But she was very conscious of the fact that she would be alone at Tye Farm tonight with Tom.

She seized her chance.

Walking up to him, she took his hand.

'Oh, Tom, dear Tom! How awful this is for you. I can't bear to think you've been treated like this by my own sister. When I think how wonderful you are——'

The man, inwardly writhing with the thought of what his wife had done to him, burning with a sense of injustice and insult, was flattered by this girl's obvious admiration and affection. Pulling himself together, he patted her shoulder, and tried to laugh.

'Don't worry about me. I'll be all right. But I'd never have thought Vicky was like that. Never!'

She retained his hand, squeezing it sympathetically. Together they walked back into the sitting-room.

From the washhouse came the mournful howling of Sooty, the pup, who had been shut up there with the dead chicken tied round his neck. And it seemed to Vicky, as she ran through the cold darkness of the night, that she would be haunted for evermore by the thought of her unhappy little Labrador. But she could not go back to him now. She dared not. She was terrified that Tom would see her and make her stay at Tye Farm. And she could not stay there any longer. Whatever happened to her now, she must get away from Tom. If he had believed her, she would have stayed. She would have done her best for him.

But he had just the same hideous suspicions about her that her mother and sister fostered. It was too much!

She ran, ran, ran over the rough roads, which were familiar enough to her in the darkness, in the direction of the Richardsons' house. Nora Richardson was kind and would understand. She would go to Nora. She would ask for protection for tonight at least. She must shut herself away from the ugliness of what lay in Tom's mind; from Freda's cold, cunning malice; and from that hateful house.

It was a good mile to The Spinneys, Charlie Richardson's farm. During the last stretch, Vicky was no longer running. There was a pain in her side, and her heart was hurting her. Her footsteps lagged. She could hardly breathe. She thought:

'I'm like a fox. I know now what it would be like to be chased by a pack of hounds. All Tom's thoughts are like hounds after me—I can feel their beastly breath. . . . But I'm not going to let those teeth tear me in pieces. I belong to myself. Not only to Tom! And something in me belongs to Digby—something that will never die.'

She was utterly spent and overwrought when she reached The Spinneys. She was thankful to see the yellow beam of light coming from the windows of the old farmhouse. They were kindly beacons. And Nora was kind. Vicky needed Nora and her understanding eyes and gentle hands.

She was accustomed to entering the house without ringing or knocking. She rushed now through the front door, gasping, shaken with the tempest of her fear and her misery.

She cried out:

'Mrs. Richardson! *Mrs. Richardson!*'

Nora Richardson, who had just come down from her bedroom, having washed and changed for supper, and was sitting by the drawing-room fire listening to the radio, heard that wild, desolate cry, through the music.

She dropped the paper which she had been reading, and, startled, rose to her feet and ran out into the hall.

She saw before her the figure of Vicky Collinson, wild-eyed, ghastly, looking half-demented. Vicky looked back at her, and first laughed and then cried.

'Mrs. Richardson! Oh, please don't let Tom get me back. Don't let Freda come near me either. I can't stand any more. I *can't*!'

Nora Richardson sprang forward and caught the girl in her arms. She called:

'Charlie! Come here.'

Commander Richardson laid aside his pipe, ran out after his wife, and found her with a fainting girl who had sagged through her arms and fallen into a little heap on the ground.

'Good God!' he ejaculated, 'What the deuce is this?'

Mrs. Richardson raised a grim face. She was holding on to one of Vicky's ice-cold little hands, chafing it. All the mother-love in her was welling to the surface. It might have been Elspeth, her own lamb, driven to her like this out of the storm.

'It's Vicky Collinson. The poor child! I knew this was going to happen. She was on the verge of a breakdown when we last saw her. That fool of a husband! Charlie . . . tell Margaret to make up a bed in the spare room as quickly as possible, and light a fire. Help me to carry her into the drawing-room. She is perished. I must get her warm.'

Richardson leaned down and picked Vicky up.

'Good Lord! She weighs less than Elspeth. I can take her by myself. You go and tell Margaret what you want.'

Vicky, who had sunk into the mists of unconsciousness, eventually opened her eyes, and found herself in the blessed warmth and peace of the Richardsons' pretty drawing-room She was lying on the sofa. Nora Richardson knelt beside her and was trying to make her drink brandy. Vicky pushed it away.

'No, I don't want it. I'm all right now.'

'Lie still, then, dear, And don't worry. I'm going to look after you.'

Vicky began to shiver again. Mrs. Richardson seized her hands and held them fast. She saw that Vicky was almost beyond self-control. Her nervous condition was pitiful. This was the result of abject misery and repression, thought Nora. The result of shutting a sensitive, emotional girl up in a place like Tye Farm with a man like Tom Collinson. Iniquitous! The man was straight and decent, but like a cart-horse in his understanding of women, and particularly out of his depth with a nervous, highly-strung girl like Vicky. The cart-horse mated to the thoroughbred! One of those mis-marriages which went on every day, every year, through the folly of human beings, groping for happiness and thrusting it farther and yet farther away from them.

'I don't want—Tom—to come and take me home,' Vicky whispered after a pause. And two big tears gathered in her eyes and began to roll down her cheeks. Such a pale, sunken little face, Mrs. Richardson thought pityingly. They make her high cheekbones stand out higher than ever.

'He shan't be allowed to take you back, my dear,' she said.

And then Vicky whispered:

'I shall never go back. I can't!'

'Then don't, my dear,' said Nora Richardson firmly; and inwardly defying all the moralists to get up and smite her. She wasn't concerned with conventions. She considered it would be highly immoral to keep Vicky chained to that man who appeared to have more consideration for his chickens than for his wife. And she felt not wicked, but righteous when she added: 'And now where can we find this other man?'

Vicky's slim fingers twined convulsively about the hand that held her.

'He came to Tye Farm—today. That was what started the trouble. My sister insulted him. And Tom—was more than insulting to me. I—it's too long a story to explain! But I didn't do what they said I did. And Tom wouldn't

232

believe me. So I ran away. And Digby said I was to go to him if I couldn't bear it. And I can't. I *can't*!'

And that was Vicky's reiterated cry, and the feeling uttermost in her, all through that memorable night of her running away from Tom. She couldn't go on. It was useless to try. If she went back, she would break. . . . Her mind would go. . . . Something terrible would happen anyhow. And she saw no use in making a renunciation. No use in trying to be noble, because she could never be to Tom what he wanted. Freda was what he wanted. It was Freda he should have married, and not her.

It was a night not to be forgotten by either Vicky or the Richardsons. Tom rang up, later on. He had a feeling that Vicky had gone to The Spinneys. Nora Richardson firmly answered that telephone call herself. It was much better, she told him, that he should not try to come here and upset his wife any more than she was already upset. She was not in a state to cope with a scene. To which Tom sullenly replied that he was fed up with the whole affair, and that Vicky had better stay away if she felt like that.

Nora Richardson positively beamed when she conveyed this message to her young friend. The lack of intelligent understanding in that boorish reply merely confirmed her belief that Tom Collinson deserved to lose his attractive young wife.

'Let him get on with it, and you just stay here, my dear,' she said to Vicky, 'and stay as long as you like.'

Vicky, almost too tired to think any more, would have let matters rest at that. But she was not allowed the peace which she so sorely needed. Soon after Tom's telephone call, another came—from Norman Park. Freda had been on to her home, anxious to let the family hear of the enormity of Vicky's fresh offence. Mrs. Waide immediately telephoned through to The Spinneys, and demanded to speak to her daughter. Once again Mrs. Richardson came to the rescue. Vicky was all for struggling on to her feet to answer the call, but Nora refused to allow it. There followed what she afterwards described to Charlie as a 'few words' between herself and Mrs. Waide.

'I've never heard such nonsense!' exclaimed Mrs. Waide. 'Vicky should return to her husband at once, and if she doesn't, then her father and I will have to come and take her back, ourselves.'

To which Nora Richardson, understanding a little further why Vicky had left her home in order to make that disastrous marriage, frigidly asked Vicky's mother if this was an age when women were forcibly 'returned' to their husbands against their will.

Mrs. Waide then said:

'Vicky married Tom, and it is her duty to live with him.'

Nora Richardson hung up the telephone, and mentally prayed to be allowed to preserve a sense of humour and balance over this affair. At the moment, all her sympathy was on Vicky's side. She tried to imagine herself forcing Elspeth back into the arms of a husband she loathed, completely failed, and condemned Mrs. Waide in consequence.

After her mother's call, Vicky went to pieces again. She cried bitterly in Mrs. Richardson's arms. She would be forced back to Tom, she said. She could see it. The family would force her, even if he didn't. And she couldn't bear it. She *couldn't*!

It was then that Nora Richardson demanded Digby Farnel's address.

'He's caused some of this trouble, my dear, and he should know about it. He must come down and see you and talk things over. I'm not going to let you go back to that life. It's killing you by inches. And I don't think Mr. Farnel will allow it, if he's in love with you.'

'What can he do?' Vicky asked despairingly.

To which the elder woman replied: 'Take you away my dear. Which I imagine is exactly what he wants to do.'

'But it would mean a divorce,' said Vicky, aghast.

'Do you think that's worse than a marriage of this kind?'

234

'I don't care what happens to me—but Digby—he can't want to——'

'If he loves you, he will want to,' cut in Mrs. Richardson, 'and I don't care how wicked I am for saying it—I think it's the one and only way out for you all.'

19

That next morning, there was a great deal of telephonic communication from Sussex to London and London to Sussex on the subject of Vicky Collinson.

Vicky, herself, was kept firmly in bed by her friend, and prevented from being harassed more than was necessary in the circumstances.

Mrs. Waide, despite all pleas from her husband to leave Vicky alone and not interfere, telephoned her eldest daughter and announced her intention of arriving on the scene. But it was Freda who diverted her from this course. Freda's evening with Tom had not been without some slight satisfaction. Tom had gone as far as sitting on the sofa with an arm about her, telling her what a fine girl she was, and what a mistake he had made in his choice between the two sisters. Freda, exalted and hopeful, laid aside her own principles, and decided that it would be a lot better for her, if her sister did *not* come back to Tye Farm. If Vicky would only go to that man—Tom would undoubtedly turn to her, Freda. Already she saw herself as his consoler, and later his second wife.

She advised her mother not to come down to Sussex. Tom was dealing with the matter himself, she said. Vicky was still with the Richardsons, and Tom had decided to go over to see her, today.

This was not strictly true. Tom, deeply injured by his wife's conduct, was in mulish mood. He had no intention of pleading with Vicky to return to him. If she *did* come back, he'd make her behave herself. Meanwhile, his sister-in-law was being a trump, and he'd never been better looked after. Worse luck she couldn't stay on at the Farm—young girl, unchaperoned, and all that. Though of course there was nothing like *that* between him and Freda. As for Vicky, she could stay away and 'stew in her own juice', before he'd humble himself to go after her.

Nevertheless, he put through a call to The Spinneys. And he spoke to Mrs. Richardson.

'You can tell my dear wife,' he said, 'that I give her till tomorrow, and if she is not back by then, she needn't come back at all.'

'Thanks,' said Nora Richardson, inwardly boiling, 'I'll tell her. And while we're on the phone, I think she's rather anxious about that puppy of hers. Might I send one of our lads over to fetch it?'

'Sorry,' said Tom, 'I handed it over to a man who wanted it, this morning. I'm not having any more of my chickens destroyed.'

Mrs. Richardson, speechless, went to Vicky and broke to her the news that her Sooty had been given to a stranger. Vicky did not even cry. She laughed.

'How like Tom to do that as soon as I'm out of the way.'

It was the sound of that unutterably miserable little laugh which put the seal on Nora Richardson's decision to communicate with Digby Farnel.

And so another call went through to London, to Digby's club. An S.O.S. which Digby Farnel answered in such a short space of time that Nora had no lingering doubts that he was seriously in love. As soon as he knew what had happened, Digby immediately cancelled every other plan and came to Vicky. In less than two hours the blue and silver racing car brought him from Piccadilly to the farm near Poynings.

He liked Nora Richardson at sight, and she liked him, too. Here was a man indeed—a charming person whom, she afterwards told her husband, she would have 'fallen for' at once had she been twenty years younger!

They sat and talked for a good half-hour before she allowed him to see Vicky.

During that time, many things were said, and Digby found himself appealing to this sweet, quiet woman who had befriended Vicky—almost like an embarrassed boy floundering a little out of his depth.

That funny, rather embarrassed look which he gave her over the rim of his glasses went straight to Nora Richardson's heart. And she liked the honesty with which he spoke.

'You see,' he said, 'certain laws are made and certain principles laid down, and one tries to adhere to them. Of course, if I had been what the world would call "straight as a die", I suppose I would not have seen Vicky again after her marriage, knowing how I felt towards her. But I was haunted by the thought of her, and I couldn't keep away.'

'That's the trouble,' said Mrs. Richardson. 'There's something about Vicky that does haunt one. She's different . . . not like other girls . . . and the most weird production for that Waide family. I think she was a changeling. I can't believe she belongs to them.'

'Well, I've only seen the sister, and one certainly can't believe she's any relation to her. But do you think I've been a cad to come back into her life? I'm sure Collinson's a good chap. Yet I can't feel a cad. I can only feel that I've got to save Vicky, both for her peace of mind and my own. When I saw her last, she was at breaking-point. It doesn't surprise me that she's got beyond it.'

'Nor me. And that's why Tom Collinson is a fool. He has tried to treat her as though she were an ordinary person, and she's not. She's extremely emotional and susceptible to kindness and all the beauty in life.'

'I know that,' said Digby with feeling. 'But tell me, Mrs. Richardson, shall I be beyond the pale if I make Vicky quit and come away with me, now?'

Nora Richardson sighed.

'My dear boy, I've got a daughter almost Vicky's age. If she were in Vicky's place today, I'd say to you—take her quickly. It'll be death in life for her if she stays where she

238

is. The world may condemn you both. That won't matter to you. And Tom will soon get over it. She's no more use to him than he is to her.'

Digby threw away the cigarette which he had been smoking. A strangely excited look came into his eyes. His heart was beating faster than it had beaten in his life before. His thoughts winged upstairs to the girl whose fate he knew lay between his own hands. There had always been a kind of fatality about Vicky and himself. From that hour when he had first seen her in that Paris train. From that day when she had fled to him in the hotel. He had wanted to save her then for himself. Today he knew he must save her because they could neither of them go on without each other. That pretty, tender-hearted child, with all her pathetic love of glamour—the glamour which she had never been allowed—was the woman whom he must make his wife. And he wished to God he had come to this decision long before the torture of her marriage to Tom Collinson began.

'Mrs. Richardson,' he said after a pause, 'if Vicky will come with me, I shall take her away as soon as you think she is fit. I'll take her abroad. None of the mud-slinging need touch her. She doesn't deserve it. Let the moralists scream. She was married much too young—hounded into it by her own unhappiness—and my cowardice. Yes, I was a coward not to take her when I had the chance. But I wasn't sure enough of myself—or her. She was made for happiness, and that fellow she married—why shouldn't he be happy too? He never could be with her. He'll get another chance when she's gone. We all will. And thank God there isn't a child or the prospect of one to complicate matters.'

'Thank God,' echoed Mrs. Richardson. 'I think that would have killed her.'

'And may I see her now?' asked Digby.

'You may, and good luck,' said Nora Richardson.

Their hands met in a warm clasp. They sealed a friendship which was never to fade, and which in later years Charlie Richardson was to appreciate as fully as his wife.

A few minutes later Vicky came downstairs, and was sent into the warm firelit sitting-room, where Digby waited for her alone.

He took one look at her. He was stricken at the change in her. There was no colour in her face. She looked as though she had been through hell—burnt up and ravaged by her own repressed misery. Like a lily, he thought, battered down by a storm. He could not bear to see her so broken.

Without a word, he walked up to her, took her hand, led her to the sofa, and drew her into his arms.

For a moment she clung to him desperately. Very gently he kissed her and stroked her hair over her shoulders until gradually some of the colour stole back into her cheeks and the old lustre into her eyes. He could feel the vitality creeping back into her body.

Then he said:

'You're mine now. You're going to be mine for the rest of your life. I'm never going to let you go again.'

That made Vicky gasp. And now the fiery red scorched her face and her throat.

'Digby! That can't be true. It can't!'

'Darling,' he said, 'when Mrs. Richardson sent for me and told me what you'd been through, I made up my mind that I wasn't going to let you go on. Your marriage was a frightful mistake. I deplore the fact that I ever let you make it. It has only lasted four months, but it's been long enough to half kill you. What you went through last night, incidentally through me, has finished it. If you're ready to be divorced, Vicky, I'm more than ready to be the co-respondent. Let Collinson cite me. I'll take you away—abroad. And you know without my telling you that, the moment the decree is made absolute, I shall marry you.'

She stayed very still a moment, her hand clasped in his, her head against his shoulder. She felt very tired, physically weak, as though she had not the strength to lift that head up again. But a divine, immense peace was stealing over her. The awful tension was easing up. The awful horror at the prospect of a return to Tye Farm, and the monotony of misery there, with a man whom she had never loved and should never have married, was diminishing.

At first she could hardly believe it possible that Digby should be here, telling her that she belonged to him and that he wanted to take her away. Yet when she gradually began to realise the truth of it, she realised also that she could not even put up the most feeble argument. For nothing mattered except him and his love. Tom would think unspeakable things of her. He would take it for granted that all the suspicions which Freda had fostered about Paris were true. And Freda and the family would join in righteous sympathy with him. They would never speak to her again. At least, perhaps poor old Dad would want to see her one day. But not the others. Flesh of their flesh she might be, but she had never belonged to them, and they had never wanted her.

But this man—this wonderful person beside her, this being who knew so much of the beauty and happiness of life—had taught her so much already, and would teach her so much more—he wanted her—again and again he told her so.

She thought of the old days at Norman Park before she had gone away with Paul Dallas to make a career for herself as a dancer. (Pathetic, blighted hope!) She thought of the man whom she used to picture in her dreams. The dream-lover who could always make her smile, and who used to hold out his arms and say:

'*Darling—I've been so unhappy. I've wanted you so long!*'

That was what Digby was saying now. And he was everything that she had ever dreamed about. How could it be wicked to accept such happiness with, or to be thankful for, this blessed, blessed content which was stealing like the elixir of life through her veins.

Digby put a finger beneath her chin, and raised her face to his.

'Will you come with me, sweet? Will you let me try to make you forget all this unhappiness? Will you let me take care of you and teach you to laugh again?'

'Oh, Digby,' she said in a choked voice, 'darling . . .'

'Will you, little love?'

She nodded mutely, because she could not say the word which she wanted with all her soul to say. But her lips against his answered enough, and he, too, was content.

What happened during the rest of the day seemed much like a dream to Vicky. A dream so wonderful that she was terrified that at any moment it might be dispelled, and that she would wake up and find herself back at Tye Farm, facing the prospect of another sinister, lonely day.

There were bound to be unpleasant moments in that day, one awful moment when she had to telephone through to her own home to ask for her luggage, and Tom answered. Then she, with one hand fast clasped in Digby's to give her courage, told her husband what she intended to do.

'I'm terribly sorry for any wrong that I've done you, Tom, and I must ask you to forgive me. But it's no use my coming back. We'd never get on. I'm going away with Mr. Farnel. You shall have the evidence. All I ask is that you should give me a divorce and try to forget me.'

Silence. There was no reply. Tom had put up the receiver without answering.

Vicky, shaking with nerves, turned and flung herself into Digby's arms. He held her close until the trembling stopped.

'Don't worry, sweet. It's got to be gone through. But it will all be over soon. And so long as it seems worth while to you——'

'You know it does,' she interrupted passionately. 'You know I adore you, but it's all so—dreadful, getting away from Tom, I mean. I wish it need never have happened this way—that's all.'

He understood how she felt and was amazingly patient with her. And he was astonished at how little he cared that he was to be made the co-respondent in this particular divorce case. He, who would have told old Jack Morgan a few months ago, that nothing on earth would induce him to run away with another man's wife. How little one knew what one was going to do in this life!

It was Freda to whom Vicky spoke next. Freda rang up. She was just on her way back to Norman Park.

'Nice news I've got to take them at home,' she said acidly, 'but only what is to be expected of you. I hear you're going off with that man.'

'Yes,' said Vicky.

'Well, Tom says he'll be glad to divorce you.'

'That's all I ask of him now.'

'I don't want to see you again,' said Freda. 'I think you've treated poor Tom abominably.'

'Do you really think,' said Vicky, with a sudden flash of her old spirit, 'it would be better for me to go back to Tom and make him and myself unhappy for the rest of our lives?'

There was a pause. Then Freda, with an eye to her own future, and a very pleasant memory of the evening she had spent alone with her brother-in-law, answered that question, not perhaps strictly in accordance with her principles.

'It's no use your going back. Tom wouldn't have you.'

And that was Vicky's good-bye from her sister. Still later, there was the unpleasantness of a harangue over the telephone from her mother. Mrs. Waide did not spare her younger daughter. She condemned her wholesale and left it at that.

Digby stood by helplessly. All this had to be got through, and he could do nothing to save Vicky from it. But when it was all over, he knew that she felt better, happier in her heart than she had felt for a long, long time.

'Nobody is ever to be allowed to upset you or hurt you again, my lovely one,' he told her at the end of that day. 'And now I'm going to leave you with your very good friend, Mrs. Richardson, because what you need is another long night's rest.'

She clung to him.

'Must you leave me?'

'Only for tonight, my sweet. Tomorrow I will fetch you and drive you up to town, and then we are going South. To France, to the sunshine. I know a little place by the bluest of seas—under the bluest of skies—where the sun will make you all brown and beautiful, and where you'll learn to live and laugh—and love me a little more.'

She hugged him to her passionately, the tears in her eyes.

'It sounds like heaven, but I couldn't learn to love you any more than I do.'

'I don't think I could love you much more,' he said.

As soon as he had gone, Mrs Richardson busied herself 'mothering' her protégée; packed her off to bed again. Vicky would want plenty of rest to get back her strength. She had got to look better when Digby came for her in the morning. Vicky smiled at her, starry-eyed. It did Nora Richardson good to see that ecstatic expression which had replaced the old hunger and torment.

'I can't believe it's all going to happen!' Vicky said. 'I can't believe I'm going away with him.'

'You certainly are, and I shall miss you,' said Nora. 'You're the only neighbour I've got round here whom I really like, and I shall certainly never be allowed to darken the doors of Tye Farm again.'

Vicky thought of Tye Farm, shuddered, then said, suddenly:

'I hope I never see hundreds of chickens again as long as I live!'

'You shan't,' said Mrs. Richardson, 'you shall eat them instead.'

Then suddenly Vicky looked tragic again.

'That reminds me. My poor little Sooty! If only I knew that he was going to be happy. I wish I knew where he had gone.'

'Ah!' said Mrs. Richardson, 'that reminds *me*! . . .'

She walked out of the room, and returned in a few moments, half-leading, half-dragging a rather cowed-looking, crestfallen Labrador pup.

When he saw Vicky, he pricked up his flopping ears, gave an hysterical bark, and bounded into her arms.

Vicky embraced him rapturously.

'Sooty! *Sooty!* How did you get here? My darling little dog!'

'That's your Digby's first present to you, my dear.'

Vicky, on the floor with the Labrador clasped to her, stared up at her friend.

'But how did Digby get him?'

'After lunch, you know he went out? Well, he managed to make inquiries in the village and found out the man who had been given the pup by Tom, and bought him back at a handsome price. He told me to give Sooty to you after he'd gone.'

A lump came into Vicky's throat. She bent her head until her dark curls were one with the silky coat of the little dog.

'How like him!' she said in a muffled voice. 'How absolutely *him,* to have thought of doing that!'

Nora Richardson turned away because her eyes were suspiciously bright, but she said gaily:

'I think if I'm right, that young man will do a whole lot of nice things for you. He's that kind of young man.'

Vicky nodded, couldn't speak. But she thought:

'Tomorrow I shall be with him, tomorrow—and all the tomorrows. . . . Oh, Sooty, Sooty, you're going to have a master whom you can worship—just as I do! And just as I shall do all my life!'

Exactly one year later, Vicky sat writing a letter under a striped umbrella in the garden of a villa near Monte Carlo. The villa which she and Digby had taken soon after their marriage, and where they were staying for the winter. The letter was to Nora Richardson. Half-way through it, Vicky sat back and looked a moment dreamily around her. Here was the beauty of nature which could almost be called perfection. The sort of beauty with which Digby had surrounded her since he had taken her away, and opened her eyes to a new world. And it was a world in which the days and nights seemed to Vicky never long enough to hold all the ecstasy which they offered.

To her right, through the green palms, she could see the dazzling whiteness of the blue-shuttered villa, against which the magenta flowers of the bougainvillea rioted in an almost shameless violence of hot colour.

It was all so hot and lovely, thought Vicky. The sun. The aching blue of the sky. And in the distance, the deep cobalt of the sea which looked like crinkled silk. Here in the garden there was shade; black, slender cypress trees, and the green canopy of the palms. Here were spice carnations and roses and azaleas tumbling over each other, a pink and scarlet cascade of colour. But Vicky felt cool and at peace. She wore white. Digby loved her in white, and there was a scarlet carnation pinned to her dark curls, and a red silk scarf around her neck. Her face and throat and arms were a warm tan. She had never looked or felt so fit, and she had never looked, so Digby unceasingly told her, more lovely.

What a perfect life it was out here, she thought! Swimming early in the morning before breakfast. Long, lazy, golden days when they walked or drove together. And if they felt like it, gay, amusing nights at the Casino, when they gambled or danced.

Sometimes they shut up the villa and went off in the car on trips, so that Digby could find fresh subjects for his cherished photography. Not that he enjoyed photographing anything or anybody more than his wife. As Vicky often laughingly told him, he must have hundreds of negatives of her now!

How gloriously happy she was! So happy that she sometimes feared it must end. So happy that she felt almost wicked and selfish. For she did not believe there could be any other girl in the world as content. She was beyond comparing this life with the old one. They did not stand comparison. She only knew that the glamour which she had sought in the wild exuberance of first youth had been false. A mirror which had cracked. But this was the image of true beauty, and it all resolved around her integral love for one man. The man who was now her husband.

She had been happy—wildly so—when Digby had first taken her away. But she had not really felt at peace until the divorce was through and she had a right to call herself Mrs. Farnel. Now it was perfect. And she had no need ever to feel compunction about Tom. For in this very letter to Nora Richardson, she was acknowledging Nora's news that Tom had brought a new wife to Tye Farm. Freda, of course! Vicky had to smile when she heard it. And shake her head a little incredulously. Freda and Tom! Freda in her place! Well, it was a place which she would fill very adequately. She would be a far better farmer's mate than she, Vicky, had been. But Vicky could not help wondering how long it would take before the first flush died down and Tom was made to wilt under the acid disapproval of his new wife.

From her mother, Vicky never heard. Mrs. Waide had positively and completely cut her out. But from her father she had one or two rather pathetic letters which told her that the old man missed her, and had never really joined in the general family 'excommunication'.

Vicky resumed her letter to the woman who was her greatest friend.

'Digby and I are longing to see you next week, and it'll be wonderful to have you and Charlie out here with us for a whole fortnight. And now for a thrilling piece of news. You know we meant to visit the Bahamas next month. We're going to put it off. Digby wants me to stay here and keep quiet. I'm going to present him, I hope, with a son and heir, in the spring. I don't think either of us could be happier. . . .'

She stopped writing again. She heard a quick, familiar step which made her look round. Digby was coming out to join her for tea. He had been writing his letters indoors.

She thought how ridiculously young and brown and well he looked as he came towards her. Nobody would dream he was so much older than herself. She thought, too, that that new ultramarine blue shirt of his, open at the throat and with short sleeves, was a good touch of colour. He had taught her utmost appreciation of colour, amongst other things. Her heart seemed full to overflowing with tenderness as he approached her. There was never such a husband! He seemed never to be able to do enough to make her happy. And there had never been such a lover! His love was still as new and exciting as ever. When he looked at her, her heart still missed a beat, and every pulse in her body stirred faster.

Digby came up behind her chair, bent and kissed her hair.

'How's my sweet?'

'Very well, indeed.'

'Finished your letters?'

'Almost. I've been telling Nora the news.'

Digby came and curled himself up at her feet, took one of her hands, and laid it against his cheek.

'Ah! *The* news.'

'Yes.'

He turned, took off his glasses with a quick, familiar gesture, and put her cool young hand against his eyes.

'I think it's bound to be an extremely handsome child, don't you, with me for a father?' he said.

She gave a little giggle.

'I'm not so sure. But I think, on the other hand, if it resembles me, it'll be ravishing.'

'"It" will be a boy,' said Digby, 'and if he resembles his mother, he'll be too disgracefully good-looking, so let's hope he takes after father.'

Vicky sighed.

'It's all been so heavenly, darling,' she said, 'that I

248

wonder if we can possibly be any happier when we have our baby.'

He put on his glasses again, and smiled up at her.

'You have been happy, haven't you, sweet?'

'You know that.'

'Well,' he said, 'I wrote to old Morgan the other day and told him that life was mighty good to me.'

'Oh, I do hope so,' she said, with a little catch in her voice. 'I've been so terrified that I mightn't satisfy you—that you might be bored with me, and——'

He interrupted:

'Quoting from Mr. Noel Coward: "Light of my life, shut up!"'

She laughed.

'All right, I will.'

'And tonight,' he said, 'I think we should have an extra drink and toast the happiness of the other two.'

'You mean Tom and Freda?'

'Yes.'

'Certainly, we will. But somehow I can't focus at all on the thought of Tye Farm and the chickens and that life over there. It wasn't life for me at all.'

'Well, with any luck, they'll get something out of it. Each man to his own taste, my darling. And by the way, I've got a piece of news for you. D'you know that Sooty went off hunting this morning, and that an irate peasant brought him back, holding in one hand a dead chicken, and in the other a gun!'

Vicky sat up, gasped, and looked into her husband's eyes.

'*Digby*, you don't mean . . . he hasn't . . .'

'He hasn't hurt the little devil at all. And I've told Pierre to keep the gates firmly shut and see that he doesn't get out again. *And* I've recompensed the man, who departed with twice the value of the chicken, calling blessings down upon me and mine.'

Their eyes met. Then Vicky burst out laughing.

'It really is funny. In the face of past history—it really is!'

'I trust,' said Digby, 'that you'll bring up your children a little better than you've brought up your dog.'

'I shouldn't think I will,' she said, still laughing.

He put an arm about her and pulled her warm, radiant young face down to him.

'A quick kiss, darling. I hear Pierre coming with the tea.'

Their lips met. Then, with a little, happy sigh, Vicky sat back in her chair, shut her eyes, and began to think about how she would bring up her children.

THE END

ROSAMUNDE PILCHER

WILD MOUNTAIN THYME

Victoria Bradshaw fell in love with London playwright
Oliver Dobbs when she was just eighteen. Now, years
later, he was a widower standing on her doorstep
with his two-year-old son in his arms. And Victoria
was foolish enough to want to take him back. Their
early spring journey to a castle in Scotland would
become an odyssey of emotional discovery . . . in a
novel about relationships as real as those you've
experienced and a love as rich and unpredictable as
dreams can be.

ROSAMUNDE PILCHER

THE DAY OF THE STORM

Rebecca Bayliss rushed to her dying mother's bed-
side only to come away shattered by more than grief:
her mother had revealed the existence of a family
Rebecca knew nothing about. Determined to find
them, Rebecca began her journey to a Cornwall
mansion and into relationships torn by passion and
greed. From her grandfather, who hid an explosive
secret, to sensual craftsman Joss Gardner, whose
past hinted of intrigue ... to a handsome cousin,
whose kisses were dangerously seductive. Rebecca
was entangled in a family mystery ... and unravelling
it held the key to her future and her heart.

HODDER AND STOUGHTON PAPERBACKS

ROSAMUNDE PILCHER

SLEEPING TIGER

For the first time in her life, Selina Bruce wasn't sure what tomorrow would bring. She had impulsively left behind her lawyer fiancé in London and flown alone to a tiny island off the Spanish coast. She was searching for the father she'd never known, but what she found was an unexpected truth about herself and the man she planned to marry. For exotic San Antonio offered Selina more than the penetrating brilliance of the noonday sun. It offered the mysterious George Dyer, who held the key not only to her past . . . but to her heart . . .

HODDER AND STOUGHTON PAPERBACKS

ANABEL DONALD

SMILE, HONEY

'Smile, Honey . . .'

That was what her mother always told her to do. She
smiled her innocent, provocative smile that still
makes the nation reach for a Kleenex when her
twenty-year-old screen triumph is repeated every
Christmas.

Now, at thirty-eight, Honey the full-time beauty and
professional personality wants to break free. But her
live-in lover has just walked out. She's surrounded
by the well-heeled media back-biter set and she's
dyslexic.

There must be an answer somewhere between the
Meditations of Marcus Aurelius and the sperm banks
of California. For Honey, liberation is going to start
with mutiny . . .

'You can tell you're in the hands of a writer who's got
our collective number. Ms Donald finds your funny
bone among the sad scenes'

She

HODDER AND STOUGHTON PAPERBACKS

MARY STEWART

THORNYHOLD

To Gilly, the house, deep in the wild wood, was an enchantment. Her very own enchantment, left to her by the cousin whose occasional, magical visits had brightened her childhood.

And as she explored, she discovered more about the woman who had come to seem like a fairy godmother to her: her herbalist's skills, her still room, her abilities to foresee and to heal.

She discovered also that the local people believed that she had inherited not just the house but the magical spell-weaving powers that lived on in the house and garden.

Slowly, quietly, she came to realise that they were right.

'The best sort of romantic novel, with memorable atmosphere and descriptive style'

Sunday Express

'A delicate love story, delightful . . . in its creation of a magical world'

Books

HODDER AND STOUGHTON PAPERBACKS

MORE TITLES AVAILABLE FROM
HODDER AND STOUGHTON PAPERBACKS

DENISE ROBINS

☐	12783 X	Infatuation	£1.95
☐	14877 2	Love and Desire and Hate	£2.25
☐	16218 X	A Promise is Forever	£1.95
☐	02435 6	Slave Woman	£1.95
☐	42419 2	The Woman's Side of It	£2.50

ROSAMUNDE PILCHER

☐	52120 1	Wild Mountain Thyme	£2.99
☐	52119 8	The Day of the Storm	£2.99
☐	52116 3	Sleeping Tiger	£2.99

ANABEL DONALD

☐	50609 1	Smile, Honey	£3.50

MARY STEWART

☐	50045 X	Thornyhold	£2.99

All these books are available at your local bookshop or newsagent, or can be ordered direct from the publisher. Just tick the titles you want and fill in the form below.

Prices and availability subject to change without notice.

Hodder & Stoughton Paperbacks, P.O. Box 11, Falmouth, Cornwall.

Please send cheque or postal order, and allow the following for postage and packing.

UK – 80p for one book, and 20p for each additional book ordered up to a £2.00 maximum.

B.F.P.O. – 80p for the first book and 20p for each additional book.

OTHER OVERSEAS CUSTOMERS INCLUDING EIRE – £1.50 for the first book, £1.00 for the second book, plus 30p per copy for each additional book.

Name ....

Address ....

....